IN THE COMPANY OF WOLVES

Brothers in Arms

IN THE COMPANY OF WOLVES

Brothers in Arms

STEVE LANG

In The Company of Wolves: Brothers in Arms

For permission requests, write to the publisher, addressed "Attention: Permissions Coordinator," at the address below.

ISBN: 979-8-9922028-5-4 (Paperback)
ISBN: 979-8-9922028-6-1 (Hardcover)
ISBN: 979-8-9922028-7-8 (Digital/Kindle)
ISBN: 979-8-9922028-8-5 (Audio)
ISBN: 979-8-9922028-9-2 (Hardback/Barnes & Noble)

Cover design by Gonzalo Rodriguez
Interior layout by Mirko Fermani
Printed in the United States of America.

Victor + Valor
4500 Williams Dr Ste212-421
Georgetown. TX 78633
https://www.victorvalor.org/

More information about the author can be found at https:// stevedlang.com
First Printing: 2017

For Steve, whom I still think about almost daily.
See you on the other side, buddy.

ACKNOWLEDGMENTS

I want to give special thanks to my wife, Brandy, who is always there for me when the road gets tough and when the words are hard to find, and to the band Mastodon, whose albums I listened to almost exclusively while writing this trilogy.

TABLE OF CONTENTS

CHAPTER 1 1

CHAPTER 2 23

CHAPTER 3 45

CHAPTER 4 71

CHAPTER 5 93

CHAPTER 6 113

CHAPTER 7 137

CHAPTER 8 155

CHAPTER 9 179

CHAPTER 10 197

CHAPTER 11 221

CHAPTER 12 245

CHAPTER 13 271

CHAPTER 1

DANTE, RAMOS, AND MAC STOOD inside Scowl Castle, contemplating their next move. Ragnok was gone, Gregor had been murdered, and the wolven brothers grieved their father's loss. The cosmic portal had been stolen again, and Mac had failed in his mission. Mac's conscience was stained with blood, and he wished he could change many of his decisions since leaving home.

"You can't blame yourself for this, Mac," Ramos said with a tear in his eye.

"Our father was a mystic and a warrior. He knew what he was doing and chose a warrior's death," Dante said.

"I'll call Saki. We have to get to the Fire Lands, but the only way is across the Death Sea. She'll take us as far as Last Resort, but we'll have to find a ship for hire." Ramos said.

"I feel your anger, brother," Dante said. He placed a hand on Ramos' shoulder. "We will avenge his death."

The three stood watching Toga in his undead mechanical struggle against the crossbow bolt, pinning him to the throne. Mac moved toward the window to look outside. He felt awe at the breathtaking view from where so much misery had spawned. Now that it was gone, the castle seemed peaceful. He could almost picture himself living there with his kids, waking up each morning to rolling fields and walls of stone six feet thick. Mac had always loved castles and daydreamed of living among the rolling Scottish countryside in a well- defended fortress as a young man.

"Mac, take this place," Dante said. "Are you reading my mind, Dante?"

"Your children will be safe here from the dangers beyond these walls."

Mac wanted his children to be safe more than anything. But he didn't know if he could survive alone in the untamed world of Eritria.

Ramos did not have to wait long for their transport. Saki had been circling overhead, following Ramos after the battle. She swooped down from the sky, and two more flights joined her. One was her size, but she had azure blue feathers and looked like a giant pigeon to Mac.

The other was purple with slick green highlights on his wings that reflected the sunlight. As he landed next to Saki, he bowed to her and then looked at the three travelers cocking his head.

"You called?" The purple bird said.

"Janx and Sabrina, meet Ramos, Dante, and..." Saki said.

"Mac," Mac said.

"They need our help to get to Last Resort," Saki said.

"Let's get going then—the wife's waitin'. Our chicks are taking flying lessons today," Janx said.

Saki's multicolored plumage faded from red to green, blue, yellow, and orange with a hypnotic rhythm as she moved. Without another word, she and her friends allowed the party to climb aboard their backs, and they were off into the clouds.

Saki and her friends carried the three to the port town of Last Resort, a burg of ill repute on the western shore of Eritria. It is known for its rough- neck residents and the irascible sailors who import and export cargo from all over the planet.

"We need to find a captain crazy enough to take us to the Fire Lands. There are monsters out there that can swallow a ship whole." Dante said.

Mac had promised to return to his children when the centaur war was over, but as soon as he learned the cosmic portal had been stolen, he knew another promise would be broken. Just like the good old days, he thought remorsefully. He had not transformed back into a human since the war with Yawl had begun, and he realized he was starting to prefer his wolven form. The children still did not know about his new ability. Would they be frightened when they saw him? Or would they be intrigued or feel safe? Bobby and Serena would have to wait a little longer. He hated leaving them, but he knew he'd have to separate personal feelings from the mission. It was like he was back in the military, and the old sense of independence was returning more every day he was away from them.

"Here is where we leave you. If you need anything, you can reach me. Just put the whistle to your lips and blow." Saki said. She used her sultry bedroom voice, and Dante cringed at all that might mean for his brother.

"Farewell, my friends. Thank you all for your aid, and I will remember your offer in my time of need, Saki." Ramos said, touching her neck softly.

As Saki and her friends departed, the three stood just outside town while the heady aroma of ocean water and rotting fish floated through the air, stinging nostrils. Last Resort was incredibly old, and there was a history of violence that came with the town. Unruly sailors and fishermen who frequented the Skull of Ranash Saloon brought most of the violence. Shabby, derelict buildings lined the streets, some leaning into one another like old men too stubborn to die.

"This place looks like Hades," Mac said.

"I don't know what Hades is, but we'd better watch our backs," Dante said.

Ships bobbed violently into the seaport across a tumultuous, windswept, dangerous bay. The rough seas caused each vessel to weave and sway toward the wharf like teeter-totters. Mac looked at the waves with dread, seasick already. His sense of self- preservation begged him to convince the party to change direction and find some other way to the Fire Lands. He wished they were in the *Poseidon* and could float through the sky in a blink. Unfortunately, the craft had been destroyed in the battle, and there was no other way. To Mac, the Death Sea looked impassable by ship, and the birds would not carry them across due to unpredictable lightning storms and hurricanes.

"It's amazing they make it to shore at all. Those waters look like certain doom." Ramos said.

"These are some of the craziest people you'll ever meet; just try not to piss anyone off," Dante replied.

"Have you ever been here before?" Mac asked. "I have, long ago when my father and I led a party of researchers to the island of Tumak Raul. They were searching for a race of druids long rumored to have vanished from the planet." Dante said.

"Where's Tumak Raul?" Mac asked.

"It's a continent to the southwest that was once a part of Eritria until the last ice age when a giant glacier separated it. My father and I nearly lost our lives on that expedition, but that's a story for another day. There's not much known about places like this town, but one thing I do know about Last Resort is that outsiders aren't welcome. However, the rough necks here have never seen a human before, so we could use that to our advantage. You're bound to draw some stares, so tell them you're a powerful wizard and banish them to the chaos realm if they start any trouble." Dante said.

Mac changed form to that of his human self. "A wizard? What should I do if they ask me to prove it?"

"Turn wolven, and that'll about scare the pants off em,'" Ramos said. "Shapeshifters are uncommon, even in a land of enchantment such as ours." Mac changed back to his human form once more.

A fishing trawler was fighting high waves just off the port, out at sea. A wave washed over the deck, plunging the boat nose-first underwater. It listed momentarily and sank to the ocean floor, dooming her crew to a watery grave. A rescue team of short pig men jumped into rowboats and began paddling out to where the trawler had gone down. By the time the rescuers had made it to the shipwrecked sailors, one pig man had fallen overboard and was lost to the stormy sea, his body vanishing below the waves. Mac could see the remaining rescuers pulling two men into the boats as they were tossed along the rough waves and began rowing back to shore.

"I don't know about you guys, but I have no desire to go out in that water," Mac said. He was shaking his head.

"Can you fix the craft that brought you to this planet and fly us to the Fire Lands?" Ramos asked. "No, that bomb destroyed it," Mac said and sighed.

"It seems, then, that we have no choice. A boat it is." Ramos said.

"Let's go into town and find out if there are any captains for rent," Dante said.

They walked into the town of Last Resort and were greeted, as expected, with suspicious stares. They walked past the Hotel Squall, where a pig man wearing a Stetson hat, cocked in front of his eyes, was sitting with his chair leaned back against the wall, snoring. Last Resort had a seedy quality, like the rundown towns in Mac's world, where safety during the day was poor and non-existent at night. Daylight grew dim as darkening clouds rolled in from off the coast, bringing heavy rain. The pigmen who had gone out on the rescue mission were docking their boat. They had rescued two reptilian fishermen who were semi-conscious from water inhalation. They were dragged onto the dock and left to lie as the rowboat pig men waved them off and headed for the Skull of Ranash Saloon.

Mac's party followed them toward the bar. Men of many races were dive patrons and could be seen crowding around the entrance. The bouncer tossed two reptilians from the bar through the batwing doors, landing in a mud puddle outside. Two men, a reptilian and a Minotaur fought in the mud and muck-filled street. They were matched in height and were equally muscular and intimidating, with bulging biceps and menacing scowls.

As the reptilian threw a jab, the Minotaur slipped it and came up with a horn to the ribs, knocking the reptilian backward into an apple cart. The cart's owner, a pig man named Lawrence, screamed in rage and joined in on the fracas; he kicked them in the shins, squealing with anger, and stabbed the reptilian in his right thigh with his dagger. While the street turned into a full-out brawl, the three newcomers walked toward the Skull of Ranash Saloon.

"Why's it called the Skull of Ranash Saloon?" Mac asked.

"Long ago, a smuggler named Ranash was caught cheating at cards by rival pirates. They beheaded him and hung his head on the saloon sign until it decomposed and fell off. It used to be called Shorty's Tavern, but Talbern Grong, the saloon owner, thought Skull of Ranash would bring in more business." Dante said.

"I'd name it something cool like The Doom Parlor or Wrath of Khan Saloon," Mac said.

"Or Skull of Mac Tavern," Ramos said, flashing wicked teeth in a grin.

"Let's just find a captain and get out of here before we get involved," Dante said.

"I agree, the sooner we leave Last Resort, the better. There's no telling what Asura is doing with your cosmic portal, Mac. If he can do it, I believe he'll open a portal to find his father, Broad Axe." Ramos said.

The closer they came to the batwing doors, the louder the raucous noise erupted inside. When they walked in, the residents of the saloon gave a cursory glance at the wolven, but when they saw Mac, all conversation stopped. They glared at him silently, suspicious and confused. Dante was unsure they could go about their business unmolested by the saloon customers, but after a moment, most of them shrugged and turned back to their business. Conversation and drinking resumed as the wolven walked to the bar, and Dante raised a hand for the barkeep. The bartender was a grizzled, old, wolven man who looked like life had kicked him in the teeth a time or two. He acknowledged Dante, nodding with feigned interest.

"What do you want?" the bartender asked. "Got any gut rot juice?" Dante asked.

"We're not here to drink, Dante," Ramos said. He turned and looked at the bartender. "We need a captain to get us across the Death Sea to the Fire Lands."

"And what would you be doing there?" A wolven man sitting at the bar beside Ramos asked.

"We're going on a trip," Ramos said.

The wolven man looked at Mac with a furrowed brow.

"What are you?" He asked. "I'm a human," Mac replied.

"Never heard of them," The wolven man returned his attention to Ramos.

"You wouldn't happen to be tied up in some foolish scheme to rid the world of Asura, would you? Because that is something I would not risk my life and limbs for if I were you. That villain does unnatural things with the dead. Best to leave him alone to rot on his island." The man said.

"We're headed to the Fire Lands on a sightseeing mission, sort of a sightseeing tour," Ramos said.

"Sure, lie to me. I'm not the one that's gonna die over there. If we make it at all, that is. You see those waves today?" He held out a hand to Ramos.

"Name's King Qan; my parents thought it would be nice to have royalty in the family, so that's the name that stuck. I'm captain of the *Gracey May*."

"Are you for hire?" Ramos asked.

"I sure am, and she's one of the best on the high seas, too. *Gracey* once saw battle in the sea war of Galk. I won her in a card game." King said, grinning with pride.

"That war was over a hundred years ago," Ramos said. "You captain a hundred-year-old warship?"

King's smile faltered.

"Sure, but that's nothing to do with how she'll handle out there." King pointed toward the sea. "I can get you to the Isle, but it'll cost you. I ain't free."

"How much?" Ramos asked.

King fixed Ramos with a shrewd expression and rubbed his chin as he thought for a moment.

"Five hundred drax." He spoke. "What? That's robbery," Dante said.

"No, we'll pay it," Ramos said. He placed a hand on Dante's shoulder to calm him. "Half now, the other half when we get there."

"Alright then. There's no harm in missing a payment if we're all dead. We can leave whenever you're ready," King said.

"There's a storm kicking up out there. Are you sure we should leave today?" Dante asked.

"Let me tell you something, boys. Those seas will never be any calmer than they are right now. There's a curse on the waters, you know. Why do you think it's called the Death Sea?" King asked.

"Tomorrow might be better," Mac said.

"We need to go, 'cause I got another paying gig in three weeks and gotta' be back here."

"In that case, can we leave in a few minutes?" Ramos asked.

"Sure, just need to get my crew, and we'll be off," King said.

He paid his tab and left the bar.

"You think we can trust him?" Mac asked Dante. "Well, if he tries to double-cross us, we'll bury him at sea," Dante said. "I think I'll have that drink now." Waiting was difficult, but they could enjoy a few hours of downtime. Mac was tired from the war with the Centaurs and longed for a week of dreamless nights after this was all over. The saloon patrons began to come and go, drifting in and out of the stormy town, while Mac's party stayed put. An hour later, King returned and signaled for the party to follow him.

"Sorry for the wait, but finding my men took me a minute. They were stuck in an all-night squipoker game." King said.

"What's squipoker?" Mac asked.

"It's a card game where they incorporate live bait and a chicken. It can get ugly; I'll explain it later." Dante said.

The adventurers rose from their chairs and followed King out the door, down to the harbor and the docked and waiting *Gracey May*. The crew consisted of a Minotaur woman and a reptilian man, both busy at work finishing preparations for the journey.

"Welcome to the *Gracey May!*" King said, smiling proudly.

The ship was a worn-down warhorse that seriously needed a carpenter's love. Her wooden hull needed repairs, and Dante could see the age of this once proud vessel.

"That's a death trap," Mac said. He turned toward his other traveling companions, who seemed perfectly at ease. "When in Rome, I guess."

"All aboard!" King said with a smile. The seas were choppy, with six-to-eight-foot swells just off the pier.

"This is going to be a wild ride," Ramos said. "But, what's life without a little adventure?"

In another hour, they were clear of the inlet and out into the deep waters of Death Sea. Up and down, *Gracey May* bobbed on angry, undulating waters until Mac leaned over the side and vomited. He grabbed the railing with a death grip, his pain, and nausea pushing him to madness for what seemed like days until the seas began to calm. At dusk, the sky turned a wild pinkish hue. As the sun faded to black a thick, grey fog rolled in from the north.

"Boys, things may get strange tonight. This kind of fog ain't normal out here. The last time I saw something like this, it was..." King said. He stopped short when they heard a high-pitched roar in the gloom. "That's bad."

"What was that?" Mac asked.

"If we stay quiet-like, it may go about its business and leave us alone," King said.

His crewmembers had drawn swords and were posted on opposite sides of the ship, so Dante and Ramos drew their crossbows, and Mac slid the plasma rifle off his shoulder and held it at the ready. The only sound was the waves lapping against the hull of *Gracey May* as they waited, breathless. Heightened tension among the crew and passengers seemed to freeze time until something moved under the water, off the port side.

"Of course, there's always the possibility that it may not leave us alone after all," King said.

"What? What won't leave us alone?" Mac asked. "The eelk," King said.

"The eelk, what's that?" Ramos asked.

"An enormous flesh-eating creature. Fun at parties and get-togethers," King said. The sea was still as they drifted in silence, rocking and creaking in the gloomy darkness.

"Maybe it went away," Dante whispered.

As if in answer to Dante's statement, a giant tentacle lashed out from the fog, shot past Dante's head, and wrapped around the reptilian crewmember's torso, yanking him off the boat.

"Yaaaaaaaaaghh!" The reptilian screamed, and then all was silent once more. Not even a splash could be heard.

"This deal just keeps getting worse all the time," Mac said.

Another one whipped past Mac, but his reflexes were fast, and he fell back while squeezing off a shot that ripped the tentacle in two. The beast uttered a loud scream, and to everyone's surprise, the fog bank began to lift, giving them visibility of the monster. Mac judged the size of the eelk to be at least fifty feet tall, if not larger, and as he stood on the deck looking up, the eelk discharged a rumbling roar. Its lower body was that of a fish, but the torso was a series of gnashing toothy mouths, each one atop the other, with hundreds of sharp teeth. Surrounding the mouths was a nest of tentacles, wriggling and squirming like snakes. On top of the torso were two large eyeballs on stalks, looking down at the ship. Mac quickly fired and hit one of the eyes with his rifle. The charge entered the eelk's left eye, splattering it with a sickly pop. Thick green goo flew as the monster thrashed in pain. A tentacle whipped Mac's foot, sending him to the deck. In the blink of an eye, he turned wolven form, dropped his rifle, and grabbed hold of the tentacle as it wrapped around his waist.

The eelk pulled him off the boat, waving Mac through the salty sea air as he involuntarily screamed in terror. Gaining control, he sliced down with his claws and pulled himself free of the tentacle, diving away from the eelk. It had been trying to move him closer to its gnashing mouth, filled with teeth. Mac dived through the air like a trapeze artist and crashed hard into the deck of *Gracey May*.

"I am not on the menu." He spoke.

Mac rolled to the side, trying to get to his feet as the ship tossed and bobbed from the commotion of the eelk. It slammed into the hull with its massive tail, knocking a hole in the side of *Gracey May*.

Dante and Ramos were firing crossbow bolts at the eelk, and as each one entered, it seemed not to affect the creature looming over them. Next, the Minotaur woman was knocked overboard by the enraged eelk's tentacles. Ramos reached for her hand, but it was too late. She slipped through his grasp and was swept to her doom by a crashing wave.

"Enough!" Dante said and began to climb one of the masts as the ship tottered side to side. The eelk swept down with mighty blows into the water, causing massive tidal waves to erupt and crash onto the *Gracey May*.

Mac saw what Dante was attempting and quickly thought of a distraction.

"Hey, ugly! Down here!" Mac said. He was screaming, and the eelk moved closer to the ship.

One decimated eye stalk hung like overcooked spaghetti as the other eye focused on Mac.

Dante reached the top of the mast and ran out onto one of the supports while Mac distracted the beast, waving his arms and jumping up and down. Suddenly, Dante dived off the mast and into one of the mouths of the eelk.

The eelk was so surprised that as Dante passed through his teeth, it never thought to bite down, and he rolled right on unharmed. Dante landed inside the eelk's throat, swimming around in a pool of disgusting, malodorous phlegm. Wasting no time, he dived down and found the entrance to the eelk's stomach, where a thin patch of flesh was blocking his access. He ripped through the barrier with his sharp claws and tumbled into the stomach cavity. The air inside was so putrid that he struggled not to wretch. With quick movements and precision, he jumped into a pool of putrescence and body parts, leftovers from the eelk's earlier victims, one of them being the shredded carcass of the reptilian shipmate taken by the eelk.

Dante swam through the pool of bile, ocean water, and filth to the stomach wall, where he ripped a hole in the lining. The contents of the eelk's stomach emptied into its body cavity. Now, he had access to the outer wall of the elk's flesh.

With a violent swipe and a bellow of rage, Dante tore into the eelk's submerged body, creating a hole large enough to fit through. As a muffled roar vibrated through the eelk's innards, Dante was knocked backward by a flooding rush of freezing ocean water. It filled the eelk's open body cavity, weighing it down and making it impossible for the sea monster to continue the fight. It began to sink as Dante swam through the opening and into open water. The eelk sunk to the bottom of the Death Sea like a rock.

Dante popped his head above the waves, only to find a mortal wound on the side of the *Gracey May*. There wouldn't be much time; she was going down too fast. Everyone except King Qan jumped into the tumultuous, freezing seawater while Dante struggled to clear the sucking gravitational pull of the eelk as it descended to the depths below.

"Dante! You made it!" Ramos said.

"You're not getting rid of me that easily, big brother!" Dante said. Dante's fur was matted with gore, and he was spitting out seawater while fighting to keep afloat.

King Qan cursed the eelk for his misfortune, his dead crew, and the ruination of his only source of income as the Death Sea filled *Gracey May*.

"Jump into the water, King!" Ramos said. "You're going to die!" Mac said.

King gave Ramos one last look, and disappeared below deck, uttering a book's worth of curse words. A moment later a trapped air bubble within the ship burped to the surface, the final catalyst in her sinking. King was never seen again.

The water became still once more as Ramos, Dante, and Mac floated in the dark. Strangely, the fog began to clear, and the moon glistened over the cold water, lighting their way.

"What a great start we're off to," Dante said. "Make jokes, but we'll drown out here without a boat. Ugh, you stink." Ramos said.

"You dive into the belly of a sea monster and fight your way out. See how you smell." Dante said.

"Ugh, I lost the rifle," Mac said.

"The crossbows are gone as well," Ramos said. After about twenty minutes of treading water, the sea began to bubble around them again.

"Something is coming!" Ramos said.

"I wonder what this monster will look like," Dante said.

"Let's get back-to-back, so it can't surprise us," Ramos said.

"What if it just comes straight up from the bottom and eats us in one bite?" Dante said.

"Can you keep your unpleasant thoughts to yourself, please?" Mac said.

Several tense seconds later, the head of a large fish rose from the water, followed by a massive metal body and large metallic dorsal fin. Water spilled out of the gills, dumping the ballast onto the water's surface, splashing as the fish breached.

"It's a, uh," Mac said. He was about to finish the sentence when a lid popped open at the top, and a green man appeared. "Submarine?"

The green man must have been something between a fish and a lizard. He had large black eyes, gill slits on the side of his head, a narrow lipless mouth, and a dorsal fin atop his head. Mac had a flashback to a show he had seen as a child called Land of the Lost, and in it, there were creatures called Sleestaks. This man reminded him of the underground-dwelling reptilians from that TV show. "Come aboard, friends! You've killed an eelk!

You're lucky I was able to find you, or you'd have been dead before too long." The green thing said.

"Who are you?" Ramos asked.

"My name is Carp. Come aboard before you drown, or a shark finds you interesting." Carp said. "I don't think I want to see their versions of sharks," Mac said.

The others nodded and swam over to a rope ladder Carp was tossing over the side of his submarine.

"Welcome to the HMS *Farley*, our king and queen's most prized vessel. I was ordered to find survivors after we saw your ship sink." Carp said.

Mac was first up the ladder, then Dante and Ramos. They stood atop the metal sub, and Mac marveled at its size. It rivaled any of the accomplishments in submarine technology he had seen back on Earth. The longer Mac was on Eritria, the more amazed he became at her people's resources and technology.

"Your submarine is a work of art," Mac said. "She sure is. I'm afraid I can't take credit, but I always appreciate some flattery." Carp nodded, smiling.

"Let's go below deck, my friends. King Rashi and Queen Shalish want to meet you." Carp said.

Carp led them down a long ladder to an empty crew bunk area, and they followed him through several passages until they came upon a grand banquet room in the middle of the submarine. A tall reptilian man sat on a golden throne next to a regal lady who was a little smaller than the man. She gazed upon the three wolven men as she sat upon her throne of gold inlaid with delicate jewels. They both shimmered with light green scales along their arms beside a yellowish horizontal chest plate. They wore no clothing except for the adornment of jewelry around their necks and wrists.

Mac stared into their golden-yellow, snakelike eyes, each dotted with a small black pupil. They were beautiful and elegant, with an air of ancient royalty. The wisdom in their gaze hinted that they were older than they looked. Carp picked up an ornate brass phone connected to a tube on the wall and spoke into it as the king and queen sat in quiet solitude.

"Six thousand years, earth man." Queen Shalish said. Dante shot Mac a puzzled look, asking *what did you just do?*

"I'm sorry?" Mac replied.

"We have been alive for over six thousand years." "You read my mind."

"When you've been alive as long as we have, you learn a few tricks." She replied.

"Thank you for slaying the eelk." King Rashi said.

"After you get cleaned up and have something to eat, we can talk about how you can get your cosmic portal back from Asura now that he has stranded you here, Colonel MacDonald." Queen Shalish said.

"Yes, and how you can help us return the Tablet of Destinies to its altar, restoring balance to Eritria." King Rashi said.

Mac and his friends were escorted to luxurious rooms lined with mahogany, where they could bathe, relax, and center their minds. Sweet and decadent incense burned in a holder on his dresser, perfuming the air with thick, musky smoke. Mac watched a single winding smoky tendril dance with effortless grace to the ceiling and spread out like the breath of a dragon. Mac sat on his bed, took a deep breath, lowered his head, and missed Carol more than ever.

CHAPTER 2

TEN MINUTES AFTER MAC SAT on his bed, he was fast asleep and dreaming. In his dream, he stood alone at the bottom step of his ranch house porch with the oppressive summer sun beating upon him. The world took on a hazy, wavering visage. A high- pitched whir of cicadas in the sugar maple trees broke the stone silence of a hot Midwestern afternoon. Mac's farmhouse was the same as he remembered before the mission to Zeta Reticuli, but an acrid, sickening, sweet odor of rotting meat wafted to his nostrils, filling him with sick dread.

The lightning-split tree stood alone on the hill, but their cows were all dead and piled around it. They lay in haphazard, twisted positions as if posed by the hands of a maniac. Flies buzzed hungrily above the decaying corpses in a free-for-all breeding ground. Mac stepped forward on feet made of lead and saw Bobby kneeling before a deceased heifer.

His son was weeping into his hands and had his back turned toward Mac as he approached his troubled child. Hands outstretched to Bobby; Mac saw them through tunnel vision as the rest of the dreadful scene faded. The closer he came, the more he heard Bobby cry for his mother and sister. His feet dragged along the ground like they had been encased in cement, just a few more feet. Mac reached out, placing a hand on his son's shoulder, and the boy jumped. Bobby raised his head and let his hands drop to his sides.

"It's alright. We can figure this out together. I'm here," Mac said. His words were slow and awkward. Bobby started to turn, and Mac prepared for a big hug, but his eye sockets were empty when his son faced him.

"They did this to all of us!" Bobby said.

Mac pinwheeled backward, tripping over a dead cow leg, sprawling in the dust, and staring into the reddish pink, gaping holes where Bobby's blue eyes once were.

"You let them all die, all those people. Why dad? Why did they put me in a barrel?" Bobby said. "I...I...I'm sorry, Bobby. I had no choice." Mac said, stammering.

An Egyptian asp slithered out of Bobby's gaping mouth, and then his son fell dead into the dust. "No!" Mac said.

In the distance, Mac could see a large pyramid on the horizon, and as he stared, it became larger, drawing nearer until his poor, dead, eyeless son and the cattle ranch massacre vanished. Mac was sitting beneath the largest pyramid he had ever seen, gazing at a triangular solid crystal capstone atop the megalith. Prismatic light glimmered within this fantastic jewel, and then a single beam shot into space, blinding his vision.

Mac shot up in bed terrified, wolven once more, sweat matting his fur, claws digging through the sheets and into the plush mattress. He was panting heavily. What was that dream about? The ranch and pyramid began to fade like clouds of cream in coffee, but he could still see Bobby's eyeless gaze and hear the accusation in his voice. The images of all those people he and his team condemned whirled around his mind in a tapestry of horror. He looked around his room to gain stability once more and tossed his feet over the side of the bed just as a knock came to the thick wooden door.

"Sir, you're requested at a banquet in your honor." A woman's voice said.

"I'll be right there," Mac said.

A banquet? He shook his head and tried to get his bearings.

He dressed in his leather pants and a black biker- style vest left for him on a chair in the corner. Mac looked in the mirror, cleared his mind, and opened the door to see a naga female standing before him. She was reptilian and fascinating, with a spine that ran from the top of her head to the base of her back. Mac thought she resembled a dimetrodon dinosaur on two legs. She curtsied before him.

"Good evening, Mac. I am Relathora, headmistress to the queen." She spoke softly. "Nice to meet you, Relathora. Are the others up and around?" Mac asked.

"Oh yes, we are awaiting your presence to begin eating. You've come from so far away and had such little rest since arriving here from your planet." Relathora bowed her head. "Right this way, commander."

Mac followed Relathora down a long wood panel hallway that smelled like lemon furniture polish and reminded Mac of fine upscale libraries. The floor was tiled with smooth ceramic squares, each depicting the diversity of aquatic life on Eritria. Fish, turtles, sea anemones, squid, whales, sharks, and it was as if, at any minute, the floor Mac walked on could pull him in. A portal on the wall showed the darkness of the Death Sea outside, and for a moment, Mac felt the entire ocean on top of him as they moved through silent shadows.

One corridor met another, and he wondered how big this submarine had to be because it did not look this vast from the outside when they were on top of her.

"This submarine seems to be getting larger." "Oh yes, she is the largest in our fleet and was designed by our master engineer, Stelos. Some have become lost here and never found. The corridors are a maze that only trusted aids of the king and queen know the secret to. It's a security measure to keep enemies from locating their royal chambers."

A magic submarine, Mac thought, and then the song Yellow Submarine by the Beatles began to play in his head. *So, we sailed up to the sun 'til we found the sea of green, and we lived beneath the waves in our yellow submarine.* He laughed out loud.

"Something funny, sir?"

"No, sorry. Just thinking of back home and the land of submarines." Mac answered.

They rounded another corner, and he could see two double doors closed against them. Beyond was the gay sound of laughter and clanging glassware. Relathora opened one of the doors and allowed him to enter a lavish dining room with a long oak table stacked with various kinds of food, from grapes and apples to a stuffed pig that Dante was carving. Ramos was talking to Queen Shalish and relaying a story of some shenanigans Dante, and he had gotten into years ago that got them in hot water with Gregor. Mac guessed it must have been a lively tale since she was throwing her head back in laughter. Dante was busy conversing with the king and explaining their plight thus far when Mac walked in and sat down at the end of the table.

"Welcome to the party, sunshine!" Dante said. He had a bottle of mead beside him on the table and was already beginning to slur his speech.

"How long was I asleep?" Mac asked.

"Longer than an hour and shorter than a week," Ramos said, hiccupping. He was drunk and half- lidded as he turned his attention back to Queen Shalish.

"Welcome, Mac!" King Rashi said. He waved to one of his servants to pour Mac a drink.

"What are you drinking? Is it that stuff you gave me when I first got here that was a bad night for the team if I remember correctly." Mac asked.

"No, thizz iz shroup, made from fermented seaweed and bananas. Good stuff, man." Dante said. One of the servants gave Mac a full bottle, and as he drank, he was amazed at how much it tasted like apricots.

"This is damned good," Mac said.

"Now that everyone is here, we can eat and discuss business," Queen Shalish said. Mac, by the way, carried herself, and she got the feeling that this lady was the one to impress.

"Relax, Colonel MacDonald. You've had a long journey and are among friends," a voice inside his head said.

The Queen was looking right at him and smiling while the others talked and drank, so Mac picked up his drink and took a large gulp. The moment the shroup passed his tongue, he felt his awareness increase, like looking at an ant under a microscope and hearing every conversation in the room amplified in his head. His heart rate increased, and he felt exhilaration just before the shroup began to cause him hallucinations.

"Not again!" Mac said.

"Gentlemen, we have important business to discuss and—since nothing happens by chance— you are all here as part of a greater plan by the creator. I'm going to be blunt. We need you three to enter the underworld of Valuria and search for the Tablet of Destinies." She said, her smile faltering.

She shook her head, looking at the table. "What's wrong?" Mac asked.

"What underworld?" Ramos asked.

"I don't do anything for the greater good," Dante said, and his face hit the table. A second later, he was snoring.

"Valuria is where the Tablet of Destinies was lost to us long ago and our ability to balance the planet's energies with it. It is the heart of this world, and it must be returned to the Tower of Kail to survive, Ramos."

"We defeated Ragnok and restored peace to Eritria, so how could this tablet fix anything?" Ramos asked.

"How many races of Eritrian's do you know of?" "Gregor has told us that the ancients came down from the sky and created four hundred or more races from the creatures evolving on this planet," Ramos said and shrugged.

"How many do you know of that exist on Eritria today?"

He thought about it for a minute. "Well, Minotaur, molemen, fairies, us wolven, reptilians, um Krill, the ice giant..."

"You can't name twenty, can you? We are all dying or reverting to our previous forms, which concerns the Tablet of Destinies. Star travelers brought tablets here.

When it was, the creators made us all to protect and guard the source of their power. Over time, their lessons were forgotten, and the people of Eritria lost their understanding of the tablet's true power."

"Is this tablet a magical artifact?" Mac asked.

Yes, and it is said that whoever holds the tablet controls the universe. Millions of years ago, there was a great war far from here, in another galaxy, between three powerful gods, but we only know pieces of the tale. Anu, Tiamat, and Marduk were powerful beings who traveled the stars carrying many devices used for planetary construction.

Among them was a set of tablets that contained enormous energy, but the three disagreed on who should control the tablets, and a quarrel began, which turned into a war. Theirs was an epic space- based war that destroyed planets with its violence. Seeing that the power was too great for any of them to control, Marduk eventually won the tablet and came here to hide it from his people. The wise followers of Marduk created us and gave us the gift of society and knowledge of our world. For a long time, our races were one culture working together for the betterment of all species. The planet prospered as a result.

That is, until one day, the tablet vanished, and the light of the pyramids faded. Instability followed, eventually leading to the downfall of the great cities. We were all plunged into a dark age, but by then, Marduk had gone, leaving only his promise to return. We're still waiting."

"But what happened to the Tablet of Destinies?" Ramos asked.

"I have sight into many areas of Eritria, but Valuria is a magical land forbidden even to my vision. I know that the tablet is down there somewhere, and if restored to the Tower of Kail, a new day will dawn on Eritria."

"If you know this, why don't you get it yourself?

Why wait for us to happen along?" Mac asked.

"That's a fair question commander. We're not warriors and never have been, and the inhabitants of this submarine are all that is left of our people. Without the tablet, we are unable to reproduce and are reaching extinction. There is also the issue of the ick to deal with," the king said.

"Ick is the result of the reptilians meddling in dark magic that they neither learned to control nor understood, and it is slowly darkening our planet." Queen Shailesh said.

"We have been flourishing; I just don't understand it. The Wolven have puppies every day, right, Ramos?" Dante said his focus was swimming back and lifted his head from the table.

"When was the last time a puppy was born to your people?" Queen Shailesh asked. She fixed them with a thoughtful expression.

"It's been..." Ramos started.

"About thirty years?" Queen Shailesh asked. Dante and I...were the last. I guess we never paid any attention to it," Ramos said, his concern growing.

"Right, and without the pyramid technology that created all of us, many other species have either reverted to their former animal forms or become extinct. The land of Oblivion, once known to us as the Fairy Lands, used to be part of the Faerie Glenn before the reptilians and centaurs began mucking around with their foul magic, and now any living creature that enters that territory is doomed to a tragic mutated existence and then death, because of the ick. It is a cancer on the land and is spreading at an alarming rate daily. Without the rejuvenating light of the pyramids, it will continue to spread and may kill us all." King Rashi said.

"You may find what you see next disturbing, but the ick spreads to Wasatch Woods. The only reason it never spread your way is that Ragnok had centaur mages stationed at the four corners of the Fairy Lands casting a barrier spell to keep it in. The ick also threatened him, and Moktar would have been consumed by it first without containment." Queen Shailesh said.

"And now all those mages are dead," Dante said. "Ragnok called all his forces to battle. We were able to eavesdrop on a conversation with his shades shortly before the war, and he planned to let loose the ick if he lost the battle." King Rashi said.

"Total war. He'd let it all die if he couldn't own the world." Mac said. "We had similar tyrants back on Earth. It seems our worlds are not so dissimilar after all."

Queen Shailesh waved a hand, and they could see the ick creeping out of Fairy Glen to the southeast and closing in on Wasatch Woods.

"You have around thirty sunsets before this malevolent force overtakes your village, Ramos and Dante."

"Did Gregor know anything about this?" Ramos asked.

"He did and was working secretly with the council of elders for the races to keep from creating a panic. The Arcane Fist were working on a containment spell to rest just beyond Ragnok's when the war broke out, and their efforts were diverted, but now, it's too late. This is what is left of the Fairy Lands," Queen Shalish said.

She waved a hand, and a screen on the wall displayed a valley of bleak gray, where the trees were dead and dark clouds gathered above. Her eye traveled over the land, and the skeletal remains of people were all that was left to signify that there had once been a civilization living there. Mac thought it looked much like the war-torn cities back on Earth, and his heart sank.

Villages and towns were devastated, and a purplish-black tar-like residue covered most of their walls, sidewalks, and cobblestone streets. This goo reached out like long, dark fingers in places, and Mac could see the substance pulsing as if it were a living creature. Her vision panned across the land, speeding northeast through Fairy Glen and stopping at a wolven settlement outside Wasatch Woods.

The creeping death attacked the houses and barns, and people who touched the purplish black ick began twitching and wandering about shaking. It grew on their flesh, devouring them alive. A mass exodus was underway as people took what they could carry and fled the oncoming plague.

"Gregor died before he could tell us about this, right? Or would he have?" Dante asked.

"When the time was right, yes. There would have been no choice but, when Ragnok got hold of that device the humans brought to Eritria, he was sidetracked by that prophecy business." King Rashi said.

"Which turned out to be true if you think about it," Dante said.

Mac placed his drink back on the table, thinking he needed to start drinking water only on this planet. Everything fermented turned out to be a hallucinogenic cocktail for him, and then Carp entered the room a moment later.

"Hello, everyone. I was detained in the psychlorama and finally found the entrance to Valuria." Carp said.

With a nod from the queen, he took a chair at the table and saw the images of desolation on the screen before them, shaking his head.

"Oh, the faerie lands. Such a shame it fell to the ick." Carp said.

"Agreed, this is horrifying. And you say it'll spread worldwide, Queen Shailesh?" Dante asked.

"If it is left unchecked, yes. The dark magic that created it can be reversed if you successfully restore balance, my friends," the queen said. "OK, but I'm curious about that psycho...what?" Mac asked.

"The psychlorama is a room where we can see the entirety of our world and hunt for secret chambers and passages lost to time." the queen said.

"The entrance is inside a sunken temple in the Bog Lands of Eritria. A city had been built atop the cavern leading to Valuria a long time ago, and when the weight became too great, a terrific earthquake ensued, and it sank into the caverns."

"That sounds like the ruined city of Lavural, the cavern spirits told me about," Ramos said.

"Yes, that's right," Carp said.

"You will seek out the Temple of Ostrid and enter Valuria from there," the queen said.

"Do you mind if I join them on the quest?" Carp asked the king and queen. "You don't mind if I come along, do you?" He turned to Mac and Ramos. "Can you fight? I mean no offense, but I have yet to run into an area on this planet where a fight of some kind isn't right around the corner." Mac asked. Before his eyes, the naga man vanished into thin air. "I'm good at item retrieval in hostile or hard-to- get-to- locations, but I never fight unless attacked physically. What do you think?" Carp said. Mac could not see Carp until he moved, and even then, Carp was a shimmering outline of the chair, floor, and tapestry behind him.

"I'd say that's a useful talent," Mac said.

"Welcome to the cause," Ramos said. "Where'd he go?" Dante asked.

Carp rematerialized on the ceiling, hanging suspended by tiny suction cups on his feet and holding the blade of a twelve-inch knife three inches from Dante's throat. Dante looked up, smiled, and then yanked Carp off the ceiling with his knife arm. Carp yelped and hit the floor with a slap.

"You're in," Dante said. The naga picked himself off the floor and shot an indignant glance toward Dante was chuckling to himself.

They all looked at the king and queen, who were chuckling and shaking their heads.

"I'm just beginning to get used to this entertainment; it's been so long since we laughed. Go with them, Carp, and save our people from certain doom. When you return the world will be changed for the better, and we will laugh in the sunlight." Queen Shalish said.

Carp's face was twisted with a silly grin. "We've been down here for so long, and I'm desperate to return to the surface."

"Well, it's good to have four again and with your talent, Carp, we may have less difficulty getting that tablet back," Dante said, and he put back another stein of shroup. Mac shook his head and still hallucinating, sipped from a glass of water given to him by one of the servants.

"Are you kidding, that's some amazing trick, Carp. I want the ability to vanish at will!" Mac said. He was swaying back and forth as the shroup corrupted his mind.

"You've received enough abilities since your arrival here, earthman," Dante said, grimacing.

"I think my tongue just went numb," Mac said. He had a look on his face as if something were wrong.

"That's when you know the shroup working, commander." Queen Shalish said.

She laughed at Mac's condition and began to laugh harder when, a moment later, Mac turned wolven and smacked his lips together like a dog that had been fed peanut butter.

That night, Mac passed out with his room spinning around him. He dreamed he was sitting once more in the field with a large Minotaur sitting beside him while Bobby and Serena played with a moleman and laughed with each other on a sunny day in the plains. The Minotaur next to him was named Gesh; he knew this instinctively, and they had just returned home from the war with Ragnok. All was well in their world, but a rift formed in the field behind Serena and Mac. They watched a translucent bubble form a portal. It appeared first as the size of a beach ball and grew larger. Mac rose and moved forward, walking through the clear doorway between worlds and standing on a sandy shoreline looking up at a dark night sky. Clouds raced by obscuring a blanket of stars. Buildings behind him shone light from their windows as vacationers settled in for another night at their chosen vacation destination. Mac knew it was Myrtle Beach from the memories he had of being there as a child.

He stood on the sand, looking at the sky as the moon shone through with electric brilliance. He looked down a moment later, realizing the water had drawn far from shore, back into the sea, and he knew something was wrong. Fish and sharks floundered, flopping and writhing on the newly formed beach as moonlight shimmered and danced in small newly formed pools. In the darkness, he was unable to see or hear the ocean. Mac stood frozen, and then he heard a supernatural roar. A wall of water, so tall it blotted out the sky, was approaching like a locomotive from heck. A mile-high tsunami bore down on him, and he could only stand still and wait for the inevitable crushing blow. His doom was coming.

He saw the outline of an offshore oil rig in the wave, trapped by the momentum of an angry sea. The wave slammed into him with the force of a bomb blast, and in an instant, his body was drawn in as the Atlantic Ocean propelled him backward. His lungs burned as Mac struggled not to breathe in the killing salt water while he watched the strand hotels grow larger and closer, and then he slammed into the Avista Resort—a captive audience to the end of the world disaster movie.

The tsunami toppled man's modern engineering marvels like tinker toys under the force of the wave. Up and down the coast, this mammoth harbinger of death swept out across the land like a terrible water dragon destroying all in its path. Mac heard screams for a brief moment as vacationers met their brutal fate, and he felt soul-sick. The shroup kept him unconscious and trapped in the nightmare for the rest of the night. He was unable to wake up or turn away. Mac snapped awake in his bed, a puddle of drool below his face. He was in human form. Dante stood over him with questioning eyes. "Bad dream?" Dante asked.

"Sort of...vivid, horrifying," Mac said. He wiped sleep from his eyes and felt the first pangs of a shroup headache pound his temples. Dante handed him a glass with blue liquid inside.

"Here, drink this," Dante said.

"What is it, more shroup? I'm done with that stuff." Mac said.

"It's juice from the elderberry, and it'll help knock out the battering ram that's about to take over your head," Dante said and nodded toward the glass as Mac took it. "I know because it hit me about an hour ago."

Mac took the offer and sat on the edge of his bed.

"I had the most vivid dream just now. I was back home, on the beach, and..." Mac said and trailed off.

"What?" Dante asked.

"Nothing...just a dream," Mac said, giving Dante a wan smile.

"Carp told me a few moments ago that we're nearing Eritria, and they're dropping us off north of Last Resort," Dante said.

"Isn't that Libmok territory?" Mac asked. "Close, but we'll be further south of them and have a clear path around Moktar to the Bog Lands." Mac put the empty cup down and sat with his head in his hands.

"I need to see my kids, Dante. They're growing up without a mother, and I don't want them to lose their father as well." Mac said.

"Courage, my friend. I have complete faith in your ability to see this quest through. Then you will see your children again. All you should know for certain is that everything will be alright. No matter what happens when we reach Valuria, you have nothing to fear." Dante said.

He put his hand out, and Mac looked up. Smiling, he took Dante's hand, and the other pulled him to his feet.

"Let's go shake the pillars of heaven," Mac said. "You have a warrior soul, Mac. I underestimated you when this all began."

"Underestimated me, how?"

"I thought you'd be the first body I had to rake off the battlefield," Dante said. He grinned, and Mac shook his head.

"Happy to disappoint," Mac said.

A moment later, Ramos appeared in the doorway. "Am I interrupting some weird love ritual? I can come back when you're finished. We're surfacing, by the way," Ramos said.

Dante swung a haymaker at his brother, and as Ramos blocked with his forearm, he started laughing. Then Dante went in for a left hook, and Ramos stopped it with his fist, to which his brother moved in for a bear hug and got slapped in the face with a clawed hand.

"Whooooo, you got moves, but I'm better!" Ramos yelled.

"This is what I call some PGA. Can we please regroup with Carp?" Mac said.

"PGA?" Ramos said. Dante's head was under his arm, and the younger wolven was trying to break free while punching Ramos in the stomach. "Professional grab ass, earth term, sorry, carry on."

"No, we need to go." Ramos dropped Dante and led them through the winding passageways.

"You know the route through here?" Mac asked. "Yeah, Carp had me commit it to memory, so he doesn't have to lead us through every time," Ramos said.

"Not that I mind helping out," Carp said. Mac jumped visibly as the disembodied voice came from beside him, and then Carp materialized.

"What the heck!? Don't do that crap!" Mac said. He transformed to wolven as a defensive reflex. "I've never seen a white wolven before. You are remarkably interesting, you Earth people," Carp said.

"Yeah, well, not all of us transform. Trust me when I say you wouldn't want most Earth people to have this ability. I think the phrase to describe this is comfortable killers."

"I apologize for sneaking up on you, but sometimes I walk around these halls for days cloaked," Carp said.

Mac felt sorry for the naga and thought about his people, who were also on the brink of vanishing forever. Then, the dream of that giant tidal wave returned to him—rolling inland for hundreds of miles before crashing and moving away with millions of lives in its wake. If there was a way to fix his world, he was desperate to find it and return home; Mac missed all the beautiful things about Earth.

"Damn, I miss home," Mac said. "What?" Dante asked.

"Sorry, just thinking out loud," Mac said. Dante nodded and shrugged as the three followed Ramos around one corner after another until they came at last to the king and queen's chamber.

"We're here, gentlemen. Before you go, I have some gifts for each of you that will aid in your quest." Queen Shalish said.

"Your Highness, we need no gifts," Ramos said. "Speak for yourself," Dante said. Ramos cut his eyes at his brother.

"I'm giving you each a bracelet of pure ogridite. Ogridite is living matter, ancient and mystical, the remnants of a race of craftsmen that dwelled on this planet millions of years ago. They moved on and left behind artifacts of great power. These mysterious relics are buried all over Eritria and, if found, give the possessor great advantages."

They each took their bracelet, placed them on their wrists, and bowed to the queen.

"How's it work?" Mac asked.

"Since these were all cut from the same ogridite vein, they are matched, and you can see each other in your mind's eye wherever you are in the universe. Just close your eyes and think about the other you wish to locate. As far as we know, these are indestructible. We have no way of duplicating the technology used to create them. They are three of a kind."

The bracelets resembled granite hoops and were smooth with infused flecks of white crystal. The queen handed Ramos a jade green bracelet, Dante received an azure blue colored bracelet, and Mac was given an onyx bracelet. Ramos put his bracelet on and closed his eyes, thinking about his brother. He watched Dante turn his bracelet over in a flash, eyeing it with curiosity.

"It works!" Ramos said.

"Thank you for the gift, Queen Shalish," Dante said.

"Yes, thank you," Mac said.

"May your journey be safe and the trouble you find minimal." King Rashi said.

Carp, garbed in shorts, a short-sleeved shirt, and a small backpack, led them to the ladder leading up to the hatch, and they ascended the rungs. Once Carp opened the hatch, warm sunlight entered the round opening, blinding them momentarily. Each man stepped out of the hole into a brand-new day on Eritria. They were less than half a mile from shore, and as the sun beamed down on them, Mac felt a renewed sense of positivity. Birds soared overhead as a school of grey fish swam by the sub, hiding from the aerial predators. Past the beach was a thick forest they would have to navigate before reaching the plains and the Bog Lands.

"You guys ready to go for a swim?" Mac asked. "I'm ready to see an end to this little adventure and get home," Ramos said.

"You are such a liar! You live for this kind of thing, Ramos." Dante said.

"You're right. What else would I be doing now if not risking life and limb with you guys?" Ramos said.

"I'm glad to be a member of your party, gentlemen. I don't get out much, so thank you." Carp said.

"Let's get it done then," Mac said.

The four dived into a calm sea and swam to the shore. The perils waiting for them on the path ahead would take all their strength and ability to work together as a team. It was another day on Eritria, and anything was possible.

CHAPTER 3

COLD OCEAN WIND WHIPPED ABOUT the soaked adventurers as they washed up on the western Eritria shore, their fur matted with knots from the salt water. It was going to be an uncomfortable morning for the wolven. Carp was the only one of the group who emerged from the ocean without freezing; his green, scaled skin dried rapidly as he looked back at the submarine. It submerged, leaving him behind on a foreign shore with men he now realized he did not know very well. He was unsure whether they were the type that, if the quest should fail, would leave him dead. It was his first time away from home. Carp looked down at his ogridite bracelet, his birthright, and he felt the strangest sensation that he would never see his loved ones again. Ramos caught a glimmer of remorse and pain in Carps eyes and suspected his secret. The king and queen were

Carp's mother and father. He stood by the young naga man as Dante and Mac wrung their fur out.

"We're going to stink like dead fish when this dries!" Dante said.

"I smell like a dumpster; what's in that ocean?" Mac asked, wrinkling his wolven snout.

"Plankonites. They're tiny critters that live in the surf and eat dead things in the ocean. You have thousands of them on you right now. That smell is their excrement." Dante said. He chuckled as Mac coughed up a fur ball in disgust.

Mac had increased vision whenever he was in wolven form, and when he looked between the hairs on his right arm, his skin was crawling with microscopic white bugs squirming and biting. "Aaaaaggggghhh!" Mac howled. How do I get them off of me?"

"Calm down; they can't take the air. They'll all be dead in a few minutes." Dante said. "However, your reaction was priceless!"

"Well, excuse me for never having had alien maggots on my body. This is too much for me!" Mac said and looked to the surf as it rolled in. He wondered how many other surprises awaited them in this brave new world.

Ramos and Carp watched the tip of the royal submarine's dorsal fin vanish below the tide. "You'll see them again," Ramos said. He placed a hand on Carp's shoulder.

"The eelk you killed was not just any eelk. He was Grayclops, the commander of the eelk legion. I don't know how you did it, but killing him might have saved what is left of the naga. And maybe even our world. If we can find the Tablet of Destinies, that is." Carp said.

"We'll find it or die trying, Carp. If your parents are right, our fates rely on returning that artifact."

"How did you know they were my parents?" Carp asked.

"I could see it in your eyes," Ramos said. He looked to the right and saw the skeletal body of a medium-sized reptile.

"Watch this," Ramos said.

Purple light emanated from his palms in a mist, pushing toward the corpse. Tendrils of violet light wrapped around the bones. The skeleton floated from the ground, forming back into the three- dimensional structure it had once been in life. The skeletal construct was a lizard about the size of a Labrador, with an elongated head and two long, sharp front teeth extending past the lower jaw. It stood, shook its head, cocked it to the side, and looked over at Ramos with curiosity.

"Neat trick," Carp said.

"Want to name him?" Ramos asked. "You're bringing it with us?" Carp asked. "He can be yours," Ramos said.

"Why?" Carp asked.

"Everyone needs a companion."

"Hmm, alright. Glorg. That's his name." Carp said.

"Hey Ramos, whenever you're finished conjuring dead pets for people, can we get on the road?" Dante asked.

"Don't be jealous of my powers," Ramos said. He snapped his fingers at Glorg and motioned to Carp. The skeletal beast complied and trotted to his new master with clacking bones.

"So strange a gift. Thank you, Ramos." Carp said. "Feel better?" Ramos asked.

"Yes, you're right. Everyone needs a friend. I'm ready to go now. I've never been this far from my people before," Carp said.

"That's OK, me neither. Looks like you're in good company, my friend." Mac said.

"Alright! Let's do it!" Carp said. Glorg followed behind Carp with the excitement of a happy dog following his new owner.

The four of them turned from the shoreline and walked toward the woods. The sound of the ocean faded behind them, and soon, there were new sounds of birds and small creatures as they entered the forest through a grove of trees. Mac felt the little white plankonites falling off him by the hundreds like dandruff. It was cooler underneath the shade of tall trees where few feet had tread, and under their feet was a soft bed of pine needles, making the trek more comfortable. However, not everyone felt tranquil; ever since the queen's story about the ick, Dante and Ramos began to feel a sense of urgency. There would be no time to fail or get lost. The vast expanses of wilderness they had explored in their youth were in danger now, and entire sections of Eritria had been wiped out by the ick already. Now, their woodland home was threatened by this terrifying evil. They knew they would have to succeed or die.

A road opened to them about a hundred feet into the forest, and after the party members glanced at each other, they hopped out of the brush and onto the single-track dirt path. A treetop canopy strangled the sunlight, thick and high.

"Where do you think this path leads?" Carp asked.

"I dunno, hopefully, out," Mac said.

"The better question is, who cleared it?" Ramos said.

"What do you mean?" Dante asked.

"Look at how well maintained it is. No cobwebs or logs across the path. It looks like someone is keeping it up. The last time I was in here, I was attacked by Syrinx, a large, angry spider. That was not such a good time. She wrapped me in her web and tried to feed me to her brood of hatchlings. I nearly died that day, and if it hadn't been for my claws and wit, they would have killed me for sure." Ramos said.

"How'd you get out?" Mac asked.

"I carried a small crystal charm in my pocket at the time, showing any that look into it their worst nightmares. I found it in the tomb of the titan Epimetheus. Syrinx had me suspended upside down, and although the blood was rushing to my head, and her silk was like steel, I could shift a bit and grab hold of the charm. When she came close again, I pointed it at her face. Instead of seeing me, Syrinx saw a large terapod coming for her, not a terrified wolven youngster suspended upside down. She squealed and ran away, taking her wretched brood with her." Ramos said.

"You think she's still in there?" Mac asked. "It's possible," Ramos said.

Carp looked through the woods, his eyes widening as if they were in a haunted house.

"I don't like this place." He said and took a step back.

"Look what you did, Ramos. You scared Carp. Carp, it will be fine, and the sun will come out tomorrow. OK, motivational talk over, let's go." Dante said.

"No, there's something evil in these woods— ancient and angry darkness. I think we should turn off this path and move in another direction," Carp said, trembling.

Mac squinted down the road and saw a sign. "What's that?" He asked.

He trotted ahead to see what it was. The sign was a narrow piece of haphazardly cut wood nailed to a six-foot tall post. Two nails held it in place; one of them had been bent halfway in and pounded awkwardly flush with the wood. Carved into the sign was an arrow pointing east, and beside the arrows were three letters, VOZ, but they were crudely crossed out, and under them, written in dark red or black, were the words *belimh sadoran droggot.*

Chills swept through Mac as he read the words out loud. What could it mean? He felt intrigued but terrified at the same time. He quickly walked back to where the rest of the party stood.

"It looks like it's pointing to a town, but the name was scribbled out, and something else painted in dark red beneath," Mac said. "Or was that...blood?"

"Let me see," Ramos said. "Me too." Said Dante.

The four of them continued toward the sign, this time more hurriedly.

"Ah, I've seen that language before in Gregor's books. It is that of the wee folk, the faeries. I think it says, *death awaits all.*" Dante said.

"That's a cheerful thought," Carp said. "Well, I welcome a challenge," Ramos said.

"Of course, death awaits all. It lies ahead for all of us, eventually." Dante said. "This is a ridiculous sign. A practical joke, maybe?"

"I think it's a warning, guys," Mac said. "I suppose it could be a trap. Is it worth the gamble when we've got no time for diversions?" Dante said.

"Eh, let's go forward anyway. At the very least, it'll probably be a place to sleep for the night. The Bog Lands come alive with predatory creatures after the sunsets. It's best not to linger here." Ramos said. "Predatory creatures hunting us in a dark forest at night. Thanks, I'll take the creepy village with the stern warning over hanging out here." Mac said. "It's getting dark," Carp said. When they turned around, he was gone. Glorg shook his head, panting without a tongue.

"Carp, where'd you go?" Ramos asked.

"I'm right here. Self-preservation is nothing to be ashamed of." Carp said. His voice came from beside Mac, unseen.

The four walked on for another mile into the deep, dark woods of the northern Bog Lands. Around mid-afternoon, Dante spotted the first of several buildings in what must have been the town of Voz. Six tiny houses formed a semi-circle around a large chapel with closed wooden-shuttered windows.

"This must be a place of worship," Ramos said. Dime-sized raindrops began to fall through the treetops above, turning the dirt into slippery mud as the four walked closer, watching their steps and trying to be quiet. When they reached the first building, Dante looked closely at the door.

"They are worshipers of Baal. Their markings are on this house." Dante said.

Painted on the door's black surface in yellow was a pentagon with an inverted triangle wrapped with barbed wire in its center and a lidless eye within the triangle.

"There's nobody here. I don't hear anything within the vicinity of this town. But there is an acrid, rotten odor nearby." Ramos said.

"Maybe they abandoned this place. Or perhaps were eaten by your spider friends, Ramos." Mac said. Ramos shrugged.

The houses were small wooden cabins, and Mac thought they looked like great escapes from city life if they were on top of the Appalachian Mountains and not in the middle of a scary forest on a foreign planet where monsters were real.

"The door's locked," Carp said. Glorg sidled up behind them, his bones clacking audibly.

"One second," Dante said. He walked a single step and slipped his index finger into the lock. Wrinkling his snout and pressing his furry ear against the door, he played with the tumbler inside. After some fiddling, there was a tiny click, and the door swung open. Foul fumes stung their noses as the air released itself from inside the cabin.

"This must be a holding pen of some kind," Dante said—a groan emitted from the dark room.

"Please...help...us." A man's voice said.

Dante crept inside, the others following closely behind him, as the odor of rotting meat threatened to turn his stomach. He stared into the darkness, waiting for his eyes to adjust to the low lighting. Suddenly the picture became clear. Three half- wolven, half-lizard men helplessly dangled from the wall, emaciated, pathetic, and near death. Their bodies were clearly wolven, and they had long, pointed ears like Dante, but their maws and hands were reptilian, scaly, and smooth. Dante never thought he'd see a wolvacaran in the flesh; he thought they were only legends. They were rumored to be a failed genetic experiment by the makers, and banished to the island of Orion, far away from Eritria.

"You're a long way from Orion, my friend," Dante said. One of them nodded wearily.

"I don't mean to be rude, but could you cut us down from here before the little demons return?" One of the Scale Paw tribesmen asked, out of breath. Dante cut them down and helped drag one of the feeble men outside into the dark chapel's courtyard.

Mac and Ramos got the other two. "What's your name?" Dante asked.

"I'm Ort; the other two are Torl and Wiln." He spoke.

"How many others are there of you?" Ramos asked.

"We were thirty strong before they captured us, but I have no idea who is still alive, and I've lost track of the time. When we learned about the trouble with Ragnok, we knew we needed to answer the call, and travelled quickly to help our wolven brothers. But when we entered these woods, a strange mist fell upon our party, and we were knocked unconscious. When we awoke, we were here, chained to these walls. I don't know where the rest of my party is, the last of their screams went silent a few days ago. So, it may be just the three of us left."

"Who put you here?" Mac asked.

"Vexanon priests. That's what they told us they were anyway. They're little devils that feed on blood to survive. They look like pale little children, but they are monsters to be sure. The lot of them need to be burned. Many days ago, they began draining the three of us, and we've lost a lot of blood. I was certain we'd die before morning came, but now you're here, and we can leave."

"Where are they now?" Mac asked. He was concerned a ghoul would jump out at any moment. "Not until nightfall. They come here to sacrifice their victims and whatever blood they don't get from them has been coming from us." Ort said.

"Let's get the rest of your people and get out of here," Mac said.

"I'll check the other houses," Carp said, bolting into the darkness.

He ran to the next house and kicked the door in, but there was nothing inside but dried blood on the walls and hungry flies circling puddles of gore on the floor. Ramos searched another cabin and found two more wolvacaran. But they were already dead. Dante checked a few more houses and found them empty, so he walked around to the side of the chapel and stumbled upon a macabre scene.

"I found the rest of the wolvacaran," Dante called.

The others soon joined him, standing over a massive ten-foot-deep burn pit dug into the ground and filled with bodies. The charred remains of Ort's people were heaped together in a stack that still smoldered from the night before. The odor of charred flesh and hair wafted up to their nostrils. The putrid odor reminded Mac of a stray cat that had gotten caught in his car's engine one muggy summer day. Mac added this charnel pit to the library of images he wished he had never seen.

"This place is death," Ramos said, holding his nose. "We must go. Mac, can you carry Ort? I'll take Torl and Dante; you carry Wiln." Ramos said.

"My brothers. My poor brothers." Ort said, barely standing from exhaustion and grief.

"I'm sorry. But there's no time; the sun is already down." Dante said.

As they left the clearing, torchlight flickered through the trees, casting eerie shadows on the ground. They heard low voices as the firelight grew brighter.

"Vexanon priests are coming," Ort said.

"We have no idea how many of them there are, so I suggest hiding until they get here and then..." Carp said.

"I smell fifteen, maybe twenty coming this way," Dante said. His nose was in the air.

"I don't know about the rest of you, but I'm not hiding from these creatures. I'll stand and fight. Look at what they did to the wolvacaran!" Dante said. He was growling as the torchlights grew closer and the voices became louder.

"Dante's right. I'll not run and hide either." Ramos said.

"These things are ghastly little monsters. You might be underestimating them." Ort said.

The aging wolvacaran man was massaging a right arm riddled with tiny rows of puncture marks. Mac saw his arm and flashed back to the underground laboratory. His guilt was greater than any of them would ever know, and the human consciousness experiments that ultimately brought him to Eritria had taken a toll on his mind and spirit.

"Stand in the shadows and wait on my command to attack," Dante said.

Mac and the others melded into shadow as the first of the vexanon priests appeared. They were, as Ort had described, about two feet tall, with round heads and dark beady little eyes. Their heads were bald, and they had pointed noses and ears with thin dark lips. Their clothing seemed Victorian to Mac.

They wore tuxedos with capes wrapped around their necks as if they were going to a play and not a sacrificial ritual. In the center of their formation, four of them carried a girl with goat legs and horns atop her head. Dante knew her as a satyr, another one of the races he had only seen rarely in the previous decade. She wore a leather vest as her only garment and was beginning to stir as the vexanon circled in front of the chapel.

They lay her in the center, just below the steps, leading up to a large wooden set of double doors, the entrance to the chapel. As the female satyr woke up, she began to panic, trying to scream. A gag placed over her mouth muffled her protests as she fought against the ropes, binding her hands and hoofed feet together. Vexanon priests stood with their torches held high, muttering in guttural, impish voices as the leader stood before them and waved for them to be silent.

"Vex! You have all come to see the risen one awaken this night." He spoke. A hideous scowl twisted his menacing face, and the crowd hissed in agreement.

"We have collected the blood of so many slaves while our god waited for freedom. We release Baal from the Chaos Realm tonight, and he will rule this world! Baal waits inside the Chapel of Blood!"

"I hate to interrupt, but I think we've heard enough," Dante said.

He launched from the shadows and bore down on the vexanon leader, tearing his throat out in a single bite. Ramos acted quickly, following his brother, rushing to the bleeding body, and immediately resurrecting the corpse. Dante rose to rip another vexanon apart, his teeth glistening with black blood. His eyes were alive with battle fury, and an insane light burned within them. Mac felt a burning inside himself, like hot coals in his stomach as a feral rage exploded from deep within. He leaped forward, tearing at the little monsters as they ran in shock, surprised by the ambush.

Mac felt a surge of otherworldly adrenaline, which was canine, animalistic, and so powerful that he could ride the wave of this sensation for a week. Mac was tearing one of them apart when he saw another vexanon biting into his leg.

"Hey, watch the teeth!" Mac said.

Mac kicked the vexanon priest off his leg and into the chapel's double doors. The doors flew open under the weight of his body's impact. After he rolled around, the little man got his bearings, took one angry look at Mac, and disappeared inside. "Yeah, run!" Mac yelled. "I'm coming to get you, little guy."

Carp, invisible, approached and knelt beside the frightened satyr girl.

"I'm here to help; just remain still," Carp said. "Mmmmmppphhhhh!" She mumbled. The satyr was struggling and began screeching.

"Call attention to us, and you'll be as dead as they wanted you to be in the first place," Carp said.

She stopped squirming and settled down. Carp reached forward, cutting her gag and bindings with his knife, and then grabbed a hand as she got to her feet.

"Thanks, I'm Sarna, whoever you are, wherever you are," Sarna said.

"I'm Carp. Watch out!" Carp said.

A severed vexanon head flew through the air and whizzed by an inch from her nose as she leaned out of the way. More vexanon had joined the battle. They could hear the groaning and twisting of wood from within the chapel as if the building were being torn in two.

"Did you hear that, Mac?" Dante asked.

There were two vexanon wrapped around his legs, biting him, while he strangled one in his fist, choking the life out of it. Bloody and bruised from battle, Dante threw the dead vexanon from his clenched fist and kicked the other two off him.

"This is fun. I could raise an entire army of the undead with these little guys!" Ramos said. He had been resurrecting them one after the other to fight against their brethren. Tiny, shambling ghouls followed Ramos' telepathic commands to attack.

"Something's happening inside the chapel," Mac said.

"I hear it, too," Ramos said.

Ramos saw the satyr kicking the vexanon and beating them with a fallen branch. Carp was nowhere to be seen, Dante had been holding his own, and Mac was standing over a pile of dead bodies. The courtyard was about a fifty-fifty split of undead versus living vexanon. Puddles of black blood pooled around tiny monsters as they fell.

"You know, Dante, you may have wanted to wait until the little guy in charge finished what he said before charging in. Now we have no idea what's about to happen." Ramos said.

"Good point; I'll take that under advisement next time," Dante said. He shrugged and dropped to his knees, crushing the skulls of the two vexanon wrapped around him.

"Hey, guys, the court's clearing out," Mac said. "Baal has come!" Said a fleeing vexanon priest. The vexanon had stopped their attacks and were melding back into the darkness. A gut-wrenching screech of wooden floorboards being stretched and torn apart came from the half-open door. It sounded like the chapel was about to fall in on itself. The three wolven and satyr were alone in the courtyard, the only movement coming from Ramos' undead infantry as they wandered stupidly around, stopping to feed on the dead.

"Guys!" Mac said.

He had been approaching the double doors when they exploded outward in a shower of splinters. A three-inch long splinter stuck halfway into his right bicep.

"Aaaagh! Son of a...!" He shouted.

A howl suddenly erupted from the darkness inside as Mac stepped back, pulling the splinter out of his arm. Two large gray hands, with long, jagged nails at the end of each finger, reached out and took hold of the doorframe. And then, a massive oval- shaped head appeared with pale yellow eyes, a crusty, diseased hollow where the nose had been, and a wide, snarling, evil grin curling at the corners. This creature resembled the clowns Mac had so feared as a child. It laughed through clenched, blackish teeth and shook as green drool dripped slowly to the porch.

"Um, I think this may be the Baal guy they were talking about," Mac said.

The creature's head moved forward, attached to a long, muscular, grayish-black neck and shoulders more expansive than the doorway.

"It's time to donate to the chapel, boys and girls. Now, where did my little vexanon friends run off to?" Baal said. He seethed in hatred. His shoulders were so broad that the monster had to twist to the side to release one arm and the other.

"Shouldn't we attack this thing or something?" Mac asked. He was backing away with slow, careful steps.

"Nah, where's the fun in that? Let's wait until it gets out and then we have a fair fight." Dante said. Ramos stood looking thoughtfully with his right hand on his chin and the elbow in his left hand. "You'd think they could have conjured you in a place that was more easily escapable," Dante said.

As if in answer, the Chapel of Blood collapsed on itself as the monster rose to his feet.

Standing thirty feet tall, looming over them, was the risen god Baal. He was lanky, skin and bones with an odor of sulfur and swamp moss. He held a morning star in his right hand. Baal wore a dirt smeared loincloth around his waist, and he glared at them with menacing hatred and an eagerness to fight.

"Time to die, boys!" Baal said.

With that, he raised the morning star overhead and, as he attempted to bring it back down, the large, spiked metal ball got stuck in a tree.

"Whaaaa...!" Baal said. "Now!" Ramos yelled.

Dante was the first to launch forward. Mac followed him as they ran for the demon's legs, claws out and teeth bared. Dante smashed a fist into Baal's left leg, breaking the femur, but as he pulled back, the demon swung down with his right fist, connecting with Dante's head, sending him reeling. Dante landed ten feet away, stood, and wavered back and forth, momentarily stunned. Mac punched the creature on his right side, and Baal wrenched the morning star free of the tree branches.

"You're going to pay the price for breaking my leg, little man!" He spoke.

Baal thrust the morning star down, missing Dante, but it landed with so much force that it knocked him onto the ground again. Ramos, still standing back, ordered his undead platoon of vexanon after Baal. Mac grabbed onto the arm holding the morning star, but Baal quickly swatted him away like a fly. The vexanon ghouls began biting on Baal's ankles and knees, gnawing through his thick flesh, forcing him to howl in pain. Mac got to his feet and ran forward to punch Baal once more. Just then Sarna came running out of the woods like she was on fire, holding in her hands a big stick, sharpened to a point on one end. With Baal distracted, Sarna sprinted forward and leapt into the air, brandishing her makeshift javelin.

She performed two forward rolls mid-air, and when Baal looked up, it was too late for him to react. He had been getting ready to attack the biting vexanon with his morning star when Sarna slammed into his chest with both hooves and struck down with her deadly stick. The pointed end made its mark and sunk into Baal's chest as her momentum carried the two of them to the ground, with Baal tumbling backwards. The morning star hung loosely in a tree just above where they fell, and the giant spiked ball was slipping on the chain.

Sarna landed with her legs straddling the monster's midsection, and before Baal could get back up, she pulled the stick out and thrust it down once more into his neck. Black ooze, stinking with grave rot, leaked out of the fresh wound, shimmering in the torchlight. Baal fixed her with a hateful gaze as he struggled to speak, his hands clawing at a ruined windpipe.

"Why won't you die!" Sarna screamed. "Grrrr, blllccch," He grunted.

She pulled the stick out of his neck and jammed it up underneath its chin and into the brain. The hideous monster stopped moving, his arms limp, legs twitching, and then perfectly still.

"I killed it! This thing murdered my whole family, and I finally killed it!" Sarna said.

She turned around, smiling at the others, just as the spiked ball above her head broke free of its restraints. Sarna had no time to react, and as a spike from the morning star rammed down into the top of her cranium, she fell underneath the large, spiked sphere. Sarna was gone as quickly as she had come into their lives.

"What in the heck just happened?" Mac Yelled. "She was the victim of outrageous fortune," Dante said.

Carp reappeared beside them, shaking his head in sorrowful disbelief.

"She got her revenge. At least she left satisfied." Ramos said.

"Ashes to ashes, dust to dust. May your soul go west in peace." Mac said, bowing his head.

Dante dug into his satchel for the funeral powder. He quickly sprinkled it over Baal and Sarna's bodies, and they watched as the two exploded in blue flames, turning to ash in minutes.

"We have to get going. Ort, has anyone survived?

Will you come with us?" Ramos asked.

"I'm afraid my friends died during the battle. But I'll go with you as far as I can. Where are you heading?"

"A place called Valuria. The entrance is somewhere in the Bog Lands."

"Are you talking about the sunken temple of Ostrid?" Ort asked.

"That's right!" Mac said.

"My people abandoned that region long ago after an earthquake rocked Lavural, our city, to the ground. It destroyed our home, so we fled to the island of Orion to rebuild."

"As students, we were taught that the earthquake you experienced was a fault over an entrance to Valuria," Carp said. Dante cut his eyes at the naga prince.

"At some point, you are going to have to get some balls and help us fight," Dante said. Carp averted his eyes and said nothing, but Ort sensed the tension and spoke next.

"I know where the sunken temple is. I can show you how to get in." Ort said. "But first, I need some food and sleep."

"Excellent, let's post a watch every three hours and get some sleep before moving on," Ramos said. "Let's cook these little critters and see how they taste," Mac said. He kicked one of the limp vexanon bodies.

After roasting four of them on a spit over a fire, Mac concluded that the vexanon priests did taste a lot like chicken but left a greasy, oily aftertaste. Mac curled up on the ground, exhausted from their fight, and fell into a hard sleep. In his dream, he was human and standing on the plains next to the wrecked hulk of his ship, the *Poseidon.* A maroon- robed figure was walking toward him. The sun shone, and a gentle breeze played on the tall grass as the figure approached. Mac tried to turn, but his feet would not move. The figure came closer. As the figure stood before him, he removed his hood. Mac smiled.

"Gregor, I'm glad to see you. This place is strange; my feet won't move." Mac said.

"Colonel, I've come to warn you," Gregor said.

His expression was grave.

"Why, what's happened?" Mac asked.

"The ick has contaminated a river that flows into Wasatch Village, the Chin River. It is the only river that runs from south to north from an underground ocean of fresh water. Its source is the Faerie Lands, and three days ago, the ick reached that water supply. Your little girl was out with Stephanie and drank some of the poisoned water."

"Oh no! I have to get back to my daughter! Is there anything that can be done? What's going to happen to Serena?" Mac asked.

"The ick's effects seem to work slower on humans than Eritrians, but it will be too late if she's not cured within the next two weeks. That is what the elders told me, and it is all I can tell you." Gregor said.

Gregor stood next to Mac and waved his left hand in the air. When he did, a magical window showed Stephanie Brandt and Serena sitting beside the Chin River while Serena stooped down and slurped a handful of the water. As the dream camera panned closer, Mac could see tiny black specks in the water that were moving like amoebas. Mac reached out to touch his daughter and warn her, but he could not pass his hand through the magical window. Serena drank as Stephanie watched to ensure the little girl did not fall into the water. Mac was screaming for Serena to stop, but it was of no use.

"How do you know this? Where am I?" Mac asked.

"You are in the place between worlds. I've come to remind you to be diligent in your quest, Colonel

MacDonald before this foul disease affects all on Eritria." Gregor said.

Gregor placed a hand on Mac and motioned for him to outstretch his right arm. Mac complied, and Gregor scratched him on the palm. When he was finished, there was a red X on Mac's palm, and then the elder wolven smiled at him wearily and vanished. Mac suddenly began to panic. What was happening to him?

Mac sat up, sweating and disoriented. Ramos instantly sat up as well. The two stared at each other, confused. Dante had been on watch and saw the whole exchange.

"What's wrong with you two?" Dante asked.

"I just dreamed that Serena drank water from the river flowing into your forest and it was poisoned with ick. I think it's real. She might die if we don't hurry." Mac said.

"I had a similar dream, Mac. In mine, the people of our village were writhing in pain, and the ick was consuming their flesh." Ramos said.

"I don't believe any of it. You were dreaming. Go back to sleep or take my watch. I'm exhausted." Dante said.

Ramos and Mac both held their right palms up, and each had an X scratched into the surface.

"No dream," Ramos said. "Gregor?" Mac asked.

"I don't understand it, but it must have been," Ramos said.

"We need to move in the morning and get this done. I have a bad feeling." Mac said.

"Well, this is another pile of crap. How can this get worse? Is the sky going to fall in on us?" Dante said.

"It's better not to ask those questions, little brother. The universe is listening." Ramos said. He and Ramos lay back down and forced themselves to go back to sleep while they could. Dante shook his head and thought about how much he just wanted to wake up in the morning and not have some vicious dilemma to ponder or vile monster to kill.

CHAPTER 4

ASURA RODE ATOP HIS LARGE iguana-like reptile on a warm summer day toward a large castle in the distance, the defeated Ragnok at his side. Lush vegetation, thick and green, blanketed the landscape, sprawling out in nearly every direction. The path they walked appeared to be maintained and was scraped out of the land in a long dirt lane that led toward the castle. Decorating the side of a cliff were carved stone faces resembling the humans that had caused him so much trouble back on Eritria. Their resemblance was uncanny from the eyes and noses to the form of their chins; the statues could have been earthlings.

The path ahead was lined on both sides with tall onyx statues of men with spears held by their sides, looking down on passersby with watchful expressions. They were polished and proud, like majestic dark gods of impossible power guarding the road. Bright sunlight glimmered off the smooth stone soldiers, giving each statue an ethereal aura. "I have two questions, my lord. That is if you don't mind," Ragnok said.

"What? Just ask." Asura commanded.

"Where are we, and what do you hope to accomplish here?" Ragnok asked.

"Revenge, Ragnok. It's cold and hard, like a hammer on a fly. I believe that with my father's help, we can achieve just that and finally put an end to wolven life on Eritria," Asura said.

"And what planet is this? Are we still on Eritria?" Ragnok asked.

"We are on the planet Telerum and far from home, my friend," Asura said. "Any more questions?"

"Do you plan to destroy Eritria?" Ragnok asked. "Even if I was, you should be grateful; the wolven destroyed your army and killed all your people," Asura said.

"How do you know your father is still alive? It's been three hundred years since you last saw him." "I concentrated my mental energy on Broad Axe when pressing the button on your device, and when the doorway opened, we came here. If he were dead, I'm not sure this creature in the box would have opened the gateway to this planet. When I was old enough, my mother explained that Telerum was the planet he had planned to escape to if the wolven or another enemy ever defeated him. Our actual location is just a guess." Asura said.

"So, you don't know for sure," Ragnok said. Asura was irritated and sent him a glare, moving on in silence.

The massive castle walls loomed over the valley, and soon they would be at their destination. Nearing the well-fortified palace, they passed a hamlet of ramshackle wooden shacks and small log homes with tin roofs. Dust began to form little clouds in the wind up ahead. A human man on horseback was approaching them from the village. His horse galloped along a dirt path cut through thick, grassy plains where a field of beautiful and fragrant wildflowers grew. To Ragnok, he looked a lot like the leader of the human tribe back home, and for a moment, he considered the possibility that humans might all look alike. The man on horseback was tall, Caucasian, and wore a dirtied white cloth shirt and tan leather pants. On his feet were black dragon- scale boots with steel spurs that jingled as he galloped toward them.

"My lord, the taxes are almost prepared for you; we only need a few more moments. I asked for two days only a day ago, but we will have your gold regardless." The man said.

Asura was cunning and wily, so although he had no idea what this man was talking about, he did know one thing: the human thought he was someone else, his father perhaps. And it was such a close resemblance that this stranger was about to hand him gold. Asura felt the familiar surge of power welling up inside him and the excitement of the possibility that Broad Axe might still live. Asura was just a hatchling when Broad Axe was cast out of Eritria.

"See that you do! I have important business at the castle." Asura said.

"That castle, my lord? You burned that long ago when you murdered, um, replaced the king and queen." The man said.

"Well, where else would I go?" Asura asked. He tried to sound nonchalant, but he knew that one false slip of the tongue would give him away.

"Why, your city in the clouds, sir." The man said. At this, Asura looked up and noticed that levitating a mile off the ground and encased in a layer of thick, white, fluffy clouds, there was a land mass the size of the Fire Lands. It seemed impossible to him that something so large could be suspended in midair without support. Jagged stalactites of stone reached toward the ground, poking through the layer of clouds. Beyond the island in the sky was a more spectacular vision: a gigantic blue-green planet visible through the atmosphere and so close that he felt that he could reach out and touch it if he were airborne.

Oceans and continents were so well defined that it seemed he was looking at the planet he stood on now, only from the sky. The sight was exhilarating but frightening, and Asura wondered how he had not seen the planet above upon their arrival. Suddenly, a black dot shot out of the clouds, making a beeline for where they were standing. As it came closer, Asura thought that a dragon was upon them, but upon closer inspection, he could see it was a large brown bat.

"Go get the gold, now!" Asura said. If his father were up there, Asura would have a gift for him.

Another human, this one darker in complexion and wearing only boots and leather pants, strode up with a black bag full of clinking gold coins. His muscular chest seemed to have been chiseled from rock, and he had abs that looked like they could absorb the impact of a battering ram. Asura rolled his eyes and thought for a moment how this man's head would look in his collection back at his castle in the Fire Lands.

"Quintus, I have the gold for lord Broad Axe!" Said the man.

"Thank you, Dale."

"Quite a prize..." Asura mumbled. "My lord?" Quintus asked.

"Nothing, just hand me the bag," Asura said.

Shadow covered the ground around them, so dark that it seemed for a moment as if the sun had disappeared as the bat passed overhead. It screeched once, turned around, and swooped down, snatching Dale off the ground in an instant. As he screamed in terror, the animal chomped down, snapping his neck. Quintus stood in disbelief as his friend vanished inside the bat. He turned his head a moment later, vomiting on the ground. Ragnok felt his muscles tightening, wondering whether he could kill the creature if it came for him next. The bat landed a few meters away, looked around at the small group, and then down at Quintus. It let out an ear-piercing screech, startling Quintus' horse, who bolted toward the hamlet.

After watching him go, Asura noticed the bat wearing a glowing jade necklace. A green beam of light shone forth, and in it, an image of Broad Axe materialized. He looked much like Asura, with the same iguana-like facial features, and he was clad in a long black robe with a velvet interior. His hood draped down his shoulders and back.

"Who are you?" The image asked.

"I am your son, Asura and I have come here to bring you home and subjugate Eritria," Asura said. He motioned to Ragnok to raise the case in his arms. "With this."

"Get on the bat and come up. If this is some kind of trick, you'll pay with your lives." Broad Axe said. His image vanished.

Asura climbed aboard the bat, taking his seat in the saddle provided. When he had secured himself, the bat took flight, hovered a moment, and grabbed Ragnok in his talons around his horse body, lifting the large centaur off the ground with ease.

"This is madness! This beast could drop me!" Ragnok yelled. The bat looked down and took to the sky with a grunt.

"I suspect if you anger it, probably, yes," Asura said over the noise of the wind. He leaned back in his saddle and enjoyed the ride.

Higher and higher, they flew toward the sky city, and so the planet beyond Telerum became larger to Asura's eyes, playing tricks with them, while Ragnok held onto the cosmic portal.

"Your life depends on that device making it to my father; you know that, right?" Asura asked.

"Yes, my lord. I have it right here." Ragnok said. The bat banked slightly right to miss a flock of seagulls, but it was not agile enough, and one of the birds crashed into Ragnok. It shook him so much that he dropped the cosmic portal device. Down, down, down it fell, and as his heart skipped a beat, Ragnok knew there was nothing left for him to do.

"You dropped the cosmic portal!?" Asura screamed.

They were in the sky above the castle where Quintus had escaped, and the metallic case was now tumbling end over end toward the courtyard. It became a speck and then disappeared entirely. Overcome with rage Asura screamed and hissed.

"Drop him!" Asura said.

The bat gave Ragnok a sly smile with an evil glint in his eyes and lightened his grip. Ragnok screamed as his body pin wheeled through the sky on his way to meet destiny. Asura passed him on the way down to get the case and nodded to his former henchman one last time. A spire on the west wing, adorned with fancy, sweeping shingles and a long steel spike at the top, caught Ragnok under his horse torso, pinning him in place. That decorative spike exited the top of Ragnok's head, making him look like a trophy. His body would remain there until the cataclysm blew it apart. Asura watched it all happening from above and thought it a fitting end for a king who'd led his people to extinction.

"Goodbye, Ragnok. You'll not be missed." Asura said.

Asura felt relief that he would never have to suffer one more boring story or excuse from the centaur leader. *Upward and onward to new adventures in a hostile planetary takeover*, Asura thought. He flipped out his long, forked reptilian tongue, gave a final glance at the dead horse-man, and landed in the castle courtyard. The scenery down on the ground was far more macabre and mysterious than from the air. Human skeletons clad in battle armor lay all about, posed in the fighting positions where they had fallen some time ago.

Asura searched for the cosmic portal while he dismounted the bat, and realized there was no place in this court where he would not step on the remains of a fallen, failed soldier. The drawbridge had been raised during this final battle, but its wooden planks were crushed and blasted inward by a battering ram resting just inside the doorway. There were other races represented here as well, and as the curious reptilian king walked around, he noticed that their skulls were distinctly like his own.

Asura finally spotted the case; it had fallen at the feet of two human skeletons that had been crucified on crosses composed of rotting logs bound together with thick rope and spikes. They faced the destroyed drawbridge with eternal expressions of disbelief on slack jaws and wide eye sockets. The crowns had been stapled onto the tops of their skulls, and they hung by the door leading into their derelict castle. Time and decay had withered their clothing to rags, and all that kept their skulls from rolling off their shoulders was a rope across the mouth and nose tied around the back of the cross. The king stood sentinel over his court with a jeweled sword hilt sticking out of his ribs and the queen a dagger planted firmly in her sternum. A gentle wind blew through the gate, whistling a toneless funeral dirge.

Asura waded through a thick carpet of bones to the cosmic portal and picked it up. The remote control was still attached, so he tested the device to avoid looking foolish in front of his father. Asura concentrated on Eritria and the troublesome, annoying, wolven leaders Ramos and Dante. He would have their heads before the end. With a push of a button, the golden rings of light materialized once again and began to spin in opposing directions as the space within wavered like a mirage and opened the portal in space-time again. Stars and planets whizzed by at the speed of light, and then he saw his home planet through the portal. The camera eye of the cosmic portal whooshed down into a deep, dark wood, where his enemies, the wolven were lying on the ground.

He had done it! The device's secret was will of thought, and now he knew it would take him anywhere he could dream. Sleeping soundly, the wolven had not posted a sentry that night, and as Asura crept through the portal and across the dirt courtyard of a destroyed, derelict chapel, he held in his hands the skull of a slain reptilian. Every so gently, he placed the skull on the ground beside Mac's head and turned to go. A *gift from a friend*, he thought. Once he stepped through the other side of the cosmic portal, the white wolven stirred, awakened by bright sunlight beaming in on him from another world. Mac raised his head, and through bleary eyes, he watched Asura wave back at him. then the lizard king was gone, and the dim torchlight around their circle was all that remained.

Asura, laughing to himself, picked up the cosmic portal and, crunching over the bones of the battle-fallen, returned to his bat mount. The bat rose slowly from the ground while Asura surveyed the castle's architecture, admiring its complex stonework. The blocks of stone were large, angular, odd shapes, cut smoothly on the ends, and had been fit together so that they appeared to be a thirty-foot-tall jigsaw puzzle. The surrounding walls were of similar construction, and although the wooden roofing was caving in—due to the slow decay of time—these polygonal-shaped jigsaw pieces seemed impenetrable.

His castle had not been built well, and he imagined these walls would stand here until the planet blew apart or a meteor hit it. The engineering it would have taken to construct such a monument to time was unfathomable to Asura. Indeed, there must have been sorcery behind it. The attackers only had two routes in the drawbridge or the sky.

"Outstanding!" He said to himself.

The bat ascended again toward the sky-city and shed much weight; the journey was far less taxing to him. When they passed Ragnok, impaled and dangling for eternity, the bat screeched at him, and Asura gave a final nod toward the glassy-eyed— forever gawking—former leader of the centaur.

"Goodbye, Ragnok. By the way, you're looking rather ornamental today," Asura said. Slack-jawed, eyes rolled back, and staring into the sky, Ragnok was beyond care.

The bat carried Asura onward and upward through billowy clouds to the island in the sky. Asura was looking at another castle beyond a wall of similar construction as the castle below, and as his mount flew past it, Asura was flying over a living, breathing reptilian civilization.

The people bustling to and from below looked just like him. The bat whisked him away to a large castle north of the city where, he hoped, he would be reunited with his father, and he could explain what had happened to him back on Eritria. The bat landed on top of the castle, where a figure stood waiting for him, cloaked in black with two gremlins by his side. Asura stepped down from the bat, wobbly from flying. As he did, the cloaked figure removed the hood, revealing a rough, rugged reptilian face. The man before him had the same iguana-like facial features and was the spitting image of Asura, but his right cheek had a long gash running from ear to chin in a zigzag.

"Welcome to the city of Osandia, son." Broad Axe said.

"Father, I've searched for a way to get to you for many years." Asura cried. Broad Axe chuckled. "Yes, indeed." Broad Axe took his son by the shoulders and held him for a moment with both claws, looking him over. "We have much to discuss, especially now that you've found a way to travel between worlds. That's interesting. You could not have come at a better time. Come inside; my gremlins will fix us something to eat, and we can get acquainted." Broad Axe said. Asura walked with him.

"A lot has happened since you left Eritria, father. The wolven and an alien race called humans have defeated my army, and they wiped out all the centaurs."

"I have seen much in my dreams over the years, and I knew you would come! Our revenge close is at hand, and that case you carry is the key. I was exiled here after Gregor, and the minotaur king Yxx overthrew my kingdom in the southwest. I would have returned sooner, but Inga hit me from behind, and I dropped the Tablet of Destinies on my way through the portal I created. I was trapped here along with my small army."

"Father, I don't understand. Does the tablet allow you to create portals?" Asura asked.

"No, I did that with my magic, accompanied by the power of the tablet. It's a strong, ancient weapon that, had I been able to use properly, would have given me dominion over Eritria." Broad Axe said.

"Not to worry, we can use this device I stole from the humans to get back there again, and then we'll find that tablet together," Asura said. Broad Axe nodded and proudly clapped his son on the shoulder. "I have something to show you that will change our fate forever, but first, we eat." Broad Axe said.

"The people on the ground below thought I was you. They gave me this." Asura said. He handed his father the bag of money.

"Protection money from our faithful servants." Broad Axe looked at the bag, snorted, and placed it inside his robe.

"How have you been trapped here?" Asura asked. "That cursed dragon, Inga, swooped down and snatched it out of my hands and then kicked me through the portal. Without it, my control of the portal was broken, and more than half of the soldiers with me were lost in between time streams." Broad Axe said.

"I was with my mother when you left. She'd told me some of what happened to you, but I had no idea Inga was involved. I've got a score to settle with all of them after what they did to my centaur and libmok army." Asura said.

"Well, it seems we won't need the Tablet for a round trip. What do you have in that case? I saw it in my dreams, and in them, you arrived with a gateway creator that could transport the bearer back and forth through time." Broad Axe asked.

"A creature lives inside of it and harnesses infinite power, reacting to stimuli from the control mechanism in my robe pocket. We stole it from the humans, and I used it to travel here by concentrating on you." Asura said. Broad Axe nodded approval.

"You have managed to travel more than a million years back in time with this...what's it called?" Broad Axe asked.

"The humans call it a cosmic portal," Asura said.

Broad Axe nodded.

"What I have in store for the Eritrians is going to be legendary in its scale of sheer destruction. We've been building an energy weapon that can destroy planets. The people here have evolved their technology to a zenith of superiority. They are far more astute than our engineers and wizards." Broad Axe said.

"The people I ran into down on the ground didn't look very technologically advanced," Asura said.

"You only met some of the outliers, peasants in a kingdom far vaster than mine ever was." Broad Axe said. "We'll ride a bat out to the energy fields tomorrow; you'll see what I mean."

They turned and walked together toward a stairwell leading to the interior of Broad Axe's castle. Again, Asura admired how close the grey limestone wall blocks fit together, and upon closer inspection, he realized there was no mortar between them. They were so tight a single hair could not penetrate the joints. The two descended until Broad Axe entered a large dining hall with an enormous, oak-constructed solid table. It was big enough to feed an army.

"That's a large table for one; who else lives here?" Asura asked.

"My men eat with us every evening, but since you just arrived, I asked that we be alone for the night." Broad Axe said.

A gremlin walked into the room and silently waited for orders. Broad Axe gave him his dinner order, and then the tiny creature took a bow, turned, and left the room.

"You were wondering what planet this is, right?" Broad Axe asked.

"I know this is Telerum from what my mother told me when she saw you being pushed through the portal. What I don't know is what that planet is above us. It's so big it looks like it might fall on our heads." Asura said.

"We are on the planet Telerum. She's a moon, and the colossal planet you see above you is Krypton. We're orbiting her." Broad Axe said.

They sat at the table across from one another, and in less than an hour, a chorus of gremlins entered the room, rolling carts with covered dishes. Asura had always been told his father was a harsh and evil overlord, a master villain. This man was nothing like the stories, and Asura began to rethink many of the deeds he had performed in his past. The killings, torture, mass mutilations. Had he done all that to live up to the image of who he thought his father was? Asura felt confusion seep into his mind and a sense that maybe his father was not the man he had thought he was. He swallowed hard and tabled those thoughts for another time, but distrust took root and grew.

"Is Krypton inhabited? Are there people like us there?"

"I believe so. Occasionally, I can see what looks like industrial smoke through the cloud cover. Maybe we'll get there one day, but before that, I have a score to settle with the Eritrians." Broad Axe said. They ate together, moving their dinner to a balcony overlooking the floating city as Broad Axe told his son about the world where he now lived. Ornate spires atop stone-constructed buildings with glass windows rose high into the clouds above. The homes and stores had been built round and squat with bulbous exteriors, and to Asura, their collectiveness looked like a strange pumpkin patch in the sky.

"The humans here mastered electro-gravitic propulsion and geo-magnetism; that's how the sky city is suspended in midair. I had two of the human scientists kidnapped once our forces were stronger and forced them to teach us how to build our island in the sky, with some slave labor from the little hamlets below, that is."

"This is either a breathtaking accomplishment or technological mastery. I wish my castle back home could float on the air." Asura said. "I want revenge, father."

"You'll have it. The weapon is almost complete. We'll go see it in the morning." Broad Axe said. They talked for hours about current affairs back on Eritria, about the war with the wolven and humans, and Broad Axe informed his son about his life on the alien world of Telerum. Tiredness crept in on Asura, as he had not been asleep in days. After his third glass of wine, he drifted into a deep slumber on the balcony of Broad Axe's castle. Broad Axe called for four gremlins, who entered like wraiths and gently carried Asura to his room. Asura entered the dream, knowing something would happen, but not what.

A long hallway stretched into the gloom ahead as the mist formed a deep fog that rolled in his direction. He walked into the fog and felt it stick to his skin; he was naked and alone. The fog turned to taffy and began to pull at his skin, but it started to burn, and he writhed in his sleep. He felt molten ropes of fire covering him, pulling him out of the hallway. Next, he was outside a house in the floating city, watching the clouds burn as debris fragments exploded into the ground like aerial bombs. Blasts rocked the night, and frightened people headed for cover. One man, a reptilian shop owner, was walking outside to see the commotion when a dime-sized chunk of fiery brimstone ripped through his skull like a marksman's bullet, and as the shocked, gawking, deadpan man dropped to his knees, a trickle of maroon rolled down his forehead, and he ended his life face down in the dirty street with half the back of his head blown out and smoldering.

Asura looked down into the face of the dead man and knew this was no shopkeeper. He was staring into the glassy eyes of his face on the ground. Asura turned to look up and was astounded to see a hail of meteors descending in an umbrella of fire from the heavens. Screams from the wounded and dying were muffled in the din of destruction and flames licking the night sky. Asura glanced back into the dead man's eyes, and suddenly, they were alive again, faint life glimmering inside black and yellow retinas. Back from the dead in some miraculous twist of fate, the resurrected Asura pleaded with him behind an expression of twisted fear. Asura felt real terror, and he could smell the odor of burned meat as it permeated the air, stinging his dreaming nostrils. The ghoul below him grabbed his robe and leaned forward. Asura could see the ground through the hole in this man's head.

"You have to get out. Get out now! While you still can!" The dead Asura said.

Asura opened his eyes and lay on his side, staring wide-eyed at the wall. His pulse raced, and for a moment, he was unsure where he was, but the sensation subsided, and he remembered he was in his father's castle. The dream of fire had been nothing more; it meant nothing. His forked reptilian tongue *thwipped* in and out twice as his breathing calmed, but it had all seemed so believable.

"You're a stranger in a strange land, Asura. You need to get a grip on yourself and see this through." He spoke. Then he rolled to his other side and fell into a deep, dreamless sleep until dawn.

He woke to a chirping bird on his windowsill when the sun was new. Asura felt like he had been drinking the night before and held no affection for the singing raptor, perched with confident salubriousness.

"Go away!" He yelled. The bird cocked her head, took a slight bow, and disappeared out the window.

He rolled out of bed and dressed as the dream faded into the recesses of his subconscious. He walked down the hallway, turned right in the only direction available, and ascended a flight of grey stone steps to a tiny arc of light at the top. Asura climbed higher in the silent morning, and at the top of the stairwell was a large flat platform overlooking the sky city and a kingdom of pyramids far in the distance. One was so large it reached into the clouds, its top vanishing like a specter. Broad Axe was already looking east toward the pyramids as if he knew his son would join him.

"You slept in." Broad Axe said.

"Odd dreams plagued me," Asura said.

"Well, we're going to the energy fields this morning. Are you hungry?" Broad Axe asked.

"No, I rarely eat breakfast."

"Let's get to it then; I have much to show you!" A bat swept in from around the side and landed a few feet from Broad Axe. They mounted the creature, and a moment later, Asura and his father were miles from the castle. The closer they flew to the megalithic structures, the bigger they became. The sheer size of the center pyramid was awesome and horrible in its enormity, and to Asura, it looked like death incarnate. What would Broad Axe need with something so large?

"Impressed? You should be. We built an energy weapon so large that we could destroy a planet if I desired." Broad Axe said.

The bat dropped them off at the foot of the great pyramid and stood by as a sentry, waiting for his master to return.

"How tall do you think this pyramid is?" Broad Axe asked.

"I don't know, somewhere between zero and a million feet?"

"Nine hundred feet!" Broad Axe said. "That's a big weapon. It is a weapon, right?"

"My boy, this is our ticket to ultimate revenge on Eritria. The future is now and in a manner of speaking, then. We're going back!"

Asura stood before the largest intelligently designed construction he had ever seen, a pyramid with four sides, beautifully crafted and broken in the middle of each one to form two separate halves, slightly angled from one another.

"Nine hundred feet tall, and one of the deadliest devices ever crafted by engineers, Asura. This weapon will make all our problems go away in short order. All we have to do is open the gateway back to Eritria when the final touches are complete." Broad Axe said.

"It's not functioning yet?" Asura asked.

A team of reptilian men and women in space suits walked out of an access shaft to their right and waved to Broad Axe and his son. They had been wearing helmets with dark shields that covered their faces and thick leather gloves to protect their hands from the environment inside the pyramid.

"Almost functioning. But my architects and engineers have assured me we will be ready soon. It's a good thing you're here, my son. I wasn't sure we'd be able to pull this off. Come over here, and let me show you a small demonstration of what we're dealing with in terms of sheer, raw power." Broad Axe said.

He walked several yards to a smaller pyramid on a stand, with a clear pyramid-shaped crystal at the top, and picked up a small round plate sitting next to it. The plate was small enough to fit in the palm of his hand and had strange runes marked on it. Broad Axe then stood a limestone block on its side and backed away. Holding the small plate, he moved his thumb around it in a counterclockwise circle until the runes began to glow. He closed his eyes and seemed to go into a trance, and as the runes pulsated, the pyramid responded, and the crystal glowed brightly. Like a tiny, imprisoned star, the energy built within the tiny model until Broad Axe opened his eyes, and a bolt of pure light shot forth, clearing the distance between it and the limestone block in a microsecond. The block was disintegrated with a single blast, and when the light died down, nothing was left but a pile of sand on the ground. Asura was exhilarated; any fear he may have had about the pyramid was replaced by a strong desire to see Dante and his friends die screaming in a rain of fire.

"We are going to have some fun with this thing," Asura said.

"Stick with me, boy. We'll rule the stars." Broad Axe said.

He clasped an arm around Asura's shoulder and pulled him in close. Asura's mind was alive with the possibilities, and suddenly, his misfortune back home seemed less critical.

"Yes, I can see your point," Asura nodded. The two began plotting the destruction of Eritria as Mac, Dante, Ramos, Ort, and Carp were waking up to a new day.

CHAPTER 5

AFTER RAMOS AND MAC WENT back to sleep, Dante searched the canopy cover alone, and realizing it was too dense to see through, he decided to climb above it and find out what time it was. It was so dark under the forest that they would never know when the morning had arrived if he hadn't climbed to the top. And time was now their enemy. He knew that if the moon were clear tonight, it would be a simple matter of reading its position to find out how much time was left, but if there were clouds, he would be out of luck.

With one last look around the camp and sniffing the air, he was reasonably sure the vexanon priests were gone and that his brother and friends could sleep in peace until he returned. Glorg looked up at him with his skull cocked to the side as if questioning the wolven warrior's next move, and Dante wondered if the creature had any original thoughts inside its empty head or if it was merely a mindless puppet of his brother's making.

"Stay put and watch out for the others, Glorg," Dante said. The skeletal lizard nodded and sat down on its hind legs.

He hooked into a nearby tree with his sharp claws and quickly scaled it. Dante was halfway up the tree and nearing the treetops within seconds. He was tired from the chaotic battle earlier and desperately needed to sleep, but he told himself it was only a few hours away and pressed forward. Closer, higher, enveloped in darkness, he hit a gigantic spider web with his head and almost lost his grip. Dante remained calm and reached inside his pouch, removing a light stone that shone with such brilliance it illuminated the dark canopy and gave him a clear view of his surroundings.

Suspended in thick, gooey steel cable-like webs were the ensnared, decaying bodies of vexanon priests, the remains of a few skeletal minotaur, and some who were so entombed in whitish gray silk they were no more than husks dangling far from the ground. The odor of death hung like a fog, but there was something else, too. Some of the withered dead smelled like an old root cellar, much different than the most recently killed. Dante could see their death gaze, their last expressions frozen as their untimely ends came. He wondered what they'd been so afraid of before death took them. Some grimaced, but most faces were twisted in silent screams, eyes wide open, staring blindly.

"OK, spiders. I had to ask what else could happen." Dante said.

Something moved in the black, skittering by his peripheral vision on spindly legs just outside the radius of his light. That sound was all the motivation he needed to move. He hoped that the spiders were averse to bright light and would leave him alone until he could climb back down and out of their territory.

"How long had they known I was here?" He spoke. His voice came out as an unintentionally expressed thought, but the sound startled him.

He climbed until his head finally popped through the treetops, and he was staring into a night filled with twinkling stars. Beacons from living beings in distant galaxies shone down on the lonely planet of Eritria. An obstruction above his head blocked the starlight, and he almost struck it with his noggin. He brought the light up and saw that it was a magic bridge constructed of wood running across the tops of the trees. The bridge stretched along the forest for miles, and he knew it might be their way out. He would tell the others, but first, he needed to know the time. Gregor taught Dante how to tell the time by reading the moon's position when he was a puppy. Reading from right to left, he saw it was halfway between midnight and three in the morning.

Dawn would arrive soon, and they could be on their way.

"We'll be back," Dante said, lowering himself down through the tangled limbs.

He had to tell the others, but first, he needed to wake Ramos up for his watch and get some sleep. He descended through shadow and light on one twisted branch after another, holding the small light crystal in his hand to ward off any curious spiders until he could be well out of their domain. He moved on swift hands and feet toward the ground, and when he stepped off the tree, the torches still burned, and there was no sign of any enemies. Glorg watched Dante with quiet interest as he walked across the camp to Ramos and tapped him awake.

"You're up, sunshine," Dante said. Ramos growled at him and opened his tired eyes.

"We never decided who would be on next watch; go wake Mac up," Ramos said.

"Nice try. There's a bridge up in those treetops above the canopy. I just climbed up there to see when the sun would rise and practically hit my head on the thing."

"A bridge?" Ramos asked. His eyes were half- lidded, and he was puzzled.

"It's true, right up there," Dante said. He yawned. "I have to get some sleep, or I'll be worthless tomorrow, but we need to check it out in the morning. It could be our fast track out of here." Dante said.

"What time is it?" Ramos asked.

"Judging from the moon's position, it's around two or three in the morning."

"OK, go get some sleep; I'll take this one," Ramos said.

Ramos stood as Dante took his place on the ground. In less than a minute, he was asleep. At first, Ramos sat under a tree, thinking about the dream he and Mac shared. Then he remembered the last time he had been with Gregor alone, before the war. Standing in his study, he had admired Gregor as his father poured over ancient tomes, ever the learner. No matter how advanced in years, Gregor had always hungered for knowledge.

"Are you going to prop up the doorway all morning or come in?" Gregor asked.

"No matter how old I get, I always enjoy watching you work, father," Ramos said.

"A war is coming. There are some complex anomalies I've discovered regarding the pyramids. They seem to be losing their power, and the implications are enormous."

"What do you mean?" Ramos said.

"There's something else coming besides the pyramid failures. It's more deadly than I thought. But I can't say anything at the moment." Gregor said. Ramos had not known what his father was speaking of at the time, but in light of the information the naga king and queen gave them, the old conversation began to make sense. Could he have been referring to the Tablet of Destinies and the ick?

Ramos was bored after an hour and decided to pass the time by raising vexanon priests from the dead and commanding them to perform tricks. Six of them together began to form a pyramid, with three on the bottom, two in the middle, and one on top. They grumbled as they balanced on top of each other, and as Ramos watched, he realized the undead were communicating with each other.

"Not mindless after all. Hmmm." Ramos whispered.

He wondered what other tricks he could do with his undead friends. Ramos waved his hand at them, and the stack began to descend and separate one after the other. The top vexanon priest jumped down, landing on his feet with a flourish, while the left- most priest on row two performed a back flip, landing on his feet, and as the right priest was leaping forward in a roll, he was snared by a single strand of webbing from the darkness above. Ramos had been lost in entertainment up to this point, so he had not been expecting the little undead creature to vanish into the trees.

"Well, that concludes this evening's show, I guess," Ramos said.

Ramos looked up as another priest was snagged from the ground and pulled into the blackness. Ramos pulled one of the lit torches out of the ground and raised its light into the tree branches. He amplified the brightness with his magic and found that the trees were alive with moving black and brown spiders, each the size of a large dog. Hundreds of them were rappelling down on steel cables of silk. Two spiders busied themselves by wrapping the undead vexanon priests, encasing them for later meals, as two more vexanon priests vanished from the ground into the maze of branches above.

The spiders, gathering in numbers, lowered themselves out of the trees like death from above, advancing on the sleeping adventurers. Ramos gathered his energy, and with a mental push, he sent the flames from his torch into the trees in a swath of fiery destruction. Spiders caught fire, squealing with the intense roasting heat as the trees blazed. Mac woke up first, jumping in surprise, struggling to figure out what new threat confronted them. Gigantic spiders skittered around their campsite, some immediately consumed in flames and running for cover.

Their chaotic escape continued to spread the fire until the forest was alight with flames and screams. In the center of the chaos was Ramos, looking up and commanding more streams of fire from his torch. He was laughing maniacally as the spiders roasted and fell over. Some of them had escaped Ramos' fiery spell and were advancing on the sleeping members of their party. Mac ran over and kicked one with his black boot, watching it splatter against a tall, thick tree. Carp was the next one awake and vanished into thin air, appearing a few seconds later, hovering over one of the spiders with a long, sharp stick. He struck down with the sharp end, piercing it through the back, wincing as green ooze shot out and splattered his legs.

"Disgusting!"

Ort woke up and struggled to his feet as two of the spiders skittered toward him with frightening speed. He was almost up on legs of jelly when a web shot out at him and ensnared his left foot. The other straddled his right leg and prepared to bite down on the tender flesh when Ort opened his mouth, and a blast of fire incinerated the spider. In seconds it became a stinking lump of charcoal, a smoldering shell of what had once been. Several others had been coming to help their arachnid brother when they saw Ort spitting flames and quickly retreated. Ort grinned and leaped to his feet.

"Get back here; the fun's not over!" Ort said.

The spiders fled as Ort flexed his arms, pushed his chest forward, clenched his fists, and spewed a stream of red-hot fire from his gaping mouth. The screaming spiders scurried into the underbrush, erupting in flames. The bushes and trees were now consumed in flames, and the forest fire quickly grew. "Ramos, we have to get control of the fire!"

Dante said.

"I don't know how," Ramos said. His voice had taken on a dark, guttural tone.

Dante looked in horror and fascination and saw the swirling, dancing purple flames emanating from Ramos' eyes like tiny streams of violet rage. The natural fuel was now exhausted, and the torch lay beside him, smoking and blackened to a charred core. The spiders were all gone, having retreated into the shadows as the night burned around them. Ramos suddenly had an idea; he grabbed one of the torches, held it high, and willed the fire from the trees and underbrush into the torch. The fire was sucked back into the torch in a vacuum, and in moments the forest was silent once again. There was nothing left but charred trees and smoke. Ramos planted the torch on the ground and stumbled against one of the blackened trees, supporting his exhausted frame on the trunk, head bowed.

"I have never seen anything like that in my life.

You're not only a warlock but a mage as well? That's unheard of." Carp said.

"Excitement's over," Dante said.

The area was clear, and thanks to Ramos' outburst, the fire had cleared the trees and brush surrounding their campsite for at least a hundred feet in every direction.

"Let's all try to get some sleep," Carp said.

"If there are any other potential threats out there, I believe they're running in any direction but ours," Dante said.

"Ort breathes fire! Did anybody else see that? He lit two of those spiders up!" Mac said.

"All wolvacaran can breathe fire; it is our last resort when in danger. Fire is a dangerous tool, however helpful it may be." Ort said. He collapsed to the ground in his weakened state.

"I say we all get some sleep, and when we wake up, we wake up. I found a bridge up at the top of these trees, and I think it may be our way out." Dante said.

"Dante's right, we're not going to be any good if we don't rest. All of us have been running on empty for a while." Mac said.

The decision was finalized, and they all rested for the remainder of that night, sleeping well into the next day. Mac's sleep was broken only once by a strange dream that the reptilian king Asura was in their campsite. He waved to Mac in an almost friendly gesture and was standing in a portal generated by the cosmic portal. Asura was half in and out of a land where the earth had a reddish tint, and the sun shone brightly, piercing his weary eyes as fresh, sweet air mixed with the doused campfire smell of the woods.

As fast as he had appeared, Asura was gone. Mac lay back down and drifted off to sleep again, knowing it must have been another strange dream. When the company woke up, Mac was lying next to the skull of a reptilian humanoid. As he held it in his hand, turning it around and around, he wondered if he had been dreaming after all and placed the skull back on the ground.

The rest of the party awoke shortly after, tired and stiff from a night on the ground; their bodies were still recovering from the battle with the vexanon and their failed god, Baal.

"We need to eat and move on before another night falls. I don't like these woods," Ramos said. Mac remembered his aching stomach, forgot all about the skull, and told his team about the odd dream involving Asura.

"That's an understatement, brother. The spiders, vexanon priests, and conjured demons from the nether regions are a bit much. This is no haven. I'm not sleeping here again if I can help it." Mac said.

"I'm feeling much better today. I think barbequing those spiders healed me spiritually." Ort said.

After they ate and ensured Ort could walk, Dante led them up through a much less dense canopy, thanks to Ramos, with Ort and the others following.

Carp needed help since he didn't have the luxury of claws, and his suction cups were covered with thick soot from the fires, so Mac carried him on his back. Mac was looking ahead at the tree in front of him, spacing out, when he looked up just in time to miss being struck in the face by a black boot. It was attached to the foot of a deceased satyr encased in a thick cocoon of webbing.

"Climb!" Mac said.

"I'm sorry, what?" Carp asked.

"Talking to myself, that's all," Mac said.

Dante arrived at the top first and saw that the bridge was suspended by long poles, some supports that rose through the trees. He lifted himself onto the wooden planks and looked around to ensure he was the only one up there. The bridge was sturdy enough to hold his weight, and as the others joined him, it only sagged a little.

"Good engineering," Mac said. Dante and the others nodded.

The bright midday sun shone upon their faces for the first time since entering the northern Bog Lands. Mac wondered what Carol would have thought of this world.

"Don't fall over the side, Ort," Dante said.

He was half joking, but as he watched the older, feebler wolven-hybrid wavering on two feet, he wondered if the wolvacaran man could survive their journey.

"Don't worry about me. I've been in tougher scrapes than this."

They walked along the sky bridge above the trees. An hour passed with no sign of the end of the bridge as the sun rode across the afternoon sky like a chariot of fire. When dusk settled, Dante finally saw a staircase leading down to the forest's edge.

"I think we're out," Dante said.

"Oh good, I was beginning to think we'd be up here for the night," Carp said.

Dante walked to the edge and looked over.

"Sure enough, it goes all the way down to the ground. Look over there! We weren't far from Scowl Castle." Dante said.

"We should have returned the way we left," Ramos said.

"Oh, come on, now that's not fair. We wouldn't have found our friend Ort here, and Baal would have eaten him." Dante said.

"That's probably true. Sorry about that, Ort." Ramos said.

"Think nothing of it. Nevertheless, I'm never going back through those woods again. I'll walk to the southern sea before that happens. I don't trust this land." Ort said.

"You might not want to do that. The land was poisoned with the ick. You'd most likely die entering that wasteland." Dante said.

"The centaurs are all gone, no?" Ort asked. "That must have been some fight."

"I'll sleep outside those walls tonight if it's all the same. That castle should be razed to the ground." Ramos said.

"Our father was killed by the treachery of Ragnok in there, Ort," Dante said.

"So sorry, I didn't know," Ort said.

"You couldn't know, but when I catch Ragnok, I'll disembowel him with a rusty hook," Ramos said.

"Camping under the stars it is, then," Mac said. "As long as we don't have to go back into those cursed woods, I'm with you all," Carp said.

They descended the staircase and walked across the fields of Moktar, a noticeably more hospitable place without the influence of centaur tyranny. Mac felt tired but grateful to be alive, and when they reached the entrance to the eastern Bog Lands, they stopped and set up camp.

"Best to go in there when the sun is up. Strange creatures roam those lands, and we have to find the Temple of Ostrid quickly. I have an idea where she lies, but our people left so long ago that, at the time, there were fields and farms. There were no bogs or high trees. Our paintings of Lavural before the dark times came are so pretty." Ort said. He seemed haunted by the memories of the times when life was easier.

"Let's find something to eat, Mac," Dante said. "It's time you learned to hunt, and I smell deer near here."

"OK, lead the way," Mac said.

"This time, I'll lead and flush out our dinner, but next time we hunt, you'll lead," Dante said. Mac nodded in agreement.

They walked about two hundred yards from the makeshift camp to where a grove of trees and bushes concealed them. Down in a pasture, not far from the tree line, were three deer feeding on berries growing from a small bush. As the hunters hunched down, Dante looked for escape routes. The deer would not run into the Bog Lands; there were dangers after dark timid deer could not escape. They had limited options for retreat: west toward the wolven camp, east, or south, right into the waiting arms of Mac.

"These deer are stupid, and even more so when scared. I'm going to flank them and drive the herd into these trees. Their alternative is to head into those woods, and nothing goes in there at night. Be ready when they run at you."

Dante slunk away through the underbrush and vanished. Mac could no longer see him, even with his advanced wolven eyesight. The deer stood there, looking skittish. His heart thumped in his chest like a drum. What if he missed them or if they took off in the other direction? There was something instinctual happening inside him. It was like he was starting to feel wolven on the inside. He'd felt stress before, but this feeling was different; it was natural. The hunter's instinct.

"Shut up. You'll do your job, just like always." Mac said, whispering to himself.

Minutes went by as Mac scanned the countryside, looking for Dante. Finally, he appeared. Dante had managed to get around the deer without them sensing danger or sniffing him out on the breeze. Mac watched with butterflies in his stomach as Dante ran slowly and then on fleet feet like an evil wind. The wolven warrior was scary fast as he bore down on the unsuspecting deer. They had no time to react before he grabbed one in his powerful claws, snapping its neck while the others did exactly as Dante predicted they would. The remaining two bolted directly toward Mac's hiding spot as Dante carried his kill in one fist, chasing them down.

Mac sat on his haunches, waiting, adrenaline firing like gasoline in a racing engine. Then he felt that animalistic hunger kick in at last. The primal instinct of the wolven was ten times more powerful than that of humans, and as the deer neared him, he leaped from hiding, almost flying. With both hands, he took the deer down by their necks. Without a second thought, he squeezed with death grips, feeling the necks break like a twig. Their bodies went limp, and when Mac landed on his feet, he had the two deer in his grasp. Seething with raw power and disorienting anger, Mac stood where he was a minute longer, the deer by his side, and howled.

"Feels good, doesn't it?" Dante said. "It feels like I'm on a drug," Mac said.

"You're not on drugs, my friend; you're fully alive in these little moments. We wolven had to learn to control this instinct, or we would have wiped each other out long ago. The genetic alterations could only civilize us so much; after all of the tampering from our makers, the wolf is still alive inside the man." Dante said.

"It feels so good. I... I don't want it to end. I want to keep going and feed off the energy." Mac said. "Hahaha! Welcome to the family, Mac!" Dante said. He clapped Mac on the shoulder, and they walked back to camp together, the deer hanging limply in the powerful clutches of two brothers in arms. Dante felt a kinship to the earthman that he couldn't explain, and that was about as deep as his sentiment would allow him to go. Mac was a solid warrior, a trait Dante respected in those he allowed to get close to him. Carp had a fire going when they returned to camp, and Ramos built a spit. Ort was sleeping on the soft grass, looking a little more like a wolvacaran warrior and not the wretch they had rescued from the clutches of the vexanon priests.

That night, they ate, laughed, traded war stories, and tried to put the reality of their situation behind them. As a special surprise, Ort passed around a pipe filled with an herbal plant that, when smoked, would enhance the mood, and give the user a second sight. As stories were told and laughter rang through the night, Mac stepped away to relieve himself by an old oak tree, closing his eyes.

Instead of seeing darkness behind his eyelids, he saw Stephanie Brandt and her daughter, Skylar, buying powders and ointments from a wolven apothecary, but Mac could not locate Serena. He thought about her, and as if in answer to his wish, she came into focus, but his little girl looked extremely ill. Her face flushed, and she sat beside Bobby on a log outside. Bobby looked concerned for Serena as she leaned onto his chest, and he placed an arm around her shoulders.

Stephanie appeared with the medicines she purchased for his daughter, but he knew the potions would not save Serena. Stephanie would have no idea what was wrong with his daughter or how to help her. Serena's only hope was their triumphant return with the Tablet of Destinies. Stephanie, Skylar, Serena, and Bobby faded away, and he opened his eyes again, troubled but drowsy from the pipe herb. He kept his fears to himself as the others continued to laugh and joke.

The party ended when everyone had their fill of roasted deer meat and passed out from the soothing power of the pipe—despite the trouble with Serena, Mac, and everyone else slept that night without dreams of horror or war. In the morning, they awoke to a beautiful sunny day. Dante packed some deer meat with him for the walk. The others followed suit, and they began their trek into the eastern Bog Lands. Dank, moist air greeted them upon entering the swamp. Weeping willows, old and defiant, grew out of the wet ground like hairy monsters blocking sight any further than a hundred feet ahead. The logs left behind by trees long dead blocked their path, and sucking mud pulled their feet down.

"How did the centaurs get through here?" Mac asked.

"Secret path. Few know of it, and we'd be traveling that way if we intended to exit, but the Temple of Ostrid is deep in the heart of this bog." Ramos said.

Ort stopped for a moment as if remembering new details about the area. He cocked his head to the side, nodded in silence, and stepped around Ramos to lead the way forward. The swarming bugs were maddening as they buzzed in the traveler's faces. The hours passed as the team made one wrong turn after another through the bog. Mac was worried they'd have to spend another night in inhospitable terrain. He'd never missed his bed back home more than he did then.

"That's it!" Ort said.

Up ahead, sunken into the muck and almost completely covered by vines and weeds, was a building resembling ancient Sumerian construction to Mac. It looked like a derelict mausoleum, and as they drew closer, he could see a black and haunting doorway like an open maw in the mouth of doom rising out of the swamp.

"This is it. If the entrance to Valuria is down there, we'll be there very soon." Ort said.

Dante noticed that Ort seemed spryer today, which made him smile and nod to Ramos, who returned the gesture. Ort hopped up onto the lip of the sunken temple and disappeared into the blackness. Dante shrugged and followed him in. Carp and his skeletal companion were next, and before Mac entered the dark tunnel, he took one final look behind them to ensure they had not been followed. Satisfied, he turned and descended into the Temple of Ostrid.

CHAPTER 6

THE WALLS BEGAN TO CLOSE around the travelers as they followed Dante's light crystal through the overturned monument. The party passed many mysterious, darkened rooms inside the temple filled with mud and debris from centuries of sunken underground. The Temple of Ostrid was now more of a subterranean cavern than a temple of worship. Shadows danced on the walls, illuminating runes carved into concrete, depicting suns, moons, and planets. Worshiping sycophants bowed before dispassionate and unaffected gods, accepting offerings from their slaves with outstretched arms.

"Be careful in here, my friends. We have no idea what may have moved in to claim this temple as home." Ort said.

"Danger in the swamp?" Dante asked. "Death waits for you," Mac said. "What?" Dante said.

"Sorry, those are lyrics from an Exodus song called Cajun Hell," Mac said, and they looked at him with blank stares. "They're a heavy metal band from my world; I couldn't resist." Still no expressions from the Eritrians. "I'll play it for you sometime."

Mac could smell a foul odor somewhere in the deep blackness, which he was getting used to. The acrid, sickly, sweet rotting of foul creatures back from the grave tingled inside his nostrils, but he could hear nothing, as visibility was limited even while using Dante's crystal. Ramos wondered if there could be another necromancer in the temple with them. Ort heard moans and grunts in the darkness ahead as they walked deeper into the sunken temple. The corridor ended at a T intersection, and Ort stopped, head cocked, listening, his nose in the air.

"I hear running water to the left, the air smells cleaner. I think the undead are to the right." Ort said. Ort turned the corner, and before anyone could protest, he was gone without a sound. Minutes passed, and the party began to become concerned. The stench of death was all around them in the darkness, and it was disconcerting even to the bravest of them. Dante had had enough of waiting, and walked around the corner, his diminutive light crystal shining like mana from the gods. Ort was not in sight, but they heard a scream from somewhere in the darkness ahead and then silence.

"Are you serious?!" Dante said. "Where'd he go?" Dante led them down one corridor, and then another as the sound of rushing water grew louder. "That scream might have been from him. Did he say anything before he disappeared?" Mac asked. "Yes, he told me he thought he knew the way out, but then he just vanished," Dante said.

"That doesn't make any sense. Why would he do that when we're all in this together? Unless he lost his mind, maybe?" Mac asked.

"Who knows why people do the things they do? If we *all* performed rationally all the time, our world might not be in the peril it's in now." Ramos said.

"Good point," Dante said.

In the distance, footsteps began to patter on the temple's stone floor.

"You hear that?" Mac said.

"They're following our scent. The undead can smell the living." Ramos said.

"Good thing they can't move very fast," Mac said. "True, but do we want to be stuck down here with them? I say we try to locate the source of the water sound." Carp said.

The light in Dante's hand illuminated macabre scenes etched into the walls, which replaced the former scenes of worshiping followers, suns, cows, snakes, and temples. Although the wall was sideways and appeared to be what used to be the ceiling, it was clear that something terrible had happened in Luvaral. Instead of gregarious, inspirational art, there were demons and fire. Wolvacaran were running from their city in what appeared to be a mass flight from something terrible. These carvings were cruder and seemed carved with more haphazard hands, as if they had been etched into the concrete from overhead.

"Something awful happened here," Dante said. "What do you mean?" Mac asked.

"You see this drawing here? The massive fire demon?" Ramos said. A man on fire was among the scattering wolvacaran, standing high over the trees. He had a giant horn jutting out the side of his head that curled down his chiseled face, and he was scowling.

"That's scary. Any idea what it is?" Mac asked. "The inscription beneath is in ancient wolven, but I think it reads: Lothrax, the fire god comes," Ramos said.

"Is that what happened to Luvaral? Destroyed by a fire demon?" Carp asked.

"I've heard of Lothrax. Gregor used to talk about him. You know, the stories you hear as puppies about monsters under the bed." Dante said. "Well, Gregor told me he'd summon Lothrax to get me if I didn't behave myself on more than one occasion. The wolvacaran appears to have a mysterious and ancient past we know nothing of."

Dante said.

"Eritria's lost civilization found again," Mac said. "If Ort were around, maybe we could ask him what all this means," Carp said. Glorg shook its head, rattling the loose bones in its jaw.

"Right. For instance, we could ask, 'was the earthquake that destroyed your city a hundred-foot- tall monster?'" Mac said.

"He seemed to know a lot about this place, almost like he'd been here before, but I wonder," Dante said. Further down the tilted wall, they could see the carving of a cloaked figure on a hill, holding its right arm out in front of itself. On one of the fingers, it wore a ring that emitted rays of light, and beyond the rays was a massive stone double door. In another depiction, the doors were open, and the head of Lothrax emerged, surrounded by fire. A detailed image of the ring was etched into the concrete wall next to the previous image. The crest on the ring depicted two entwined snakes, one eating the other, and the winner had two jade crystals in its eyes. "Cool ring," Mac said.

"I'm guessing whoever wears it can summon the big guy. You think that's what Ort went off to look for?" Dante asked.

"It's possible, and come to think of it, I'm starting to think his whole story about coming to help us was a lie. The wolvacaran abandoned Eritria a long time ago and cut off all ties with the other tribes. Why would a wolvacaran suddenly betray that hatred for us?" Ramos said.

"Maybe his plans were not as well-intentioned as we thought," Mac said. "If he gets that ring..."

"Anything's possible. The ring would be a nice artifact to have, though." Ramos said.

A sudden scratching of feet in the dirt from behind startled the three from their art appreciation. "There is no escape from Mermadon!" A voice said.

It came from behind the party, and as Dante turned, his light shone on the half-rotted, gangrenous face of a satyr warlock in a black hooded robe. The dark wizard was blind, with milky white retinas, and as Dante's light illuminated him, he could see an army of ghouls coming up from behind the satyr. They were easily outnumbered.

"Merma...who?" Ramos asked. He readied himself instinctually to take on the mob.

"We'll fight them together!" Dante said.

"Get out of here. I'll hold them off and meet you down the hall." Ramos said.

Ramos wore an old necklace Gregor had given him that contained the power of short-distance teleportation. He smiled and winked at Dante, pointing to the amulet around his neck. Dante nodded and patted Ramos on the shoulder as his brother turned and shot a bolt of purple light from his hands into the cluster of enemies behind them.

Four undead were obliterated by the blast of energy, and their ashes covered the warlock with dusty gray powder.

"Get them!" The satyr said, commanding the horde.

Dante, Mac, and Carp ran down the corridor, guided by Dante's light, and after a short distance, all three of them hit the floor with their bottoms and accidentally slid down a chute. Damp moss had grown over the wall, making their descent slick as ice. The sound of rushing water grew louder as they flew down the slide, not knowing what peril awaited them.

"Oh, Crap!" Mac said. He was in the rear sliding hard as his feet kicked Carp in the back.

"I hear rushing water ahead!" Dante said. The roar was building in the darkness.

"Me too...an underground river?" Carp said.

Dante held the light crystal in his hand while the bumps and jolts along the way made the light strobe. Then, the light was gone, and roaring, rushing water filled the dark. Mac felt his heart beating like a bass drum, and Carp began to scream. Seconds later, Carp disappeared in front of him, and then Mac was free-falling into space with the deafening blare of millions of gallons of water gurgling somewhere beneath him. He did not know how far away the water was until he splashed into the icy lake. As a half-gallon of water rushed into his open mouth, he coughed and sputtered, struggling to keep his head above water. He felt himself begin to pass out as little white dots started to granulate his vision. Then he saw a white, translucent figure up ahead, glowing with light. The figure looked into his eyes with sadness and love.

"Carol?" Mac said.

Numbness began to settle into his arms and legs. As Mac drifted toward the light, his care and fear began to subside. She was close now, and he would be with her soon. As Carol's outstretched hand guided him toward her, he let the water carry him away. He swam toward her with near-frozen arms and legs, exhaustion sapping his remaining strength. As his extremities lost all feeling, he was on the dry ground again. Or was he out of the water now? Carol reached out to him, and he looked into her beautiful eyes again. He rolled onto his side and belched a quart of water out of his lungs; the searing fire was all-consuming. He struggled to inhale and found his chest would not cooperate.

"Breathe!" Carol said. "I ca..." Mac said.

"You will die if you don't breathe, Mac!" Carol said.

Consciousness was fading as he smiled stupidly at her. She slammed him on the back with her fists, and more water erupted from his mouth. And then, he found he could breathe a bit more comfortably, spitting more of it out on his own.

"You left me no choice!" Carol said. She was angry, but endearingly, he'd forgotten about until now. He closed his eyes and took a deep, free breath.

"Thank you, Carol." He said and smiled. "Carol? Huh?"

Dante stood over him, looking puzzled. "It's me, brother."

"Oh, wow, that was a heck of a thing!" Mac said. "Welcome back, buddy," Dante said, lifting him off the ground.

Carp swam ashore a moment later, unharmed. A tiny dim light at the end of the cavern illuminated the darkness just enough for the three to see each other.

"I forgot how good a swim feels," Carp said.

They heard a growling roar from the darkness above as Ramos exited the Temple of Ostrid. He made a loud splash into the rushing water.

"I'll go get him," Carp said. He swam away while Mac wrung out his wet fur.

"It seemed so real; she was standing right here," Mac said.

"You have to get a grip, Mac. Your wife died in another world, but you're still alive, and we need you to fight with us to save this planet." Dante said.

"You're right," Mac said. "You'll see her again one day."

"Yeah, I guess I will," Mac said, a small smile slipping out.

"We must not dwell on the dead until we join them. We need to fight for those alive while we can."

"I know."

"Good," Dante said, pawing Mac's fluffy wet head.

Carp swam ashore with Ramos in tow, and the two stood to join Dante and Mac.

"What happened when we left you?" Dante asked.

"I used my skills as a necromancer and directed the undead to attack the warlock and each other. The entire event was rather amusing. Then, I used my amulet to teleport away, and the next thing I knew, I was sliding down a tunnel."

"This power you have now surprises me more and more all the time," Dante said. He was shaking his head in disbelief.

"I'm glad you made it here in one piece," Mac said.

"There's a light at the end of this cavern, so I think we found what we came for. Has Ort shown his face yet?" Ramos asked.

"Not since he left us," Mac said.

"Maybe he sensed the danger and ran for it. I don't know." Ramos said.

"Yeah, or maybe he's a coward and a liar," Dante suggested.

"Let's get moving. The faster we get the tablet and put it back in place, the better, and the sooner I see my kids." Mac said.

They walked about half a mile to the cavern's exit. When they arrived, the beauty beyond was more than any of them could have suspected. The underground river cascaded over the side of a waterfall a mile high into a lush, fertile valley below. Mist rose high, creating a white fog with a rainbow dancing in the center like a multi-colored, inverted grin. Forests covered the ground to the east and west, but vast canyons decorated the landscape to the north in massive natural rock formations speckled with burnt sienna, beige, and red. A brilliant sun shone down on Valuria as Mac and his friends stood dumbfounded on the precipice of an uncharted world underneath the surface of Eritria.

"This is the most beautiful place I have ever seen," Mac said.

"It's like poetry," Carp said.

"If this is where the Tablet of Destinies was lost, we are going to have a difficult time finding it down there," Ramos said.

"Look to the far east. See that tower? There must be a city over there." Dante said.

A crystal city had been built in the heart of the jungle, the walls of which were creating moving prismatic rainbows that resembled a light show. The city, obscured by the forest itself, was surrounded by a stone wall cutting through the trees. As a layer of clouds passed by, they saw a tower constructed of metal and ivory on the horizon. It was easily as high as the waterfall, perhaps taller, with a large crystal atop the mysterious structure gleaming in the sunlight.

"Wait, look over here," Ramos said.

The four walked to the left side of the waterfall, and as if by magic, a stairway appeared on the side of the cliff face.

"Stairs!" Mac said.

"Hah! A way down." Carp said.

The stone steps were approximately three feet wide and descended in a spiral down the cliff face. "Anyone afraid of heights?" Dante asked. He was looking over the cliff face with fear and suspicion.

"You're not telling me *you're* scared, brother?" Ramos asked.

"I'm not a huge fan of high places either, but what choice do we have? Our only way back is forward." Mac said.

"There is no way back if we don't succeed," Carp said.

"Watch your footing," Dante said and took the first step.

The others followed behind him silently, carefully watching their footing on the narrow descent. Mac's pulse became heavier the further away from the safety of the ledge they climbed.

Pebbles beneath his feet rolled over the side, disappearing into the ether, and each time he looked over the edge, vertigo threatened to send him plummeting. His stomach was tightening in knots, and in the back of his mind was a sick sense that, at any moment, he could jump to his death. Down, down, down they walked, carefully stepping down the stairs.

"There are birds in this world," Dante said. Far from the ground, the party looked north and saw a flock of pterodactyls heading east over the forest about a mile from them.

"I think I'll feel better when we're on the ground," Mac said.

"We'll be there soon," Ramos said.

Mac turned to Carp and saw that he looked paler green than usual; his face was stone-like.

Carp stiffened with each downward step. "Just...keep...walking," Carp said. His voice was pinched and thin.

An hour later, they reached the tree line. Each party member took a deep breath, a sense of calm washing over as the spiral staircase vanished into the side of the cliff.

Dante was first to the ground, then Ramos, then Mac and Carp.

"I think I know what happened to Ort," Mac said. He was looking at an outcropping of rocks and a crushed body caught between two of them in the river's flow. Ort's muzzle was missing, and the top of his skull had been visibly dented in.

"There's no way Ort survived that fall. Poor guy, well, I feel like an...what's the expression from your world, Mac?"

"Ass?" Mac said.

"Yeah, that," Dante said.

"We'd better get him out of there at least. It doesn't seem right leaving his body like that." Carp said.

The other three nodded, and in silent reverence, they quietly dislodged Ort's body from the rock and allowed the river to sweep him away. Mac said a few kind words for him out of habit, and the others, unfamiliar with this custom, nodded approval when he finished.

"Well said, Mac," Ramos said. "Thanks. Where to now?" Mac asked.

"That city seems like a good place to start," Dante said.

"How do we know the locals are friendly?" Mac asked.

"Have you ever known locals to be friendly toward outsiders? Present company excluded." Ramos asked.

"Not usually," Mac replied.

"Be on your guard. If it looks like a duck and quacks like a duck, it's a duck." Dante said.

"That's funny; my commander said the same thing before I left Earth," Mac said.

The four walked east into a lush forest of tall trees and vibrant flowers weaving their way between the dense foliage.

"There has to be a trail somewhere," Carp said. Then he spotted a large pert blue flower, about the size of his head, with yellowish purple petals opening outward in a warm greeting to passersby. Four red styles extended past the petals, each topped with a purple stigma coated with a glittering powder that hypnotized the naga prince. The flower's sweet aroma teased his nostrils. It drifted on the wind like perfume, drawing Carp closer.

Snaking along the ground, between his feet, were the flower's vines, and the closer he came, the more the sinister foliage wrapped around his legs, making his movement more difficult. Carp was oblivious to his peril; he was lulled into a hypnotic trance as the carnivorous plant emitted powerful pheromones. Dazed and stunned, Carp grinned as the bulbous head of the flower opened in a frightening display of teeth, sticky white sap dripping from within the petals. Mac had been walking ahead of Carp and turned back just as his naga friend's head was about to vanish into the monster plant's open mouth.

"Carp!" Mac said. "Carp! Watch out!"

An arrow whooshed by Mac's ear a moment later, spearing the flower, and a second one cut it at the base, dropping the bulb to the ground. The vines released Carp's legs, and he looked around in confusion like he'd been walking in his sleep.

"What happened?" Carp said. "We're under attack!" Dante said.

Carp jerked upright, scanning the surroundings for a threat. Nothing moved, not a tree or a frond, as if the shooter had been a phantom.

"I think we should proceed with caution," Mac said.

He felt the tiniest prick in his neck. Instinctually, he placed his hand on the irritated area. When he pulled his hand back, he was holding a small dart. Then suddenly, Mac felt as if his feet were attached to cement blocks, and his head had become marshmallow fluff. The world around him went dim, and Mac fell face-first into a bush.

A second later, Dante dropped to his knees and toppled sideways. And then, Carp and Ramos followed them, crashing to the ground.

Sometime later, Mac's eyes fluttered open, and for a moment, the splitting pain in his head blotted out all emotion. His mind was convinced he had just been on a three-day bender, but he could not remember the last time he'd done such a thing.

"Welcome back," Dante said.

Mac looked up and saw the hazy figure of Dante sitting across from him. To the right of Dante sat Ramos and Carp, chained to the wall.

"Your vision will clear up in a few moments," Ramos said.

"Where are we? What happened?" Mac asked. I'm not sure. I felt a sting in my neck, passed out, and woke up here like you," Ramos replied.

As his vision returned, he saw they were interred inside a rock dugout that had been converted into a prison. The way out was barred, and it looked like they were trapped. The walls of their cell were reddish brown. The room's height from top to bottom was about seven feet tall, ten feet deep, and roughly ten across. Had they been able to stand, Ramos, Dante, and Mac would have had to stoop in his wolven form.

Footsteps came from outside the tiny cell.

Mac's head felt like tiny people were inside his skull, ramming the bone with jackhammers, an apparent side effect of the poison dart. Shuffling feet and conversation from down the corridor were getting closer. Bright daylight from somewhere told Mac they were being held in an outdoor cell. Then he remembered the canyon they had seen from the waterfall and saw that the walls were made of similar stone.

"Do you know who did this?" Mac asked.

"I think we're about to find out," Carp said. He quickly vanished.

Before them, on the other side of the bars, were the strangest creatures Mac had seen yet on Eritria.

The man looking in on them stood five feet tall, with a ring of horns around his head that resembled a crown of thorns. The horns appeared to be solid bone, and they were fixed to his head. His skin was brown, and his beady little eyes glared in on the party with mistrust and interest. His canine molars jutted out like spikes on the top and bottom of his jaw. Mac thought the man's mouth looked somewhat like a bulldog, but overall, the creature reminded him of pictures of storybook demons he looked at as a child. With well-muscled, lean arms and a talisman (a small orb with five stars encircling it) hanging around his neck, he stared at them as if they were creatures in a cage at the zoo.

"I bet childbirth was rough for this guy's mom.

Those horns had to hurt." Mac said.

"I'd watch what you say; we don't know if these creatures understand English," Dante said.

"Who are you? What do you want? Why are you in Valuria?" The man asked. His voice was gruff and direct.

Dante noticed the spear this man was holding was just like the centaurs' tridents, and it could easily reach them through the bars. He tried the manacles chaining him to the wall, but they wouldn't budge, and he could see Ramos and Mac doing the same.

"We're from the overworld of Eritria, and we became lost when we fell down a hole while searching for a temple in the Bog Lands," Dante said.

"You are trespassers on slog land. What is your relationship with the Sisters of Agama? Are you assassins?" The man asked. His trident poked through the bars, and he seemed more agitated. "We don't know who you're talking about. We came from the waterfall, high above your valley, and now we need to find the way back out." Mac said.

"Can you let us out of here, please?" Carp asked. None felt the need to mention the Tablet of Destinies or their actual business in Valuria to their captor. Mac wondered when he would get the opportunity to kill this man. The man regarded them for another moment until he revealed a hidden key. It was a long iron skeleton key with a demonic skull on top and two notched teeth at the bottom. With a sideways tilt of his head, he decided to free them, opening the rusty door. After Mac, Carp, Dante, and Ramos were unlocked and stood again, the slog led them outside into a bright, sunshine-filled day.

"I am Verdant, of the Hathor slogs," Verdant said. Verdant and the four adventurers walked into a gathering area within the canyon, where many tables had been set up for a celebration. Bowls of fruit, roasted pigs, and transparent orange and red liquid carafes rested on the tables while a spirit of happiness filled the air. Slog citizens were smiling and talking amongst each other as the newcomers entered the crowd. High canyon walls surrounded the clearing, a perfect home for the cliff-dwelling slogs. Their homes were apartment-style buildings crafted from the cliffs but fortified with stone blocks and steel, accessible by swinging wooden-planked, rope sky bridges. The people of Hathor bid them hello as they passed by carrying bread, baskets of meat, and bottles of wine, depositing them on the long tables.

"What's the celebration?" Ramos asked. "Today, the king's daughter, Weana, is getting married. The ceremony is about to begin." Verdant said.

"After the ceremony, we shall gather around the speaking flame and discuss your arrival. Until then, enjoy the festivities," Verdant said.

Verdant walked with them to the canyon's end, where a pavilion had been built on a beach by the ocean. Crashing waves rhythmically rolled onto the golden sand, receding as new waves took their place. Seagulls flapped in the breeze as salt air touched the nostrils of each party member.

"Is there an ocean in the center of this planet?

Now, I've seen everything," Mac said.

Mac watched as the water stirred just beyond the breaking waves. A giant tidal wave began to grow, and underneath it was the outline of something large and mysterious. And then, a shark the size of a double-decker bus leaped from the water, snatching four unsuspecting gulls in a single gulp. Mac had never seen anything so large swimming just offshore. It must have been more than seventy feet long.

"Did you just see that?" Mac said.

"I saw a wall of teeth shoot out of that surf over there," Ramos said.

"That was horrifying!" Mac said.

"OK, going into the water is probably bad," Dante said.

The ceremony began, and a slog in a light blue robe lined with dark glyphs on his lapels asked everyone to take their seats. Two long lanes of chairs were set up for the wedding, so Mac and the boys sat in the back to watch the spectacle. Slogs entered from the sides, avoiding the green and purple swirled pattern carpet rolled from the last chair to the beach pavilion. The slogs moved almost automatically as they took their seats, and when the final slog was seated, a flute began to play from somewhere high on the cliffs.

Weana and her groom appeared, walking arm in arm down the aisle. She walked with grace, giving the strangers graceful nods while passing. Her horns were decorated with flowers and gold rings, and her dress was a violet charmeuse, strapless and divine. The robed slog man they had seen earlier stood before the crowd at the end of the lane and waved his arms around as he spoke to the bride, groom, and crowd. They could not hear what he was saying, but they kissed when the ceremony ended, and everyone left their seats in wild applause.

As promised, when the sun went down, and everyone had food and drink, the slog leadership council invited Mac and his friends to sit with them and smoke a weed they called jump. A campfire was built in the center, and all the people of this council took a seat. After the first puff, Mac immediately felt like his head was a balloon floating off his shoulders. "This is nice," Mac said. "Stars, in an underground world? Far out."

His mind began to drift, and as he gazed upon the stars, they drew him closer. He could feel their tiny lights even from far away.

"Well, he's gone. We'll see our buddy Mac again once he's come down."

"He stays like this?" Verdant asked.

"Mac is from Earth, and Earthlings, from what I can tell, have difficulty handling their inebriants. He's checked out on us more than once since he arrived." Ramos said.

Mac heard the conversation from a distance, although he was sitting right next to Ramos.

"No, I'm still here. I need to get my bearings." Mac said. His voice sounded disconnected and dreamy.

A taller, more foreboding-looking councilman entered their circle around the campfire and took a drag on the talking plant pipe. He glared at Mac. "This is our shaman, Omnious," Verdant said. Omnious was wearing cloth shorts with cargo pockets and a silk shirt with a dragon pattern, not unlike something a modern-day beach bum would wear. He reached inside one of the pockets, pulled out a piece of folded-up parchment paper, unfolded it, and held it up to Mac's eyes.

"Tell me why I'm dreaming about this place. For three nights, I have been haunted by it, and the strange people I see suffering in my visions all look like you," Omnious said.

Mac looked closer, squinting through his hazy vision. His eyes widened when he realized that the drawing depicted a crude map of Earth.

CHAPTER 7

MAC WAS STUNNED. He couldn't believe his eyes. Africa, Europe, and North and South America were depicted accurately, and Omnious even colored the continents green and brown. More people than Gregor seemed to have been dreaming of Earth on Eritria. Who else knew about his home planet? How could they even find it, especially when they only had primitive technology? Mac reached out to touch the artwork and felt the unhappy sensation of homesickness. The oceans were colored deep blue, and he could almost see the clouds passing by as Earth orbited in her procession through the cosmos. "That's my home planet, but how could you...?"

Mac said.

"I see visions of the past and future," Omnious said.

"Then you probably know my world is dying," Mac said.

"I have seen your planet's imbalance with nature, the nightmare you made your world. Have you come here to do the same thing to our planet?" Omnious asked.

"Of course not; at least that's on in the minds of our leaders. We're escaping to try and reforge a new world. To start over the right way. Humans lost their way long ago; we were taking too much from the Earth without giving much back. I think we just got caught up in following leaders with selfish agendas, ordinary people who could be bought by multinational corporations for their support when they took office. Reason and common sense left my people long ago. It was also too late by the time we'd realized how far it had all gone wrong." Mac said.

"What do you mean?" Verdant asked.

"I mean, my people, the humans, are some of the more intelligent beings in the galaxy, but for some reason, we have something I can only describe within us as self-hatred, and that hatred is often projected on other people. I want nothing more of their wars and ignorance, and I agreed to come on this mission to try to build a better home for my children. A chance to start over." Mac said.

"Humans are hairless and odd-looking creatures, but we're getting to like them. And just because your people brought themselves to the brink of extinction, that does not mean other creatures in the universe don't do the same thing," Dante said.

"Dante has a point. But you look like the wolven, Mac. How can that be?" Verdant asked.

"I was attacked by a libmok when we arrived, and through a blood transfusion with their father, Gregor, I gained the ability to change between forms," Mac said. He demonstrated his ability for the slogs by shifting into his original form. "We won't all make the journey, though. The people who paid for this little adventure will undoubtedly choose who stays and who goes."

"But if those same leaders who helped destroy your planet come here, won't they just do the same?" "They'll have to play by new rules here to survive. Truthfully, only time will tell how the people from Earth adapt to Eritria, but I'm hoping for the best." Mac said.

"What is your story, Mac?" Omnious said. Mac looked around and saw that the slogs were captivated by his tale. He worried about saying too much, but the effects of the plant he smoked were lowering his inhibitions.

"I was in charge of a project that was supposed to find life somewhere else in the universe, a new home for humanity, but I retired before we found the answer because our methods were unsound. We murdered our people to find this planet, and I just couldn't be a part of it anymore. The nightmares we cooked up in that underground facility still haunt my dreams," Mac said, trailing off.

He heard the words coming out of his mouth and could not believe them. The narcotic effect of the drug was letting some of the skeletons out of his closet, classified information, and causing diarrhea of the mouth. He hesitated a moment, realizing what he'd just revealed.

"How were you able to find Eritria?" Omnious said.

"We used drugs to dope up homeless people with no families to miss them. The drugs heightened their consciousness to a level none of us had ever experienced. They became more like astral travelers than humans. We used the power of suggestion to guide them and force their consciousness into the far reaches of space. It was cheaper than trying to do it with a crew and ship. Besides, we had no idea where we'd go when we first began. We knew our army had also captured a spacecraft from the Zeta Reticuli star system. And before the pilot died, he told our interrogators he had seen life in this star system." Mac said.

"That's when you began to torture and maim your people?" Omnious asked.

"That's when we altered the program and began to search this galaxy quadrant. Which did require extra.. .effort." Mac said. Old habits die hard, and Mac had been trained his entire career to deflect when asked a direct question about a mission. He couldn't believe he was defending his own wrongs. "Omnious, are we here to interrogate our guests?" Verdant asked.

"I'm just trying to get a good idea of who we're dealing with here, Verdant. We know about the wolven and their ways, but the Earthmen certainly seem to have a violent and bloodthirsty past." Omnious said.

"You're right. But I was sent here to ensure that was all in the past. Doesn't everyone deserve a second chance?" Mac asked.

"That remains to be seen. Don't be surprised if this planet casts out your race just like your Earth did, but you're OK with us. Welcome to Hathor, Mac from Earth." Omnious said.

Mac felt guilty. Could he ever redeem himself from his past?

"Thank you, Omnious," Mac said.

"You seek the Tablet of Destinies, correct?" Omnious asked.

"What you search for was probably destroyed long ago during the great war between the sky gods Ninerta and Anu." An elderly lady declared. "Sashu, that war is a myth," Omnious said. "Just because something happened long before you were born does not make it a fantasy," Sashu said. The wrinkles in her pale little face showed much hardship. Her horns had been filed back with age, less sharp than the younger slogs.

"It does not make it true either, Sashu," Omnious said.

"Be that as it may, the Tablet was assumed to be the energetic catalyst of our planet's sudden evolution. From the stories sent down through the ages, we must conclude that it was hidden to stay protected from enemies of the sky gods." Sashu said. "We were told the Tablet was used to create our races above ground through the use of ziggurats and the pyramids," Dante said.

"Indeed, it is an object of great power, capable of many things, and when used for good can bring about life. But when evil hands touch it death and desolation are what it leaves behind." Sashu said. "That is what we have been told since the dawn of our time."

"Nobody knows for sure if it still exists, do they?" Ramos said.

"What if we came here for nothing? If we can't stop the spread of the ick, we're doomed." Carp said. "My people are almost gone." He lowered his head. "The ick has infected my daughter. We are desperate to find this artifact." Mac said.

"We feel the effects as well. The white tower is no longer glowing as it once did, and our magic is fading." Sashu said.

"The Sisters of Agama may know more than we do, but they are not to be trusted. In recent years, they have been less hospitable to outsiders and even the slogs. We used to be on good terms with them, and then, one day, our relationship fell apart. They began to kidnap our people for their nefarious purposes. You humans seem to share this trait with them so that they may help you, Mac from Earth." Omnius said. Mac ignored the dig.

"That's true. How many more slogs do we have to lose before we fight back against them?" A slog man asked.

"They're too powerful, and their technology is far more advanced than ours. I'm surprised the sisters let you get as far as you did without taking you hostage. Surely, their queen had watchers in the woods." Another man said.

"Dante and his party were walking toward their city when we overtook them in the forest," Verdant said.

"You would have more than likely been captured and placed in the mines to dig silver and gold for Queen Resha had you gone to that city," Omnious said.

"Look, I don't know about this feud you share with these sisters, but we have to find this tablet and get it back in place. And it sounds like we all suffer from the same malady, so I say we work together." Dante said.

"We wish we could help you, but our people have not unfolded the mystery either," Omnious said.

"Maybe the Sisters of Agama have taken them for themselves. Or perhaps they know where we can look." Mac said.

"Excellent point," Ramos said.

"I propose we go investigate their city and play dumb about what we know," Dante said.

"Be careful. If the sisters discover your intentions, they may capture and enslave, or tear you apart, Dante." Omnious said.

"You let us worry about that. We've been through worse. Besides, our future relies on success here. If I have to tear through every one of these so- called sisters to get what we need, then so be it." Dante said.

"We will have to proceed with caution. The world depends on our survival." Ramos said.

"Although I don't know the meaning of that word, brother, I see what you mean. If the sisters know something, we need to be clever and stealthy to get the information," Dante said.

"Do what you must, but we can't go with you. It's far too dangerous for us." Verdant said.

"The sisters are wicked and terrible, with dark magic that exceeds any power we've ever seen," Sashu said.

"Be that as it may, we have to leave in the morning," Ramos said.

The rest of the evening took a turn toward more pleasant conversation as they passed the pipe and discussed the long history of Eritria, both above and below. Dante and Ramos told stories of the recent centaur war and Ragnok their king. Mac told them about the eelk and their confrontation with the monstrous sea creature. The slogs, in turn, described the many mysterious caves, caverns, secret underground rivers, and their history as a nation. Mac fell asleep sitting up, and Ramos was not far behind him as the day's activities caught up with him. Verdant guided them to the cliff dwellings with spare rooms for the party. High above the ground, the apartment complex was only accessible via a cable-driven elevator that doubled as a transport device and security because there was only one way up or down.

"You have only one way up? Please say there are stairs somewhere or a ladder." Carp said.

"Stairs are a security risk, and we need protection from the predatory animals here in Valuria. We had them once, but dengue panthers from the jungle could climb them too easily. We suffered violent attacks inside our homes some time back." Omnious said.

"We'll be leaving at dawn," Ramos said as the elevator reached the top of the cliff.

"I wish you luck on your journey, friends, and I pray you find what you're looking for," Sashu said. She bid them farewell and took the elevator back down.

Ramos and his party stood a hundred feet from the ground on a path cut out of the cliff face. The path glimmered in the light of the torches nearby, tiled with gold bricks. Mac estimated that the walkway to their apartment dwelling was easily worth several million dollars back on Earth. Verdant led them to separate apartments within the complex, and the evidence that these people were great builders and engineers lay everywhere. The slogs' homes were designed masterpieces, with glass exterior windows in each room, wooden blinds, complex original paintings on the walls, and vases filled with pretty flowers. Each party member was given his place to spend the night, too.

That night, Mac dreamed of the underground laboratories where manmade horrors abounded. In tonight's macabre matinee, he could see his last test subject: the woman who came to him looking so crusty and dirty that the collection agents had mistaken her for a man. The testers and acquisition crew preferred men to women. This was because it was always easier if the researchers did not have to think about the possibility that they might be murdering someone's mother.

In their haste, two overworked special operations men from New Jersey had bypassed the usual delousing shower, shaved the subject's head, readied the patient for injections, and before any of the testers realized their recent acquisition had breasts, the needle was in her neck, and the twenty- something Ms. X was on the final journey of her soon-to-be short life. The tranquilizers and paralytic they had given her during processing prevented speech and movement, but not the ability to understand what was happening.

Mac had seen one face after another drone in and out of their laboratory over the years, and after a while, they all blended like perfumes at a department store counter. Mac had discovered her sex a short time later, after taking a closer look, but by then, it was much too late. In the dream, he could not move his mouth to talk, and when he looked down, his feet were buried in concrete up to the ankles.

The final phase began as her brain fluids mixed with the serum. The subject's face contorted into a grimace, out of her mind, no longer conscious or aware but still alive. Stars flashed on the screen as her mind drifted into deep space. Saturn passed by as blood ran from her eyes. Her body began to convulse until she expired as Mac watched the screen go blank shortly after going Pluto.

The woman slumped forward, and then she raised her head toward Mac, glaring at him with bloody, empty sockets.

"You did this!" She spoke. Her mouth was filled with cobwebs, and as she opened her mouth wide, tiny black spiders skittered out while she talked to Mac.

He shot up in bed, sweat coursing down his face, and maw in rivulets, fur knotted, breathing heavily. The final vision had burned clear into his eyes: her body being liquefied and poured into a fertilizer barrel. The stacks of steel drums filled a football stadium-sized warehouse in the underground facility. He wiped his face with the blanket and threw his legs over the edge of his bed. *No more sleep tonight*, he thought and went to the window. It was half-light outside; the sun was beginning to rise. As Mac looked skyward, he realized the stars far above were crystal stalactites dotting the ceiling of Valuria. He leaned forward and tried to picture Carol's face, but the details were fuzzy. He wished he could rid himself as easily of the images conjured in the catacombs.

The Valurian sun shone its first rays on his face as the new day dawned. They would leave to find the sisters this morning, and Mac would be one step closer to reuniting with his children.

Far below, Mac could see the slogs setting out plates and food for breakfast and could not help but admire these people for their closeness. Dante and Ramos were already down at the breakfast area, walking and speaking together as Mac watched them, feeling his growing kinship with them widening. Mac dressed and entered the elevator to join them at one of the long tables. Carp was already up and had filled his plate with some vegetables resembling turnips and beets.

"We need to leave after we eat," Dante said. "You're right. The longer we're down here, the further the ick spreads." Ramos said.

"I'm worried about Serena. I'm not sure how long she has to live with that ick crap growing inside of her." Mac said.

"Yeah, and soon the ick will spread to every corner of our continent wiping out what's left of the vanishing races," Ramos said.

"If this Tablet can reverse the damage before I lose my little girl, I'll be forever in all of your debt," Mac said.

"I think we are all equally in each other's debt, Mac. This foul magic may be what killed most of the faeries, driving them underground." Carp said. He pushed the vegetables around the plate with his fork. "Who are the faeries?" Mac asked. "We've got legends of them back on Earth as little winged creatures that grant wishes or something like that,"

Mac said. Dante raised his eyebrows.

"We have entirely different faeries than you do, my friend. We call them the little people behind closed doors, but don't tell them that to their faces, or they'll cast a spell to rip out your eyes or make your kids sick. They are a grouchy, hostile race of people who are better left to their own devices." Dante said.

"Dante's right. We traveled to their land once, long ago, and nearly didn't make it back. They lure the unsuspecting into their fairy circles and feed on life energy as you dance yourself to death. We were fortunate enough to escape one before it was too late. But that's a story for another day. Once this is all over, we can explore, and I'll show you where they live, Mac. As long as we don't go too far into their territory, we should be alright." Ramos said.

"I'll take you up on that," Mac said.

After the four finished their meal, they found Verdant sitting with his wife and children at one of the long tables.

"We're leaving to find the sisters," Dante said. "May fortune's light shine upon your faces, and the darkness never touch your back, my friends,"

Verdant said.

"We'll set this world right again once we find the Tablet," Ramos said.

"Beware of the dark queen. The sisters are not to be trusted." Verdant said. He stood and balled his hand into a fist, bumping his into Dante's, and then made his way around the party doing the same. Many of the slogs regarded the party as fools who were sure to get themselves killed on a mission of madness. They looked on with expressions of disbelief, even though Verdant, a distinguished community member, believed in Mac and his friends.

"The name of their city is Calvalor, which means *fortress of pain.* Be careful, adventurers." Omnious said. He had been standing behind the party. Ramos turned to face him as he lowered his robe hood.

"Thank you for your hospitality, chief," Ramos said.

"You are perceptive, Ramos. I never mentioned that I was the chief." Omnious said.

"One leader knows another, Omnious. May we meet again." Ramos said. He extended his right fist as Omnious bumped it with his own.

"I am sorry we can't do more, but the sisters' magic is far stronger than ours. The light of our society is diminishing, and we are weaker than we once were." Omnious said.

"You've done enough, Omnious. Thank you again, and may we meet on the road of good fortune again." Ramos said.

Ramos raised his hood, and the party walked into the wilderness where archers would guard them as far as Calvalor. A road led them away from Heathor, snaking through the forest. Dante could smell the archers in the trees, but he still did not trust the slogs, and as they walked toward Calvalor, he wondered about the Sisters of Agama and what kind of reception they would find upon their arrival.

Wolven were warrior priests, and since the last war with Broad Axe, they had been masquerading as peacekeepers, farmers, and recluse forest dwellers. The

Sisters of Agama would have a whirlwind of ferocious canine aggression on their hands if they thought they could get the best of Dante, he thought.

"These sisters must be more shocking to look upon than the slogs, as ferocious as they've been made out to be," Ramos said.

"If you need me, I'm still here; I think I'll vanish for a while, though," Carp said.

"Good idea. We need a man in the shadows." Mac said.

The dirt road merged into a stone trail after about an hour into their trek. A sweet scent wafted to their nostrils as they continued. Multicolored flowers lined their path, and shifting vines decorated with attractive blossoms.

"It smells like a botanical garden here," Mac said. He felt his uncertainty dim, and calm washed over his mind.

"The flowers, they smell..." Mac started. "Stay away from the forest," Carp said. "Look to the right."

Ensnared in the vines was a small pig struggling to break free as the greenery wound tighter around its body. A thick vine had wrapped around the neck, preventing it from squealing. The struggle was over a moment later, and the pig went still. A large purple flower lowered as the vines worked like hands to deliver the pig into its hungry mouth. Violet and yellow petals closed over the little body, and for a second, Mac could see teeth springing up from each colorful petal as it enveloped the pig. Mac looked around and saw that the same flowers surrounded them.

"The plants here are quite deadly. I know, firsthand." Carp said.

"The sooner we're topside again, the happier I'll be," Mac said. A long green vine slunk out of the forest and tickled his toes.

"We should keep moving..." Dante said. He looked down at the vine nearing Mac's foot and shook his head in disgust. "...before we become a part of the meal plan for the Valurian forest." They heard a sound in the forest. It was natural, but it wasn't birds. It sounded like female voices. The melody drew them along, guiding, soothing, and easing their mental stress.

"Does everything here have a narcotic effect? Where is that singing coming from? It's so...relaxing." Mac said.

Around the next bend, the men found their answer. A four-story-tall iron gate suddenly confronted them. This gate was the only visible opening in a two-story stone wall so long it disappeared into the forest in both directions.

Beyond the gate, the adventurers could see a city of crystal and glass. Golden bricks lined the path beyond the gate and made up a large fountain in the middle of the road. In the fountain's center was a large pterodactyl cut from crystal, spitting water from its mouth into the pool below. Mac tried the gate, but it was locked.

"Well, this is not a good start," Ramos said.

"We could brute force the gate," Dante said. He looked at Mac and Ramos, shrugging.

While the three stared at each other, trying to figure out their next move, a tall, human-looking woman in a red robe walked down the path toward them. Her steps were lithe, and she moved with such grace as if she were on a floating cloud.

"Carp, keep quiet," Mac said, whispering out of the corner of his mouth.

Long blond hair draped over her right shoulder, past a long, slender neck and lower, covering her breasts. The robe she wore was low-cut, exposing the buxom beauty's rather attractive cleavage. Mac felt himself staring, but unlike gazing into the sun, he found it difficult to look away and knew he had been busted when he met her eyes. He looked up and saw her smiling at him with a knowing glance, and then she moved her eyes over the entire party. "Welcome to Calvalor. The four of you must be quite weary from your journey. Please, come in. You there, transparent in the bushes, have nothing to fear from me."

Carp materialized with a sheepish grin.

"You don't have to be ashamed, my friend. We sense many things in this realm. Many unseen forces that lurk in shadows are visible to our eyes. However, there is no need to hide, for you are friends. My name is Sister Agatha, and you are all guests of the Sisters of Agama. Come inside and meet the queen," Agatha said.

She waved her hand, and the iron gate opened wide for the party to enter. With a final glance at each other, the wolven and their not-so-invisible naga prince walked through the entrance and into a city unlike any they had ever visited before.

CHAPTER 8

SISTER AGATHA LED THEM DOWN the golden path, past the pterodactyl fountain, through a garden of flowers and ripe vegetables, and into a shining crystal city where the buildings gleamed in midday sunlight. Each shop, home, and apartment were constructed of thick, frosted crystal. Mac studied the construction as they walked by. There were no crystal bricks or stones; it appeared that the crystal walls had been poured rather than carved or extracted from a quarry. "You have a lovely city, sister Agatha," Mac said. "Thank you, traveler. Calvalor is a wonderful home for our people. Lady Resha, our queen, desires to meet with you all." Agatha said. "She knows about us?" Dante asked.

"Oh yes, she watched your descent from the waterfall," Agatha said.

"But how?" Carp asked.

"We have many eyes in the sky and..." Agatha said.

"The pterodactyls," Ramos said.

"Correct, that's why we have a crystal sculpture of the great winged sky dwellers. Our queen can see through their eyes."

"Really?" Ramos asked.

"Well, we must keep our eyes on the evil slogs." Something was off with their current situation. Ramos sensed it, although he had no evidence. As much as Valuria appeared to be a paradise under Eritria, all was not well.

"Evil slogs?" Ramos asked.

They approached another fountain, where a tall brunette woman greeted them, dressed in a flowing green gown adorned with jewels. Her features were soft and supple, and she had a royal demeanor. The way she carried herself, her straight posture, and her smile told them that her life was one of luxury. Like the siren's song, Mac could hear the cheerful singing voices of many women as the lady approached them. "We'll not talk about them; this is a time for celebration. Queen Resha, our guests have arrived."

Agatha said. She bowed to her queen.

"Welcome to Valuria." Queen Resha said. "Thank you, queen," Dante said. He bowed to her, and the others followed his lead.

"Come inside my castle and rest for a bit. I would like to hear about your home above ground.

And what brings you to our land."

"Of course, your majesty. Thank you for welcoming us into your home." Ramos said. "Our society has never left Valuria, and we rarely receive visitors, so we're eager to learn about the overworld." Queen Resha said.

She walked ahead, and as they neared the castle, two more lovely ladies guarded the entrance. Their wings were white and spread past their shoulders like the depictions of heavenly angels, Mac thought. In each hand was a polearm with a blade curved as a scythe affixed at the end. The two guards smiled charmingly at them, setting Mac off balance.

"Welcome to Calvalor." The sentry on the right said.

It seemed strange to him that these people were the evil women the slogs had warned them about, Mac thought. He had a hard time believing these were the same people. Maybe the slogs had lied. He decided to rely on his military intelligence training: keep what he had been told close to the cuff and wait for further evidence to appear. He figured it was like playing chess, although he was still unsure who the pawns were.

Queen Resha brought them into a large circular room with a circular crystal table in the center and carved oak chairs pushed in around it. Ramos entered the room first, quickly noticing the pulse of some great power from within. His eyes glowed purple involuntarily as the power tugged on his soul like a tractor beam, and he could feel himself being pulled toward the floor. He stopped walking momentarily and backed out of the room, feeling the surge of energy release him as he left the doorway.

"Is there a problem, Ramos?" Queen Resha asked. "Your eyes are smoldering, warlock. I hope we don't have anything to worry about." She laughed. It was a good-natured giggle, but something behind her words gave him pause.

"No, no, sorry. I just felt...faint for a moment. Long journey, I guess." Ramos said. Dante looked over at his brother with concern because he, too, had seen the purple fire in Ramos' eyes, but as his brother walked back into the room, the glow did not return. The queen, who had shown a sense of humor about the event, cut her eyes at Ramos with interest. He looked over, and she flashed him a warm smile, but he could hear her voice inside his head.

"*Sit, rest, and leave your problems outside, warlock. Allow the calming energy to ease your cares, and we will be well met.*"

Ramos took a breath and found a seat at the table, allowing the queen to sit first. She motioned for them to be seated, and then a moment later, some servants, beautiful, winged angels, brought in heaping plates of fresh vegetables. The wolven brothers looked at each other with disappointment, as there was no meat, but being gracious guests, neither wanted to offend their host by turning down a free meal in their honor. They would hunt something later.

"For the meat-eaters in our party, we have a special treat. Although we do not eat meat ourselves, Regina, one of our hunters, was kind enough to bring us a fresh kill this morning," Queen Resha said. Ramos wondered how she knew they would need meat before the wolven arrived.

The servants carried a large bowl of seasoned, charbroiled meat and set it on the table. Mac thought momentarily that he caught a glimpse of a slog horn in the bowl, but her spoon turned too fast for him to be sure. The maiden who served the dish smiled at everyone and left the room without another sound.

"Everyone, please, eat." Queen Resha said. She clasped her hands and watched as empty plates were filled, hungry guests were fed, and once each guest had taken their portion, she filled her plate.

After all, bellies were full; the queen asked everyone to talk about themselves and why they had come to Valuria. Ramos felt like they were being put on the spot, and he knew he should keep his reasons to himself. He regretted not discussing with the group that they'd need to keep their business private even if asked directly. As the queen centered her questioning on Carp, he began to feel nervous that he'd ruin the secrecy of their quest.

"We've come in search of the Tablet of Destinies, Your Highness," Carp said.

He looked at Ramos, wondering whether he'd said too much. Ramos confirmed it by shaking his head and rolling his eyes. Carp gulped, realizing what he'd done, but continued to speak.

"I am Carp, son of the king and queen of the naga. To stop the spread of a killer virus and the extinction of all life in Eritria, we've come here to get the Tablet and put it in the Tower of Kail." Carp said and paused.

"Go on, don't be afraid. We'll not harm you in any way, my friend." Queen Resha said. Her attention focused on Carp.

"The Tablet of Destinies was lost long ago, and we think that Inga, the green dragon, brought it to Valuria. We noticed that populations were declining all over the planet, and it was not until we learned about the Tablet and its power that we connected the dots. Now, a new entity poses a threat to our planet: the ick. It's a dark magical force that was contained until the centaur mages keeping it quarantined were killed in the war, and now the disease is loose, and it may be too late for my people, even if we do find the Tablet."

"I see." Queen Resha said.

"I know about the Tablet and its great power. It was once contained within these walls. That was before it was stolen, of course. Didn't Omnious tell you they stole and hid the artifact?" Queen Resha asked.

"What?" Mac said. His head spun; had they been tricked so easily?

"The slogs are a minimalistic society. They seek to eliminate all magic and industry that does not involve sharpening sticks and stones to beat each other. Simpleton savages! The Tablet used to sit in the Tower of Kail, powering the network of pyramids above ground, keeping the balance of power in our world and yours. Inga did bring it down and give it to my people, the Egren, but the slogs snuck in and stole it like thieves in the night." Queen Resha said.

"I can't believe this. We were right there. I knew we shouldn't have trusted them." Dante said, pounding his fist on the table.

"Is the Tower of Kail the one with the large crystal top we saw coming down?" Ramos asked.

"The very one." Queen Resha said.

Queen Resha opened the palm of her hand, and a ball of pure white light floated from it. A candelabra chandelier hung above their heads, and as the ball of light passed each candle, a tiny flame ignited the black-tipped wicks. A moment later, a black-winged beauty standing about seven feet tall entered the room. Mac watched her cross and felt his heart skip a beat. Her skin was alabaster and smooth, like a porcelain doll, with eyes of swirled orange and black, reminding him of Halloween colors. Her lips were a shade of midnight that glistened in the light as if pure darkness had kissed her.

Her lower lip pouted, and she walked with a sexy sway that gave Mac goosebumps. She glanced at him for a second, as if reading his thoughts, and shot him a quick devilish slight curl of her lips that widened his eyes. She wore a black leather bustier with red threading and black leather pants that ended at her bare feet. Her outfit was intoxicating, erotic, and dangerous, and he wanted to know more. Mac was entranced, and all thought of Stephanie Brandt vanished like dry leaves in a summer fire.

"Hi there, wolf boy." She spoke. The woman blew him a kiss and fluttered her dark wings. "Oooh!"

"Lilith, leave our guests alone. What did you find in the mines?" Queen Resha asked.

"More of the workers died overnight. I don't know what else to tell you. You know we're having problems with the ick."

"So, the ick is affecting Valuria too..." Carp mumbled.

"Gentlemen, meet your guide, Lilith. She'll help you find what you seek, what we all search for," Queen Resha said.

Mac wanted to try to say something but knew it would be inappropriate.

"We can start our search in the morning, but we don't know where to begin," Ramos said.

"Lilith knows every inch of the hills, valleys, and caves of Valuria. She'll help you."

The raven-haired beauty shot Resha a get bent look, stiffened, and shook her head.

"Thanks, mother," Lilith said. She turned to go, and Ramos looked from her to the queen.

"I'd follow her if I were you." Queen Resha said. Ramos and his party did as suggested, but before they left Resha's chamber, he noticed that the queen wore a ring on her right hand identical to the one they had seen on the mural in the Temple of Ostrid. It depicted two snakes eating each other's tails, glaring back at him with jade eyes. He filed it in his mind and would tell Dante later. The party followed Lilith out the door of Queen Resha's castle and down a long path toward another large crystal and stone building.

Guarding the structure were two stone golems chiseled from basalt to resemble giant vampire bats. They were gazing skyward, their mouths half open, fangs displayed menacingly, and they looked like they might take flight at any moment. Beyond the golems was a set of stone stairs that led down in a spiral toward the darkness.

"Where are you taking us?" Carp asked. He was getting more nervous.

"What, you're afraid now? You just climbed down a mile-high waterfall and escaped the slogs." Lilith said.

"It seems somewhat disconcerting that you're leading us into a stairwell that descends into the earth. I'm just concerned that this may not be the direction we need to go." Carp said.

"It does seem like a rather convenient way to get rid of trespassers. You got a dungeon down there or something?" Ramos asked.

'There's no hidden agenda, and nothing's going to happen to you down here." Lilith said. Mac was staring at her breasts. "Eyes up here, soldier." She was smiling and shaking her head.

"Sorry, I was uh..." Mac said.

"Besides, it would never work between us; you've got way too much hair for my taste," Lilith said.

"Hah, that's where you're wrong. He's a hairless human from planet Earth!" Dante said. He put his hand over his mouth and snickered.

"A what?" Lilith asked. Her eyebrows rose in a knowing glance that Mac failed to catch.

"Show her, big guy," Ramos said.

"I'm not a carnival freak! I won't switch back and forth to appease your sick sense of humor, Dante. I prefer this form for now, so thanks, but no." Mac said.

"Oh, come on, show me," Lilith said. She was clapping her hands in front of her face.

Mac stared at her for a minute, her black, orange eyes captivating him with a hypnotic pull. He concentrated and slowly turned into a soft, fleshy human. Within twenty seconds, he was standing before her, exposed. Instead of looking away, she smiled.

"You're a cute one! Maybe we can work something out. How do you feel about girls with wings?" Lilith said.

"I never considered it before, but you're very..." Mac said.

"Alright, stop tripping over your tongue. Let's go; I have to show you something and don't worry, I don't bite," Lilith said. "Unless you want me to." She looked at Mac, who blushed and quickly returned to wolven form.

Lilith led them down into the dark. With a wave of her hand, torches attached to the wall lit one by one as she passed. Minutes later, they were at the bottom of a long spiral staircase, entering a great room. This chamber was so large they could not see the top, even when Lilith ignited every torch.

"We're here, boys," Lilith said.

On the wall were three giant murals that stretched around the massive circular room.

"We'll begin the tour over here. If you've never heard this tale, you're in for a treat. We don't bring many guests down here." Lilith said.

Mac nearly tripped over something in the dirt, and thinking it was a rock, he looked down to see he had kicked a large femur bone. Several more bones lay around them, and his alarm was growing. The first mural depicted a bearded man standing atop a pyramid temple, holding a rectangular object above his head. People in a courtyard far below were kneeling, bowing to him while the sky filled with winged creatures that looked quite like the Sisters of Agama. Rays of energy from the rectangular artifact disintegrated the army of winged creatures as they approached the man.

"This is the Marduk mural. A great battle between the titans took place in the world above ours long ago." Lilith said.

"How long ago?" Mac asked.

"Over two million years. This is the story of Marduk, Tiamat, and Anu: The Anunnaki sky gods who came here and modified our ancestors." Lilith said.

"I've heard those names before. The naga queen explained some of this when we met with them on the submarine." Mac said.

"Marduk gained control of our planet using this device and defeated those who sought to use it for war. The Tablet of Destinies is so powerful a weapon that he who has it controls the universe. Tiamat, the queen of Andromeda, also sought to wield this power and tricked Marduk into allowing her to see the Tablet. She had a ship waiting and stole the weapon from him before he could stop her." Lilith said. The second mural showed a ship leaving the planet as they walked alongside it.

"Anu, who also sought the power for himself, engaged Tiamat in a great space battle near your part of the universe, on a planet named after the queen. After her destruction..." They moved to the third and final mural. "Marduk tracked Anu down and killed him on this planet."

The mural depicted a collection of tablets in Marduk's hands, which he smashed atop a mountain. Then, it showed him walking down a valley with one tablet under his arm. At the end of the mural, he walks into a tall white tower, and in the final image, light emanates from the top in all directions.

"Having hidden the tablet far beneath Eritria, Marduk boarded a ship and left the planet. These murals represent what we've been able to translate from the ancient clay tablets and scrolls." Lilith said. Her story finished, and she turned toward them. Mac stepped over something sharp on the floor, and when he looked down, he realized it was the ribcage of a human-sized skeleton. To his right were the skeletal remains of a slog.

"What is this place?" Mac asked.

They looked around the dimly lit underground chamber. A tall, barred gate appeared in the wall to their left where there had been none before, and when Mac turned back around, Lilith was already moving toward the stairs leading up.

"It's a trap!" Mac yelled.

"I hate to leave you down here, but if I don't, the queen will feed me to the pterodactyls. You have to understand this is just self-preservation." Lilith said. Before she could get to the stairs, the doorway vanished, and in its place was a smooth wall. Lilith turned to the wall and felt for a door, but she could not find one. Suddenly, Resha appeared in the center of the room.

"Welcome to The Crucible of Shadows. Where you will battle to the death and receive a hero's honor when you die." Queen Resha said.

Dante ran at the queen and dived through the air, rolling as he flexed his muscles and readied his claws. Expecting to hit the queen with full force, he over-rotated. She vanished, and then he flipped, landing on his feet, and sprawling across the dirt floor.

"Ah, ah, ahhhh. Not that easy, wolven."

"So, you were just going to leave us in here to die?" Ramos asked. Enraged, he turned on Lilith as purple flames danced in his eyes.

"The queen made me do it! I had no doubt you warriors could defend yourselves from what is coming, but she threatened to kill my surrogate parents. They're the only real family I've ever had, I'm sorry." Lilith said. She was talking to all of them but looking at the forty-foot-tall gate and the gaping maw of darkness beyond.

"I'll kill you!" Ramos said.

He hurled a violet ball of fire at her, but she leapt nimbly into the air, hovering on wings as the fire missed her. Dante ran toward her next, and although Mac wanted to kill her for trapping them down there as much the others, the gate was opening, and his eyes were transfixed by it.

"That doorway behind you is a portal to another world, Ramos," Lilith said. Her eyes were widening with fear as she watched the gate creak open. "Um, guys, I think we may have company soon," Mac said.

"I'm trying to tell you your fight is not with me but with the Cyclops," Lilith said. She flapped her wings in the half-light.

"Can we get out through there?" Dante asked. Ramos became tempted to throw another fireball at Lilith, but he stopped when a deafening roar exploded from the black tunnel past the gate, shaking the gigantic room.

In the next instant, light filled the large chamber, revealing to the party where they were.

"We're in an arena," Ramos said.

High above the murals were grandstands. The sisters had piled in above them and were now seated as they quarreled with Lilith. Mac looked up and thought his eyes were playing tricks on him. Their appearances changed, and the sisters were more demons than angels now.

"They got ugly quick!" Mac said.

"Harpies," Dante said. "I should have known by the smell of rotten meat when we entered the city." "What? I didn't smell anything." Mac asked.

"That's because you were too busy looking. These women are among the undead. I'm surprised *you* didn't catch it, brother." Dante said. Ramos looked at him with a sheepish grin and shrugged.

"Well, they were pretty," Ramos said.

"So is she, and look at the mess we're in now," Mac said. He tilted his head toward Lilith.

"I'm not one of them. I was captured by these monsters and forced to work for them. They would have killed my family if I didn't." Lilith said.

Harpies were staring down at them as the roar grew closer. The once beautiful Sisters of Agama had grown pale, and their teeth were longer, more like daggers in their mouths as they grinned with wicked delight from their safe perch high above. "Lilith, we thought you would like to see your family one last time before the monsters tear you apart." Queen Resha said.

Lilith had no time to counter with witty banter before two bodies were heaved over the side of the wall above them. They both landed in the dirt with a hard thump, neither moving.

"Mom...Dad?" Lilith said and flew over to them.

When Lilith saw the bodies, to her horror, it was indeed her mother and father, with both of their throats sliced open from ear to ear. She dropped to her knees in grief as she stared at the dark maroon smiles that cut into their necks. Their wings were broken and torn, sticking out in jagged angles. Lilith reached out and cradled her mother's head in her lap as it popped off in her hands. Eyes wide with disgust, terror, grief, and rage, she let out a howl in the arena, answered a moment later by another, closer roar from the deep dark. The harpies began chanting something inaudible.

"I'll kill you for this, Resha," Lilith screamed.

The queen began to laugh.

A second later, a thirty-foot tall, hulking man kicked the gate open and rushed into the room, kicking Dante, the closest to the gate, across the arena. He slammed into the wall with a thud as the invader stood with a dual-bladed battle-axe in one of his hands. He was well built, muscular, and looked like a wall with legs. His head was bald, and the giant's mouth was filled with sharpened teeth. In the center of his forehead was a single red and blinking eye, and as he surveyed the room, his mouth twisted into an evil grin.

"Let the games begin," Mac said.

Without a second thought, he rushed toward the behemoth. The Cyclops shuffled into the center of the arena and gave an ear-shattering bellow, but he did not see Mac running up from behind. Carp vanished and crept outside the fray to determine what to do next. The young naga prince felt helpless in this place; how could he ever be a hero when he was so weak? He missed his mother and father and wanted to cry. He knew the other men would look down on him, but his fear of this new threat sent him into hiding.

He sat against a dark wall section, slid to the floor, and wept for his sorrow. With their attention focused on the Cyclops, Carp was the least of wolven worries, and none of the men had expected much from him in any event. In the group consensus, he was a third wheel, and if he did prove to be of some worth, so much the better. His talent for vanishing from view—discovered almost immediately—and to the disappointment of his new friends, he lost Carp further standing in the group. The big boys had work to do, and Carp could tag along for the ride if he stayed out of the way.

Ramos conjured a purple ball of fire, casting it toward the Cyclops, who saw it coming and quickly stepped out of the way. He turned his massive battle axe to the side and hit the fireball like a baseball into the stands, vaporizing three harpies and setting one on fire. She screamed and ran through the crowd, but this only caused a wave of cheers from the spectators. Mac was on him from behind, and with a slash of his claws, he tore into the Cyclops' Achilles heel, but the tendon was like iron as he tried to pull it apart.

The Cyclops howled in pain and back-kicked Mac across the arena. He hit the ground with a thump, and the back of his head took a brutal hit. Stars floated before his eyes as he stood back up, his clock sufficiently rung.

Dante ran forward and almost met the business end of the double-bladed battle-axe with his head but ducked in time to encounter the hilt on his shoulder instead. He heard a bone break and, for an instant, felt the pain.

"Blinding him is the only way to get an advantage!" Lilith said. She yelled as her wings carried her high above the arena.

"Get down there and fight!" Queen Resha said. All in attendance began tossing stones at her. One of them hit her in the temple, and he felt her wings falter, the blows threatening to send her to the ground.

"She may be right; this thing is too big, fast...and strong," Mac said.

Dante was on his knees in front of the Cyclops, and he could see the monster raising his battle-axe for a final blow when the young chief used his good arm to punch the Cyclops in his knee. The bone shattered and sent the one-eyed giant reeling, giving Lilith the opening she needed to change the battle's outcome. Gathering her strength, she flew at the Cyclops' head, teeth bared, spear-tip fingernails at the ready. When she was close enough, she landed on the Cyclops face as he stumbled backward from Dante's attack. Lilith, quick as grease lightning, reached out with her left hand, plunging it into the Cyclops' eye, destroying the red orb as he screamed in agony. With a grimace, she freed her hand and waved a fist full of yellow goo.

Lilith tried to fly away, but the Cyclops snatched her by the wings and flung her to the ground like a discarded toy. Black blood seeped from the open wound in his eye. No longer able to see, he began to stumble. As he did, his foot came down next to Dante's left foot, almost crushing it under his boot. Dante yelped in pain and rolled out of the way, getting quickly to his feet. With a torn foot, smashed knee, and his only eye gone, the Cyclops staggered around and fell on his axe when he tripped over a pile of bones on the floor. The blade sliced through his chest, cutting his heart in two as his body weight drove the axe further in. The Cyclops gave a final chuff and rolled over onto his back dead.

"Mine!" Ramos said. He rhythmically waved his hands as the violet light passed from him into the Cyclops, resurrecting it.

The Cyclops twitched and rose to his feet once more as the queen looked on with horror, suddenly caught off guard. Before she could react, Ramos commanded his new pet to throw the axe at her. End over end, the blade sliced through the air between them and hit the wall behind her seat. The wall crumbled, and she fell off her pedestal into a pile of rubble forty feet below. The dagger queen Resha kept in her belt fell on the ground as she struggled to regain her footing and clear the ringing in her ears. Carp had been observing from the other side of the arena, and now was his chance to make a difference. He seized the moment and ran toward the rubble pile where the dagger lay on the ground. Closing in, his camouflage faded away.

He bent down and grabbed her dagger. Although he was visible now, she never saw him coming, and he plunged the knife deep into her neck. Queen Resha reached behind her, slapping at the knife, trying to turn, but Carp twisted the blade and, grasping her left arm, spun her into the Cyclops. With a push from Carp, Resha stumbled forward as the Cyclops swung his retrieved battle-axe into her like a golfer and split the queen of the harpies in two. The pieces of Queen Resha landed next to Lilith, and in the last seconds, the queen's mind could process data; she watched helplessly as Lilith spit in her face. "Die!" Lilith said. She knelt forward and removed the snake ring from Resha's finger. "I'll take this back, thank you very much."

The gaggle of harpies flew into the air, shrieking with terror as they watched their queen's demise. They flew for their clandestine exits, escaping to the surface in a screaming mass. The battle was over. Lilith collapsed on the floor and began to cry over the loss of her mother and father; she was unable to look at them in their mutilated condition. Her heart was broken, and as she sat, Lilith kicked Resha in her lifeless head with the heel of her foot.

The other party members approached her, standing around her in a semi-circle.

"I'm so sorry for what I did to you guys, and my surrogate parents still died," Lilith said. She masked her face behind gore-covered hands.

"Hey, I might have done the same thing if my family was in jeopardy. I came forty light years from my home planet to protect them after assisting in the murder of thousands. I'm no saint." Mac said, offering her a hand up.

When she accepted, he pulled her into him, and it felt like a homecoming as she submitted to his embrace. In his wolven form, his strength matched hers, and Mac knew he needed her. He knew what loss was like and wanted to help her. He would make her laugh, be her fool. Mac was in love again for the second time in his life. For a moment, he considered Bobby and Serena's reaction to the beautiful, pale, raven-haired, winged woman from another world as their stepmom. Would they take to her so easily? Lilith turned her head into his chest as he held her for another minute.

"I don't mean to sound crass, but we have no idea what else is going to come out of that hole back there, and I'd rather not be here when it does," Ramos said.

The Cyclops bent down and lifted them out of the arena, placing the wolven, Carp, and Lilith in the stadium seats. Then, Ramos released him from his service, and the Cyclops fell to the floor next to Queen Resha. They followed the tunnels back up to the surface and winced as daylight stung their eyes. There was no sign of the harpies as the adventurers emerged, one member stronger.

"Carp, you did an excellent job! You killed the queen." Ramos said.

Carp smiled, embarrassed. "Yeah, great job, kid," Mac said.

"Are you coming with us, Lilith?" Dante asked. He looked from Mac to Lilith and saw they were holding hands. "I'll assume you are!"

"There's nothing for me here. I'm the last Egren." Lilith said. She was far from sounding like the sexy minx they met upon arrival, and after helping them fight through the horror show down below, Lilith was welcomed with open arms into the quest for Eritria.

Mac explained that they were in Valuria to reverse the destructive power of the ick and the disease it had unleashed on the Faerie Lands and that if they did not get the Tablet back to the Tower of Kail, it might mean the end of life as they knew it.

"Where do we start looking for the Tablet?" Mac asked.

"Falworn cavern, that's where we start," Lilith said.

"Where's that?" Dante asked.

"Under a mountain of stone and fire," Lilith said.
"Sounds like fun. Lead the way, Lilith." Dante said.

CHAPTER 9

ASURA HAD BEEN INVESTIGATING THE pyramids for weeks while the reptilian army trained for a war Broad Axe had promised them was coming.

Legions of reptilian men and women sparred in the fields, wielding swords, knives, and polearms of varying shapes and sizes. As each day passed, Asura learned more about this planet's technology. He knew he would need to use it to regain control of the earth, which he was entitled to rule. One morning, Asura and his father walked along the pyramid fields together, admiring the artisanship of the great structures.

"A new age is dawning, my son." Broad Axe said.

"Do you think so?" Asura asked.

"I can feel it in the air, like electricity! With your cosmic portal device and the strength of our army, plus the great pyramid, victory will surely be ours! If the resistance is too high and we can't take it back by force, well, we'll blow it to pieces and move on to the next world. Now we can travel to any planet in the universe *without* using the flying ships of the Telerum people."

"Total war on Eritria," Asura said. Broad Axe seemed troubled.

"What's wrong? You have something on your mind." Asura said.

"I was contacted by the Telerum Prime Minister last night through the holoscope. He revealed some disturbing news from the village of Metat." Broad Axe said.

"Oh really? What was it?"

"A viral outbreak has begun in a village not far from here, and the Telerumian's think it began when you came through the portal." Broad Axe said.

"What do you mean? I wasn't sick with anything before coming through the portal. It cannot be the ick; it was contained in the Faerie Lands until Ragnok's mages were called to war." Asura said.

"Nevertheless, the timing of your arrival and the proximity of the virus outbreak is too coincidental."

"What kind of virus?" Asura asked.

"It's a flesh-eating bacterium. The Telerum people have no resistance against it. They don't even know where to begin." Broad Axe said.

"Well, if it's so deadly, and they suspect it was me, how come you're not sick?" Asura asked.

"I don't have an answer for that, but I am telling you there may be trouble for us on the horizon. The Telerumian's outnumber us by a large margin, and do not forget that it's their technology we're using, which they've already mastered. We cannot afford to fight with the humans on this planet and fight against those who oppose us in Eritria; wars fought on two fronts are a much harder win. It would be folly."

"Why? I say we fight them all and let the gods sort their dead." Asura said.

"You are so young; you must not be familiar with the practice of diplomacy. Wait until you're almost a thousand years old, like me." Broad Axe said.

Asura grimaced with disdain but didn't let it linger. "You once told me that the relationship between Telerumian's and reptilians was tenuous at best. I fail to see how this is a problem." Asura said.

"What do you mean?" Broad Axe asked. "Take me to where they say the virus started," Asura said.

"Very well; it's not far from here." Broad Axe said. He summoned a pair of bats, which were airborne in minutes.

Lush green trees and lakes of azure blue dotted the countryside, and far below them, Asura began to see the first of the more advanced settlements Broad Axe had told him about. Flying discs raked back and forth over farmers' fields, planting crops, watering the land, and picking ripe fruit from trees. Their homes were constructed of stone with thick wooden shingles on their roofs.

"Why do you wish to come this way?" Broad Axe asked.

"I wanted to see for myself what mischief I'm being accused of, that's all," Asura said.

They neared the area where Asura had first entered Telerum. They could see the spot where the cosmic portal had burned the grass in a large black circle. Not far from it was a small, abandoned village. He had not seen these villages when they had first arrived from Eritria, and while trees obscured a few of them, this one was out in the open and must have been behind them when he entered. There was no sign of living people as the machines and androids performed their daily functions on pre-programmed auto-routines.

"I think that's it." Broad Axe said. "Let's go down," Asura said.

They landed by the entrance to the village and were greeted by nothing but grave quiet and the smell of dead bodies. Most of the home's doors swung open a crack, creaking in the breeze. Asura dismounted his bat and stepped down into a patch of tall grass.

"Let's have a look around, shall we?" Asura said. Broad Axe shrugged, dismounted, and followed him into the village.

Two scout ships passed by above the reptilians, monitoring their movements.

"You think that's them, Loran?" One spoke. "That looks like Broad Axe, alright, but I don't know who the other is. It could be the one who brought the virus, and I don't want to go anywhere near that reptilian if he is. Let's report back to headquarters and let the commander know, Radgar." Loran said.

Asura looked up into the sky and watched them go. When they disappeared, he dropped the hood of his robe to get a better look around. They entered the first house on the left, and Broad Axe almost wretched from the stench inside.

"Ah, the sweet smell of death," Asura said. He walked into the three-bedroom house to find its former residents collapsed one atop the other in the living room. Large black boils had broken out on their arms and legs. Deep holes pocked their faces, reminding Asura of water lotus seedpods back home, and the holes crawled with hungry maggots. The rot had taken hold of their bodies fast, and their skin was thin, stretched out, and blackened with decay. Their death gaze revealed the pain and suffering they had experienced before death mercifully took them. Dried pools of blood ran out from beneath the pile.

"My gods!" Broad Axe said. "This can't be because of you." Broad Axe said.

"Where you see a horror show, I see an opportunity. Have you seen the giant pyramid on the horizon?" Asura asked.

"Yes, but that's the Telerum High Command. They'll never let us use that. In fact, they've even threatened *us* with it in the past." Broad Axe said.

"Is it operational?" Asura asked.

"Yes, I've seen them use the light weapon against the planet Krypton, but only once, when they were at war. It can destroy and wipe out a fleet of star ships with one blast."

"Those scouts are going to report back that they saw us down here, which means they'll more than likely come back," Asura said.

"You're probably right. What's your plan?" Broad Axe asked.

"It's fluid, but are you ready to burn your boats to reclaim Eritria?" Asura asked.

"I'm open to suggestions."

"I plan to infiltrate the Telerum high command and kill them all."

"We just discussed this. We can't fight a war on two fronts, especially if we want to defeat our enemies on Eritria." Broad Axe said.

"If what I have planned works, there won't be a war with the Telerumian's," Asura said.

As they walked outside, a ship arrived, much larger than the previous two scouts' small craft. It was triangular and metallic black with a circular hole in the center. A spiral door opened from the docking bay of the giant ship. Asura stepped back inside the house for a moment, and when he returned, a white light appeared from within the ship and enveloped the two reptilians.

"Was this part of your plan?" Broad Axe asked. Asura smiled and cut his eyes wickedly but remained silent.

Asura looked at his father with disgust. The so-called great warlock had become weak with age and his lavish lifestyle. A seed of clarity crept into his mind as he realized that his ultimate plan for Eritrian domination might not involve a continued alliance with his father.

As the light surrounded them, paralyzed their limbs, and carried the two up inside the ship, Asura contemplated his revenge on Dante and his clan. All he had to do now was get free. Asura looked up into the light as he was lifted silently into the belly of the Telerum air force graviton. Broad Axe was across from him, fearing that Asura's hatred had twisted his mind into an unnatural state.

Five minutes later, Asura found himself in a prison cell with transparent walls and immovable constraints. Broad Axe was also in his cell, and Asura could see his father sitting there helplessly. How pathetic, he thought. He heard the thumping boot heels of Telerum soldiers coming down the hallway, and it would not be long before his accusers were in sight. Asura tried to use his magic, but as he concentrated on conjuring a force blast, all that appeared was a pitiful green charge between his fingers, like an electrostatic discharge, and nothing.

He thought the cell they held him in must have had some anti-magic property. Rounding the corner were two Telerum soldiers dressed in black uniforms, each wearing a patch depicting two red and black hammers, posed like walking legs on their lapels. The first was a man with short cropped brown hair, and the second was a woman with long blond hair, braided and slung over her shoulder; she was pretty for a human and demure with smooth skin. Her smile was more like a victorious crap-eating grin, and he wanted to tear the lips off her face.

"Welcome to Telerum, Asura. You're under arrest by the Telerum High Command for spreading an unknown viral infection among our people, " the blond woman said. We found your friend stuck on top of Abaddon castle, and the analysis of his blood showed a strain of necrotizing fasciitis that attacked the living tissue of our people."

"I've done nothing wrong here, so what if the centaur had an infection in his blood? I assure you it had nothing to do with me," Asura said. A sharp prick in the heel of his foot caused him to jump. "Ouch!"

The needle descended as rapidly as it had come out of the floor, and when he looked up, the Telerum woman held a small, rectangular electronic device in her hand that was a little bigger than her palm.

"You carry the same strain as the centaur, but we tested Broad Axe, and he came up negative." She spoke.

"You listen to me. There are hordes of reptilians waiting on the other side of that portal, and when I..." Asura said.

"Silence. You are to be judged and incinerated for your crimes against our planet." She spoke. The gold braid slinging down across her right breast looked like a noose. Asura could not wait to hang her with it.

"Just do as they say, son. It'll be easier this way." Broad Axe said.

"What happened to the great warrior warlock king I heard about when I was young? You've had your balls clipped, father." Asura said. He hissed at his Broad Axe as the elder looked away in shame.

"We would have had a much harder time finding you if Broad Axe had not turned you in, Asura." She spoke.

"What?" Asura said, eyes burning.

Broad Axe was being freed from his cell by the man with short hair.

"Betrayed by my own father," Asura said. "I'm sorry, son. They promised to leave my sky castle alone if I helped them." Broad Axe said. "When I get out of here, I'll kill you first, daddy. Maybe last, I don't know." Asura said with a sneer.

"I wish it could have been different, Asura." Broad Axe said.

"Me too, enjoy your last days alive, traitor," Asura said.

Asura was taken to the Telerum capital city of Calou, which would later be named Mount Sharp by humans from the planet Earth in another epoch. Now, it was a thriving metropolis with a three-mile-high pyramid in the center that spanned the better part of fifty miles from corner to corner at the base. Asura, sitting shackled in his cell, was given a small porthole from which to view the city as they arrived.

The sheer size and advanced Telerum technology surprised him. Silver disc-shaped sky ships commanded the air, glass towers rose high above the Telerum soil, and rectangular apartment buildings dotted the cliff faces as Telerum citizens enjoyed another day above the topsoil. Asura sat and watched as he contemplated revenge and the destruction of these people. He had hoped that his father would be the man of legend, the great warrior warlock Broad Axe, raiser of the undead, commander of the underworld. But what he found when he arrived was a tired old fool, willing to roll over on his son for fear of retribution from humans.

"This will not stand," Asura said. He paced inside the cell as the soldiers walked down the hallway.

On the command deck, the blond woman looked at her partner with concern as they watched Asura on the screen, pacing back and forth, his eyes glowing red.

"Dran, he's dangerous. I could feel the hatred radiating off him like a hot iron when I stood outside his cell. If we weren't blocking his energy field..." She spoke.

"Don't worry Lainey, soon he'll be on trial by the council, and in a couple of days, this will all be a distant memory. They'll probably incinerate him inside the great pyramid." Dran said.

"I hope you're right. Broad Axe is easily controlled because he fears the army, but his son appears fearless." Lainey said.

They watched him wave his hands around, muttering to himself. To Lainey, he looked like a demon, and her skin crawled just looking at him. She coughed a few times and felt her forehead. It was beginning to get warm, and she noticed red splotches on her skin.

"Lainey, stop worrying so much. You look like you need a break anyway; are you not feeling well?" Dran asked.

"I think I'm coming down with a cold or something."

"When we get back, go to sick call and get looked at. If you haven't got your health, you haven't got anything." Dran said. His own head began to throb with a headache, and he felt warm. "You know what," he said, "I'll even go with you and get checked out too."

Asura sensed eyes on him. There was a camera somewhere, but he couldn't see it. He looked out the window again. They were beginning to land in a large metal hangar that had big glass windows. The sign above the building read *Municipal Entrance*. The side of the craft opened, and his cell was loaded onto the back of a vehicle he would have known as a truck had it been explained to him. Telerum citizens stood around gawking at the reptilian they had read about in their newspapers that was causing so much havoc in outlying villages.

Asura smiled as he passed, shaking his head from side to side as he gladly spread the virus. His cell had been quite indestructible, and with only one way out, through the sealed bottom, he had been given air holes through which to breathe. It was these same air holes that allowed the virus to escape his cell. Asura almost started laughing, and a moment later, when Lainey came around to make sure he was still secure, he saw black rings under her eyes and red blisters forming on her cheeks.

"You'll be detained until trial, Asura. The judge will hear your case before the high council, and your fate will be decided." Lainey said.

"You would be amazed at the horrors I have seen and survived in this life, human. You'll also find that I'm less easily dealt with than my father. I'm afraid he has become less than he once was." Asura said.

Lainey's eyes began to water, and she sneezed onto the glass cell. Her vision wavered, and she staggered for a moment as one of the onlookers ran over to grab her arm. Lainey sneezed again, passing the virus to that man, who passed it to three more people in the crowd. He then passed it to his wife and three children who gave it to six more people. By that night, half of the Telerum capital was infected with a flesh-eating bacterium that, while dormant on Eritria, found the Telerum atmosphere a perfect environment to awaken and mass multiply. Asura sat in his cell, waiting patiently as the people around him died by the thousands over the next few days.

Asura was largely forgotten and sat in prison alongside dying inmates.

A last measure of the Telerum guard was to open the cells of the condemned and allow them to have some last vestige of freedom before the end took them. One man, a reptilian he recognized from his father's legions, was in the cell across from him. It was every man for himself as the holding cells were opened, and this man was running for freedom when Asura stopped him.

"I recognize you. Mortah, right?" Asura said.

"Yes, I'm Mortah. You are Asura, Broad Axes' son. How can I help you?" Mortah asked.

"Get me out of here. These Telerumian's have cut off my ability to use magic, and I need your help before you go." Asura said.

Mortah looked around uneasily.

"No one here will punish you for helping me; they'll all die very soon. What services do you perform for my father, Mortah?" Asura asked.

"I am a gardener and handyman. I fix broken things." Mortah said.

"Then why are you in prison?" Asura asked.

"I was late on my taxes. Our requirement for freedom is that we pay the Telerumian's a piece of everything we earn. I didn't pay on time, so they put me in here after a chase from the imperial guard."

"So much for freedom of the reptilian race. They've got you all doing their work for them, paying fees to live on the planet you are fixing? That's not right. How'd you like never to pay taxes again and become a prince?" Asura asked.

"I would like that very much," Mortah said. "Get me out of here, and I'll give you an entire continent on Eritria, and you will rule the people of that land," Asura said.

Mortah thought it over for a moment. "How do I get you out?" Mortah asked.

"There's a trapdoor underneath this cell. If you can get behind this box and push it over, I can get out. It's that simple! It's really the worst design ever devised. But please, help me. I've been holding having to defecate for two days." Asura said.

Mortah got behind the cell and pushed with all his might, but he was getting nowhere. He stopped when more reptilian prisoners ran past and recognizing Mortah they paused to help.

Five reptilians aided in the freedom of their new leader, and Asura promised them all positions within his new regime in return for releasing him. They would all have land and power in his new kingdom of Eritria.

Death had come to Calou, and as Asura walked free once again, he stepped over the lifeless, pockmark-riddled, rotting body of Lainey. She'd died slumped against a wall while the virus moved like lightning through her division of officers. Most of the people he walked by looked as if large chunks of their bodies had been melted by acid. Dran had died at home in the arms of his wife as they piled their children around them at the very end. Watching with helpless horror when the holes appeared in his children's faces had been the worst part for Dran.

They were so deep and black that it was as if each puss-filled socket held the incubating larvae, an impossibly horrifying insect ready to spring forth. The pain each had experienced before death twisted their faces into a wicked smile that remained well after rigor mortis set in. Asura smiled at the corpses as he passed them by.

Asura walked out to the landing zone, where he had first been processed for his short time as a prisoner. In a few moments, with the help of his new henchmen, Asura was riding inside one of the Telerum flying discs and on his way back to the sky castle. He and Broad Axe had a score to settle. Looking back at the massive pyramid, its crystal gem capstone gleaming in the sun, he felt butterflies in his belly at the thought of erasing the troublesome wolven from his life forever. It would be worth the sacrifice if he had to blow Eritria up to make that happen.

Time would give him victory, and once he had control of Broad Axe's army, he would rightfully rule once more. As the castle came into view and grew closer, Asura stood with his band of refugees, raised the hood of his robe, and smiled. His eyes glowed like hot coals in a fire.

"Gentlemen, we are about to shake things up a bit for dear old dad. Are you with me?"

"We are with you until the end, Asura," Mortah said.

"I, Rankor, speak for the entire fire eye clan. We will fight at your side as well. My people only need to see me at your side, and with the king dead you will be our new king." Rankor said. The other reptilians nodded agreement.

"You are the king," Mortah said. All the reptilians let out a whoop of unity.

"The king is dead, long live the king," Asura said.

CHAPTER 10

THE HARPIES HAD ABANDONED CALVALOR and were nowhere to be found as the party emerged from the underground arena. Mac felt like they were walking through a ghost town; dozens of evil eyes lurked and waited in the shadows, watching them from well-found hiding places. With every footstep, Mac wanted to break into a run, anything to get as far from this city as possible. But he maintained his bearing and walked with the group.

"Without Resha, it'll take the harpies some time to regroup, but they will eventually select a new queen. When that happens, we need to be long gone." Lilith said.

"They didn't build this city like Queen Resha said they did?" Mac asked. He was walking beside her at the back of the pack.

"No, the Egren did, long ago, back when the sky gods first constructed the tower. The Egren were the creations or children of those people, and they were left here to guard the planet. The two Resha tossed into the pit with their throats cut were the last of that race." Lilith said.

They reached the entrance where the crystal pterodactyl fountain stood, and as they passed by, Lilith took hold of the raptor's beak, pulling down on it. The water stopped running, emptying the basin, and a stairwell appeared inside the fountain. Dante and Ramos looked at each other curiously. Mac nodded, and Carp looked at each other with mixed interest.

This journey had been taxing for Carp, and with so much death, he felt emotionally depressed. Stabbing the winged woman took everything he had, but if he stood by, she might have hurt him or his friends.

"One last stop before we leave. I think you boys are going to enjoy this." Lilith said and started walking down the steps.

"Nice ring, by the way. We've seen that inscription on a mural in the Temple of Ostrid." Dante said.

"I've held this ring for longer than I care to think about. It's one of the original lost artifacts and contains great power. Should it ever be used, a demon of great destructive energy would be summoned from the chaos realm." Lilith said, leading the party a few more steps down the stairs.

Ramos looked around the arsenal and found the hilt of a sword. He picked it up, turning it around in his hand.

"Broken sword," Ramos said. He squeezed the hilt and with slight pressure, a three-foot long blade of flames extended from a two-inch slit in the top of the hilt. "Whoa!" He waved it around to show Dante.

"Now who's being careless? Watch out with that thing." Dante said.

"This is quite the weapon," Ramos said.

Carp looked through the shelves of weapons and found a small pistol about the size of a child's toy.

"This looks about my size, but I doubt it'll do much," Carp said. He turned it over in his hand and shrugged.

"Be careful, Carp, that thing is more powerful than you think. Inside that gun is a crystal designed to harness the power of our universe in a single blast of fire. If you shoot that in here the ceiling will cave in and kill us all." Lilith said.

"I've always preferred claws over weapons, but I could get used to this," Dante said. He pulled the bow back again, listening to the electrical charge of his lightning arrow as it vibrated energetically between the metallic bowstring and arrow rest. He relaxed his left hand and allowed the string to go back to its resting state as the arrow vanished.

"All Egren were trained in the use of these weapons long ago. Sadly, the harpies invaded our city in the middle of the night, with such a strong force that we were unable to defend ourselves in time and those left alive were enslaved to work in the silver mines. "

"I'm sorry to hear that," Mac said.

"It's ancient history now, but since I brought you to the weapons cache, I would be eternally grateful if you could help me defeat the harpies once we find the Tablet of Destinies."

"Well..." Ramos said. "I'm in," Mac said.

"Are you sure you're thinking with the right head?" Dante said, grinning. He fixed Mac with a knowing stare, and Lilith blushed.

"Yeah, I'm sure," Mac said. He had been irritated by the question, but Dante had a point. "I'd be happy to help you, Lilith," Dante said.

"I'll come along as well," Carp said. He pointed his gun, tilting his head sideways, one eye closed, and pretending to fire as he spoke. "Keep the gun in the center of your body, straighten your head, look down the sights, and open both eyes as you squeeze the trigger,"

Mac said.

"Ah, okay. I'll do that from now on." Carp said.

"We should keep moving before the enemy regroups and attacks again," Ramos said. He dropped the sword hilt into the left pocket of his robe.

"Take what you want, and we'll be on our way," Lilith said. She picked up her own recurve bow and walked ahead of the team. Mac stared at Lilith, hypnotized by the sway of her hips. Dante snickered, shaking his head.

"You're going to get yourself in trouble," Dante said.

"I may already be. Why are you interested in her or something?" Mac asked.

"Uh, no...she's all yours. I like my women with a lot more hair. But watch out, I feel this lady is more deadly than she lets on." Dante said. "I heard that," Lilith said.

"She has excellent hearing, too," Dante said.

The planet's core sun dimmed as it began its daily afternoon pass in the sky above. Mac still could not wrap his head around this bizarre paradise and how magnificent it was. Birds he never thought existed thrived down here, some with bright rainbow plumage, others that were orange and pink. Mac considered Valuria a gigantic petting zoo where the animals might eat you if you got too close.

"Eritria's a lot like that," Mac said, mumbling.

"What?" Dante asked.

"Oh, nothing. It's just that this planet is so wild; it's a lot to take in. Earth was governed by so many rules that I think my people may have a tough time adapting to the lack of structure and technology, that is if we can ever get the cosmic portal back and bring the rest of them over. I've had my struggles adjusting to the people and pace here." Mac said.

"How many more of you are there?" Dante asked.

"Millions or thousands, I don't know. My dreams have been dark lately, and I'm afraid it may already be too late for them. I thank God I could get my son and little girl out in time." Mac said.

"You miss them," Dante said.

"Yeah, but I've been in the military for so long that I'm conditioned to get the job done regardless of my personal feelings. It's like putting a sheet over a chair to preserve it while you're gone for a long time. That's what I do each time I leave my family, but ever since I lost Carol, it's been tougher. When she was raising them, I always knew they were in good hands." Mac said.

"The wolven will continue to look after your family while we're gone, brother. Now that the centaurs are dead and the libmoks are scattered, your children are in the safest place they could be. Far safer than we are." Dante said. He clapped a paw on Mac's shoulder and smiled.

"Serena is sick with the ick. Gregor showed it to me in a dream the other night. I think she might die if we don't get the Tablet soon." Mac said.

"Well, we'd better go get it then, right?" Dante said, grinning at Mac.

They walked up the steps to find a small contingent of harpies waiting for them at the gate.

"Surestra, what do you want?" Lilith asked, holding the bow by her side.

Having disposed of the previous façade of beauty, Mac thought these winged monsters looked like demons now. With pale, sallow skin, flinty evil eyes, rotten noses, long, unwashed, greasy hair, and fangs instead of canines, these wretched creatures were frightening. His children would scream at the sight of them. Their leather halters hung on a frame of thin bones, and the ghoulish women could have been mistaken for walking corpses.

"We crown the new queen tomorrow, Lilith, and then we come for you," Surestra said.

"That's fascinating, move out of the way," Lilith said. Three harpies blocked the way, and as Surestra stood fuming, the other two looked at her with uncertain eyes.

"You think what we did to your parents..." Surestra said.

Lilith fired a bolt of pure electric fire through Surestra, opening a bowling ball-sized hole in her chest. Mac could see daylight and trees through the hole as the heat cauterized her wound. Surestra gasped once and collapsed to the ground. The others scattered to escape, but not before Dante fired his bow and struck one of the harpies in the head, vaporizing everything from the mouth up. She fell to the weeds, where she lay twitching as cadaveric spasms caused her muscles to fire uncontrollably.

The other took to the sky and began to cast a bolt of flames at Lilith as a last resort, and as she did, Ramos brought her headless friend back from the dead. The headless, dead harpy flapped her wings in a jerky, unstable motion as if a drunken puppeteer were guiding her appendages, twirling around until she charged her compatriot. The headless harpy grappled her sister, and the two tumbled to the ground in a heap. Ramos' eyes glowed with their telltale purple hue as he controlled the corpse. Dante pulled back the bowstring and fired an arrow at the struggling pair, opening holes through both bodies. Ramos released his control over the repossessed harpy, and she dropped to the ground, limp and once again very dead.

"Let's get out of here before more of these show up," Mac said.

Lilith led them down a path through the woods that, had they not been with her, the team would have missed altogether. In the distance, they heard the screams and cackles of angry harpies within the city as the sound reverberated off the crystal walls, echoing into the afternoon air. Lilith looked back once and kept moving through the forest.

They walked for hours without speaking as they struggled through the thick bushes and overgrown branches. If Lilith decided to disappear into the forest, they would be lost in the jungle of Valuria. As their beautiful guide led them deeper into the woods, she discovered a deep cave's dark and foreboding mouth just before nightfall.

"We should stop and rest here for the night," Lilith said.

"Aren't we safer from the harpies if we enter the cave?" Mac asked.

"The people who originally inhabited this land went underground to escape a massive cataclysm when the land died above ground. They have existed in tunnels and vast cities beneath our feet for more than ten thousand years. They are not known to be friendly to outsiders, so we may need to tread lightly." Lilith said.

Mac thought it was another oddity: a world within a world, within a world.

"So, why are we going in there?" Carp asked.

"Because that is where Inga, the dragon, hid the Tablet," Lilith said.

"I thought Marduk brought the Tablet down here, and slogs stole it. Which story are we supposed to believe?" Mac asked.

"Both. There's more than one Tablet." Lilith said.

"What? That can't be true." Mac said, shaking his head. He shook his head. "There are two down here?"

"That's right, and my hunch is they are both inside this network of caves and tunnels. All we have to do is find them, which won't be easy. There are things, creatures, living in there that do not like to be disturbed." Lilith said.

The party agreed with her decision and made camp outside the tunnel entrance. As Mac stood considering the mouth of the cave, he thought he saw something move within the darkest part of the tunnel, but he was not prepared to chalk it up to a trick of the eyes.

"See anything in there?" Dante asked.

"No, I just get a weird vibe from this place," Mac said.

"Well, I'm dying to try out these new weapons.

We'll probably be indebted to Lilith after this." Dante said. He looked his bow over again.

"Hey, Lilith, do you know what the people who went down there look like?" Mac asked. He began to gather firewood.

"From what I was told, they were about six feet tall, with white fur and long snouts. And the males have strong, curving horns on each side of their head." Lilith said.

"That sounds a lot like a ram," Mac said.

"Adya, my surrogate Egren mother, said they were peaceful until a disagreement arose in their society, and then opposing factions formed; that's when the fighting began," Lilith said.

"Sounds like my people," Mac said.

"One faction went underground, and the other perished up here when some horrible event wiped almost everyone out thousands of years ago. It was a period of darkness for every one of Eritria and Valuria." Lilith said.

"We had a similar period of darkness when something in our distant past caused the sun to vanish for several years. Humanity was almost wiped out. I'm here because we're at that point again." Mac said.

"Are you sure it's safe to camp at the mouth of this cave?" Carp asked.

"My mother told me that the rams underground have a sensitivity to light from being out of the sun for so long; no we don't have anything to worry about from them until we go down into the cave," Lilith said.

Mac thought there was one flaw in her theory. When the sun went down, there would be nothing stopping an army of creatures with light sensitivity issues from emerging from that cave and killing them in all in their sleep. "I'll take the first watch tonight," Mac said.

"I just said..." Lilith said.

"I know, but to be safe, we need a lookout. Harpies out here, rams in there, we've got to watch our back and front." Mac said.

"Mac has a point. I'll take the second watch." Dante said.

Ramos took third, and Carp would watch them during the final hours until sunrise. Nighttime came over the party after their camp was constructed, and they sat by the campfire, each of them lost in thought. Lilith brought a small provision of meat for their journey into the tunnels, so she shared a small portion of it, just enough to quiet grumbling stomachs.

Campfire smoke blew around them in the gentle breeze, transporting Mac back to when he would go camping with his father as a child. Ghost stories around the circle just before bed replayed in his mind, and he smiled. Those had been good times. It was more straightforward; he had always thought they would go on forever. But what's great about being a kid: you're so eager to be an adult, but time seems to crawl as your new mind learns about the world around you.

A day can seem like a week, and when you grow up, it seems time will never slow down again. Mac had felt time speeding up for over twenty years, with a sensation that he was on one of those moving walkways in the airport, speeding up to get...where? Bobby and Serena crept into his thoughts, and he wondered what they might be doing right now. Although he was scared for his little girl, he knew he needed to stay focused on their mission. But he couldn't help but think of the ranch and being back there with his family. The stars twinkled overhead as his mind drifted.

After dinner, a small meal consisting of meat and beans, Ramos reached into his bag and removed a tiny green orb, which he tossed into the flames. It rested on the coals for a moment and then began to emit green smoke with an odor of chamomile and honeysuckle. The smoke enveloped the party, surrounding them in a light green bubble, that eventually turned clear.

"This is a protection spell that will allow all of us to get some rest. I don't know why I didn't think of it before. This bubble will let air in and out, our campfire smoke too, but anything or anyone who tries to enter the bubble will be blocked." Ramos said.

"That would have come in handy a long time ago, Ramos," Dante said.

"I only have two of these. I was saving them for so long; I guess I forgot about them." Ramos said. He shrugged and reached into his robe bringing out another small orb.

Ramos tossed the second orb into the flames, and this time the smoke was pink and vaporized almost immediately.

"What's this?" Mac asked.

"We're about to go on a vision quest," Ramos said.

Mac could no longer hear the words coming from Ramos' mouth as he felt himself drifting into the ether. Ramos was still speaking, but he looked like a character in a silent movie until he faded from vision altogether. When Mac looked up next, he was back on Earth, sitting by the ocean. There were huge hotels floating in the water as the hot summer sun beat down on him. Mac squinted and wished he had a pair of sunglasses. To his right, Dante sat looking perplexed at the ocean full of manmade structures.

"Are we still on Eritria?" Dante asked.

"I don't think so, at least our minds aren't," Mac said. But this did not feel like a dream, and as he reached out to touch Dante, the wolven warrior's body was solid.

"This is Ramos' magic at work," Dante said. Gentle waves washed up on the shoreline as Mac and Dante surveyed the devastation along the South Carolina shoreline. He recognized one of the destroyed structures as the Avista hotel by its horseshoe shape, and Mac knew immediately where they were: North Myrtle Beach. A hotel that had been torn in two poked out of the salt water at an angle, mostly submerged. One of the former vacationing residents was hanging over the balcony, trapped in place by a dresser that had pinned him or her to the railing. Cars, buses, trucks, and one or two golf carts rested in the sand, half-buried as Mother Earth absorbed them into her body.

"Where are all the Earth people?" Dante asked. Mac looked at him and shrugged.

They stood up and turned around to see the foundations of the former vacation rental towers pockmarking the beach with exposed plumbing pipes, shattered walls, and hundreds of decayed corpses. The tidal wave that had washed inland had caused unrecoverable devastation. They left the beach to walk through the destroyed town that had once been Ocean Drive. Mac felt as if he was in a surrealistic nightmare, but it seemed so real, and Dante was in it with him.

"Do you feel that?" Dante asked. "Rumbling. Something is coming." Mac said.

An earthquake vibrated beneath their feet, and the broken city vanished as it quickened. Rushing toward them was the Great Pyramid of Giza, and as Mac looked down, he saw that he was standing in the desert with Dante still beside him. In this scene, a large crystal had been affixed to the top of the pyramid, and not only had the limestone blocks been restored, but the outer casing stones had also been replaced. As the two stood staring at the brand- new pyramid, a group of figures approached them in the desert. Waves of heat gave them the appearance of wavering mirages in the hot sun, and they were carrying something with them.

Mac looked down and saw that he was holding a white stone tablet with odd etchings upon it, and when he looked back up the men were much closer. The object in their possession was a rectangular wooden box with two figurines affixed to the top, and they carried it on two long wooden poles. They stopped before Mac and Dante, gazing at them with knowing, peaceful eyes, nodding to the tablet. These men were incredibly old, judging from the wrinkles on their faces and hands.

Mac thought they looked like they had been alive for as long as the planet. They set the box on the ground and nodded to the tablet in Mac's hands. He stared at this alien object, the Tablet of Destinies, then turned it over to the man in front, the one in charge. These were the men from far away Ethiopia, carrying the Ark of the Covenant with them. When Mac offered the tablet, the man took it and placed it inside the Ark. They nodded, thanking Mac and Dante, and continued forward, disappearing inside the great pyramid.

"What do you think they're doing in there?" Dante asked.

"Repairing Earth," Mac said.

Within moments, a powerful pulse of energy emanated from within the pyramid, sweeping out and around them in waves that knocked both men to the ground. Next, a light beaming from the pyramid's capstone shone in all directions, producing a white-hot ray that nearly blinded them. This light shot out across the desert, getting brighter until it faded, and as it did, Mac and Dante woke up from their slumber to see that the rest of their party was still in deep sleep. The protection bubble was still around them, and they hadn't moved.

"Was that real?" Mac asked.

"I have no idea, but we both saw it together, whatever it was," Dante said.

"Dante, I think I have another purpose after this is over. Will you come with me to Earth once we save Eritria?" Mac said.

"I will travel to the ends of your Earth for what you and your people have helped us do. You have my word, brother." Dante said.

"I think we can save my planet from destruction and start over before it's too late." They both slept for the rest of the night in a dreamless slumber, waking only when the rays of morning's first light touched their faces. Mac sat up and wiped the sleep from his eyes, and Dante grinned at him as if they had shared a secret.

"Did that happen last night?" Dante asked.

"You mean the two of us standing in the desert of my planet? I think so. I don't know. It sure seemed real enough." Mac said.

The two said nothing more about the previous night's adventure, but as everyone else woke up, Mac thought about the pyramid and the Ethiopian men with the Ark. Could his vision have been the solution for saving Earth? Within the hour, everyone was up and had a full stomach. With no more ado and time running short, they entered the mouth of the cave.

"Egren came in here before looking for the tablet and never returned," Lilith said.

"Oh dear," Carp said.

Dante activated his light crystal as they walked further into the darkness. Something moved in the black up ahead, but when Dante shined his light down the tunnel, nothing but their shadows could be seen.

"This place has a creepy factor of eleven on a scale of one to ten," Mac said.

"Just make sure your weapons are ready when they attack," Lilith said. Mac raised his rifle to the ready position.

"You mean the rams?" Carp asked.

"Enormous army ants live down here too," Lilith said.

"You saved that information for now?

Thanks a lot!" Mac said.

"I thought you needed to get the Tablet. Whether there are enormous killer ants down here or not, the Tablet is here somewhere." Lilith said.

"That's a Good point, but I still don't like you keeping an important piece of information from us," Mac said.

For over an hour, nothing happened as they walked through one tunnel after another. Finally, they began to hear voices and whispers in the darkness.

"Watch out for the colony. They know you're here." Someone whispered.

Mac turned to see where the voice had come from and was shocked to see the hairless face of a sheep woman standing five feet tall with pink eyes two feet from him. She had come from one of the adjoining tunnels, and now looked left and right nervously as she waved for them to follow her. That's when Mac heard something clicking further down the tunnel, like fingernails tapping on a desk.

"They're coming!" She whispered. "Follow me."

"This smells like a trap. Who are you?" Dante asked.

"Suit yourself. I'm going now." She said and vanished the next instant.

Mac looked down to the tunnel on his right, and sure enough, in the light of Dante's crystal, was the head of a monstrous army ant. It hissed as it sniffed the air with its feelers, discovering the location of the intruders. The creature's mandibles were pinching wildly as it advanced on them. While Dante was frowning, Mac raised his rifle and fired into the ant's face. It exploded in a rain of white goo that splattered the tunnel walls, but the sound was loud, and now more ants were coming up the tunnel toward them.

"Crap!" Mac said. It was all he could think of saying, and then they turned and ran down the tunnel toward where the sheep had fled.

She was waiting for them by a ladder leading up into another tunnel, and as they climbed, they could hear the click and clack of hundreds of feet closing in.

"We have to be quick! The colony will not stop until all invaders in this tunnel system are dead or evacuated," she said.

She climbed the ladder and looked down on the wolven as they rose. Carp was in the rear and falling behind. One after the other, they reached the top of the ladder as the ants swarmed the tunnel, a reddish-black ocean of death. Mac was almost to the top when Carp joined him on the ladder, but the naga prince dropped his gun and jumped to get it.

"Forget it! Let's go!" Mac said. Carp looked up and nodded acknowledgment, but as he reached up to climb, an angry mandible clenched around his foot, pulling him and screaming into the blackness.

Mac stood at the top of the ladder, helplessly watching as the cluster of black insects surrounded him. Struggling and squirming, he disappeared in the frenzy, and just like that, Carp was gone. Glorg was swept away in the fracas as well, ending the undead companion, Ramos, who had risen for Carp.

"Mac! Come on!" Dante yelled from above. "They got him," Mac said.

"What? No!" Dante said. "He dropped his weapon."

The ants began to claw at the bottom of the ladder. They climbed over each other in a collective ladder of writhing bodies.

"There's no time; we have to go," Ramos called from above.

"I'm sorry, Carp. I'm so sorry." Mac said.

He turned and climbed upward. His militaristic mind told him to forge on and forget the dead. He couldn't turn back now, not so late in such an extended mission. Still, it felt like his heart had become numb with each new tragedy.

Once Mac cleared the ladder, a stone was pushed over the hole, blocking the ants' further advance.

The ram girl stood before them in the tunnel. "They'll have to double back and find another route. I'm Shiraz. Let's go; my people can help you with your quest." Shiraz said.

"Can they help us find our friend?" Mac asked.

"Once the colony has you, little else can be done. Feel some hope that he is still alive and their prisoner because if he is, he will be taken before the queen, and she will decide his fate." Shiraz said.

"So, he could still be alive?" Mac asked.

"Yes, it's possible. Please, we must go." Shiraz replied.

They ran down one tunnel after another, going deeper into the earth until they finally approached a heavy, round stone door. Shiraz uttered a word in sheep, and the door slid open. A ram on the other side bid her hello, patted her on the shoulder in a brotherly gesture, and then rolled the rock behind them. Past the door was another short tunnel, and then it opened to a magnificent underground city with dwellings carved from the stone walls and a ceiling that rose at least two hundred feet.

Carp would have appreciated another civilization that lived below the surface. Would the naga fade from existence without him? The sound of his crying filled Mac's mind. You don't know crap yet; he could still be alive. Stop it! He thought.

"Welcome to Ramm," Shiraz said. "My father is King Leto. Come on, and I'll introduce you."

She led them to a large carved stone castle and entered the front door, passing by two eight- foot-tall rams with their hands on the hilts of large two-handed swords. They looked down on Shiraz's guests with suspicious eyes but let them pass.

"Good morning, Ragg," Shiraz said. Then she nodded to the other. "Geral."

"Good morning, Princess Shiraz," Ragg said. The two nodded back and then returned their eyes forward.

Inside the castle, Shiraz led Ramos, Dante, Lilith, and Mac to the king's chamber, where a muscular, frowning ram sat on his throne, staring at them without flinching. His great horns were massive and curled around the sides of his head like a helmet.

"Welcome adventurers, saviors of Eritria. You are welcome in my home, for it is the Tablets of Destinies you seek. And we, the caretakers of these magical artifacts, have been waiting a very long time for your arrival." He spoke.

CHAPTER 11

ASURA, MORTAH, RANKOR, AND TEN other free reptilians flew the Telerum disc-shaped craft back to Broad Axe's castle. In his mind, Asura's aspiration toward forming an allegiance with his father had been abolished by Broad Axe's cowardice. And now, Asura would assume command of the legions on Telerum and then return to Eritria to rule once more.

Asura admired the sights as they traveled back to Broad Axes castle. The countryside on Telerum was mostly large groves of trees with red patches of earth interspersed. Farmland and industrial plants chuffing smoke and steam puffed plumes of grey and white into the afternoon sky. While Asura admired the Telerum technology, he had no idea how most of it functioned. As a ruler, he commanded any number of subjects who could operate the machinery or tell him how it worked if he ever cared to know.

"Do you know how to operate the giant pyramid back there?" Asura asked.

"One man might: Obedon. He is a mechanic who worked inside the pyramid for many years before his sentence was lifted and the Telerumian's released him. Had he not been the son of a monarch, he would have been executed for his crime, but he may have helped us." Mortah said.

"Interesting. What did he do?" Asura asked. "He was ordered by the Trelador Syndicate to kill the human Telerum tribune, Pius, and failed. Telerum authorities caught him just before he was about to pull the trigger." Mortah said.

"I like him already," Asura said.

"He is also a lieutenant of Broad Axe's, and with a show of strength from you, he may join your rebellion," Rankor said.

"Our cause is that of all Eritrian reptilians. We're going home at last, and when we do, we will not just take the continent of Eritria, but the entire planet. Did you know that long ago, when the sky gods came to Eritria and created creatures with the ability to reason, we were the first species?" Asura said.

"No, Broad Axe never mentioned it," Rankor said.

"Our people were slaves to these gods, who used us to mine precious gems and minerals for their benefit. Over time, we figured out what and who we were to them, and the reptilians revolted against this tyranny. From the murals and drawings, I've seen, they looked a lot like the humans on this planet, only taller."

"What happened when our people revolted?" Rankor asked.

"The gods realized they'd made us too much like them, had given us too much knowledge, and our rebellion against their tyranny threatened their way of life. So, they attempted to wipe us out with a virus and did a fantastic job of killing almost every reptilian in Eritrea. After our near destruction and exile to the Fire Lands, they started over and created the wolven.

They were not created as slaves but protectors of Eritria in case the reptilians ever attempted a resurgence. Our time is now, and the wolven are joining the extinction list very soon."

"We will fight beside you, Asura," Mortah said.

"We'll need Obedon to operate the pyramid when the time is right. " Asura said. His team of mercenaries agreed, and they prepared themselves for the coming fight.

They saw the castle in less than an hour, and Asura could feel the adrenaline flowing through him. Broad Axe had become weak in his old age, and to Asura, he seemed foolish and cowardly. It was time for a change of leadership. Ever since he'd decided, he'd been anticipating this moment.

The reptilian saboteurs were less than a hundred yards from the castle when they slammed hard into an invisible force field. Standing on a levitating platform near his castle was Broad Axe, and he glared directly at Asura's ship. A two-handed battleaxe was slung over his back, but he used his magic conjured in both hands to put up a wall of energy before the reptilian attackers.

The flying disk lost control and careened into a cliff below the floating city. Asura opened the exit hatch just before impact and leaped out, placing a magical protective bubble around him as the ship crashed into the side in a brilliant flash of light. The ship and his new crew were destroyed so fast that none of the men aboard felt a thing, and as Auras clung to the side of the cliff, he heard his father's voice inside his head.

"You didn't think it would be that easy, did you?" Broad Axe said. He was communicating telepathically.

"I had hoped it wouldn't be, father," Asura said.

Broad Axe appeared above him on the floating city and looked down at his son, shaking his head.

"When you get together, come on up, and we can either finish this foolishness or talk about how you and I will take this and many other worlds. Together." Broad Axe said. He vanished from sight.

Far below him, the crumbled pieces of his stolen ship were falling to the ground, along with his dead crew. The crash so tore them apart that even if he had resurrected them to fight Broad Axe as undead soldiers, they would be little more than quivering masses of shattered bones and skin.

Asura was ashamed and infuriated that his hastily stitched-together plot had failed so quickly. With grunts and groans, he began to scale the cliff, eager to finish it. Broad Axe was waiting for him when he reached the top, sitting on the edge of his floating platform. "You kept me waiting." Broad Axe said. His battle axe lay beside him on the platform, and he was eating an apple.

"So, do we fight?" Asura asked.

"That depends on you. Are you ready to stop being a hothead and listen?" Broad Axe asked.

"I'll listen," Asura said.

Broad Axe waved his hand, and a chair appeared out of thin air right behind Asura. He tested the chair with his hand and took a seat. Like a petulant child getting a lecture, Asura sat frowning while Broad Axe eyed him sternly.

"First off, great plan. I like the way you poisoned the Telerumian's and stole their vehicle. Second, my plan had always been to come to break you out, but I had to do it with diplomacy. You were fortunate with that viral strain, but if they decided to turn the pyramid weapon on this castle, the entire reptilian race would have been wiped out, along with half the countryside, all because of you." Broad Axe said.

Asura hadn't thought of it that way. But how did his father know so much?

"You don't live a thousand years without learning how to survive, Asura. Did you know I had five brothers?" Broad Axe asked.

"I did not," Asura said.

"In a power struggle, we all turned on each other, and I killed them one by one until I was the ruler of the Fire Lands and then the continent of Eritria, before Gregor took power away from me, that is."

"And that's when you came here," Asura said.

"That's right, and we started again. When we return to Eritria, son, we can do the same thing, but you must let me be in control. There is no room for two rulers; it confuses the people, and my power is much stronger than yours."

"But I ruled Eritria," Asura said.

"So, did I remember? Besides, you also lost an entire army to the Wolven, and now you have no soldiers left," Broad Axe said.

His father had a point, and in less than an hour since arriving at the Sky City, Asura had been turned from a heroic conspirator and future king to a failed coup leader with a dead crew and was now being scolded by his father.

It was a bad day for the once-powerful lizard king of Eritria.

"Ah, fine. I'll follow your lead." Asura said. "Good, I want you by my side, not creeping up on me with a knife to do me in." Broad Axe said.

"So, what's your plan?" Asura asked.

"We are going to use the pyramid to destroy the wolven while not killing ourselves and take that entire planet back. And then, we'll colonize Telerum in the past." Broad Axe said.

"What do you mean?" Asura asked.

"We're living in Eritria's distant past here on Telerum. It took me a while to figure it out, but we traveled back in time when we fled Eritria. We'll adjust time by a few hundred thousand years." Broad Axe said.

"You could create a paradox that kills us all," Asura said.

"No, I already thought of that, and what we're going to do will blow even your cynical mind."

"I'm all ears," Asura said.

Broad Axe was grinning as if he had just stolen the keys to the castle. "Come with me and bring your cosmic portal." Broad Axe said.

"Think of this as a game that harnesses the power of time travel."

Asura picked up the cosmic portal case and followed behind his father. The reptilians were erecting a forty-foot-tall statue of their king, Broad Axe, and at the base was a doorway. Above the doorway were the inscribed words:

INTO DARKNESS, OUR LORD BROAD AXE AND HIS SON ASURA TRAVELED TO DISTANT LANDS, AND UPON THEIR RETURN, THE REPTILIANS SHALL RULE SPACE AND TIME.

THIS STATUE IS A TESTAMENT AND TRIBUTE TO THEIR GREATNESS AND WILL REMAIN IN THIS SPOT UNALTERED.

"Interesting statue. It looks just like me." Asura said.

Broad Axe cut him a sideways glance. "Yeah, you're right. We need a way to get back, sort of a placeholder for memory. If this statue is still here, we can come and go through the doorway created by your device. We'll need them all to see us when we return because when we come through here again, it will be the end of a thousand-year prophecy." Broad Axe said.

"Where are we going first?" Asura asked. "Home. Now, concentrate on the Fire Lands and the last thing you saw before you opened the cosmic portal." Broad Axe said.

Asura closed his eyes, thought of the undead ghoul he'd left behind in his chambers, and pressed the button. The gate opened, and after seeing space unfolding before them, Asura saw into his throne room. The shambling undead dragged his left foot to where they stood like a lost dog.

"We'll step through together." Broad Axe said.

They turned back to see the sky city as it was one final time. A crowd gathered as the two walked through the gate.

"Remember the inscription on my statue. Eranic, my lieutenant, is interim king, and his bloodline will watch over our people until my return," Broad Axe said. Asura, close the gate."

Asura did as he was told, and the doorway winked shut, leaving them alone in his throne room with the rotting animated corpse following them around.

"OK, now give me the controller." Broad Axe said.

Asura handed him the small remote, and Broad Axe closed his eyes and drifted back to the image of his statue on Telerum. And then he pressed the button. When he opened his eyes, the doorway was open, and several women in robes were kneeling before them. When they saw Broad Axe and Asura on the other side, one of them began to weep.

"Our savior, Broad Axe, has returned!" She spoke.

The woman to her right fainted as the father and son walked back through the doorway.

The landscape had changed dramatically since they'd left. Now, there were millions of reptilians, and three sky-cities had adjoined the original.

"Welcome back!" Broad Axe said. He put a clawed hand on Asura's back.

"What happened?"

"While we were gone only a fraction of time, the time here flashed forward a thousand years. I gained a psychic connection with the creature inside this box, and it told me what to do." Broad Axe said.

"And our people had time to mass produce in preparation for your return," Asura said.

"Exactly!" Broad Axe said.

"That was pretty smart," Asura said. "That was genius!" Broad Axe said.

Asura nodded, and for the first time he could remember, he smiled, too. They had their army, and Broad Axe was now a god. They stepped back to Telerum, and Asura closed the gate.

In the time they had been gone, and because the original humans on Telerum had all been wiped out by Asura's devastating virus, the reptilian industry had sprung up all over the countryside below them. Huge factories, apartment complexes, spaceports, and resorts existed in the sky and on the ground. Flying ships of all shapes and sizes travel through the air from the ground to sky cities and out of the planet to Krypton above. A rotund reptilian in a black tunic and black leather pants walked over to them and immediately knelt before Broad Axe and Asura.

"My lords, you have returned! What a glorious day for the reptilians! I am Speculon, high priest to the acting Chancellor of Reptilia, Brax." Speculon said.

"Stand up, Speculon, and take me to Brax." Broad Axe said.

"Reptilia. Much better name than 'Telerum.'" Asura said, smirking.

Word spread quickly that Broad Axe and Asura had returned to rule Reptilia once more, and as they passed through the streets, people bowed to the ancient ruler. He had become a legend in the years since they'd left, and now, instead of a division of reptilians at his command, Broad Axe would address a nation of his people. But first, he needed someone to explain how much had changed since they had gone and find out where loyalties lay.

After a few thousand years, the leadership of Reptilia might not be as awed by their return as the reptile people. As they walked, Broad Axe pondered the state of things. There were going to be some management changes, but would examples also need to be made?

Speculon showed him a more updated version of his original castle, this one with menacing gargoyles posted like sentries along the rooftops. It gave the castle a more severe look that Broad Axe thought much improved the old haunt. They passed by two wide-eyed sentries who stood out of the way as Broad Axe and Asura walked by, their mouths dropping as they each exchanged a brief glance with their king. They climbed a stone staircase until they reached the throne room. Sitting on the throne with a leg propped over the side of the arm was a tall, skinny, handsome reptilian with the king's crown tilted on his head, women sitting at his feet, and a maiden feeding him grapes.

"Good news travels fast, my lord," Brax said. He did not move an inch to acknowledge Broad Axe, who was becoming perturbed.

"On your feet, Chancellor." Broad axe said. "You've been gone a long time, Broad Axe. Things have changed your worship. We never thought you would return. Well, I didn't, and now that you're here, you should know that things are being handled just fine." Brax said. He stood up to face the elder reptilian with a smug smile.

"I've come to regain control of my kingdom, and you will not stand in my way. Submit to me as your one true king or leave." Broad Axe said.

Brax snapped his fingers, and a lightning bolt crashed into Broad Axe, sending him to the floor and ripping a fiery hole in his robe. Asura immediately retaliated and fired a bolt of green energy into Brax, knocking him back onto the throne. His head snapped back against the hardwood, but he got right back up and snapped his fingers again, sending three bolts at Asura, who sidestepped them, catching one in his hand and holding it until it dissipated into nothing but static discharge.

"Nice trick, Asura," Brax said.

He was just about to snap his fingers again when he was thrust into the air, turning upside down. Broad Axe held him in an anti-magic bubble and walked up to the balcony, where hundreds of reptilians had already gathered in the courtyard. They had all assembled to glimpse the great Broad Axe's return. Broad Axe stood above them with Brax held in his magical grasp, and as he began to speak, Brax floated out over the city, terrified out of his mind.

"My friends, we have been gone long ago, but it was for a purpose. Our homeland on Eritria awaits us, and I can promise you that when we return, which I'm sure many of you have waited for, we shall return as victors. The power you feel here on Telerum will be ten times stronger on Eritria; you'll think faster, fight harder, and raise your families where you were created. There will be those who wish to stay behind, but of you who wish to join us, do I hear aye?!" Asura asked. The ground rumbled with the resulting affirmative reply.

"AYE!" said a crowd of thousands.

Broad Axe waved Brax to the side and let him go. He dropped out of sight over the sky city to a decisive end on the hard ground far below. His broken body would be unrecognizable in a day or two, just a vessel that once contained a weak soul.

In the underground city of Ramm, Mac, Dante, Ramos, and Lilith all said a word for their lost friend, Carp, just before being shown to their sleeping quarters. The fact that two of these Tablets existed made Mac's heart race, and his shared dream with Dante the previous night now seemed even more real. Could Earth be saved after all?

Shortly after being shown their quarters, King Leto requested their presence for dinner. Starving and exhausted, the four joined the ram king and his entourage at the table, where a great feast awaited them. They served soup first, which, to Mac, had an odor of curry. If he used his imagination, the meat floating in it looked like it might be chicken. He considered asking what the meat was but decided to keep his appetite intact. While everyone ate, the king began to speak.

"You may have heard many stories about these Tablets, but what I'm about to tell you is what we have documented in our historical records. Broad Axe, a warlock king of the reptilian people, stole one of the Tablets from the Tower of Kail to use against the wolven. After he was defeated, we became the caretakers of the Tablets when Inga brought the stolen one back down here to hide it from the reptilians." King Leto said.

"Inga brought the tablet back here. Why wasn't it replaced in the Tower of Kail?" Ramos asked.

"We had no idea that the absence of the tablet would cause so many problems. The issues you see today were gradual, and it was not for many years that we discovered the threat to life on this planet." King Leto said.

"But in all this time, no one else could have replaced it?" Dante asked.

"We wanted to, but there are three factions down here competing for the power in those artifacts, and if the Sisters of Agama, slogs, or the ant kingdom were to have even one of them, it would mean certain disaster." King Leto said.

"So, you kept them hidden away until a worthy recipient came along to set things right again," Mac said.

"Right, and now here you are. We are entrusting these relics to you. May the gods be with you on your journey.

"What about the other Tablet? You said Broad Axe only took one." Ramos asked.

"The ant queen, Shulan, held one of them in her lair, and at the request of Inga, we led a raid on the ant kingdom and took the tablet from her by force. I lost many soldiers in that battle. It's a long story but had Shula kept it; the ant army would have eventually threatened Valuria and the overworld." King Leto said.

"How did Inga get here?" Dante asked. "She came in through a tunnel in the volcano above our city. It is a treacherous path and secret to all but the ancients of this world." King Leto said.

"How do you survive the ants, King Leto?" Mac asked.

"We have a system of tunnels with the rolling doorways you saw when Shiraz saved your lives. The ants can't get through because the doors only roll from the inside, and our walls are carved out of solid volcanic basalt rock."

"Have they always been here?" Lilith asked. "The ants appeared when my father became king hundreds of years ago. Their colony tunneled through when the ant kingdom expanded. The war was protracted, and many people were lost before we figured out how to beat them back." King Leto said.

"I don't mean to rush you, sir, but we need to get those Tablets and be on our way," Dante said.

"Of course, but you'll have to place the first Tablet back inside the Tower of Kail to save the people of Eritria." King Leto said.

"Where does the other Tablet go?" Ramos asked.

The ram king had fixed his gaze on Mac. "With him." King Leto said. He pointed at Mac.

"With me?" Mac asked.

"You have your world to save." King Leto said. "Two worlds far apart will be joined in brotherhood as one when the Tablet is replaced, and our work is done. That's a rhyme my mother used to tell me when I was little, and it stuck in my head as I waited endless years for your arrival."

"The dream," Mac said, "Were we there?" Dante asked.

The king motioned to a servant who brought a small brown wooden square box. The top was decorated with dark iron and had an elaborate clasp on the front. King Leto took the box and held it in his hands before opening it up and reaching inside. He pulled out a crystal-clear orb and motioned with his hand for Mac and Dante to come closer. As they did, their eyes became transfixed on the object, and it drew them in as images filled the orb.

Dante and Mac saw that they were on a wooden ship crossing the desert, and beside them on the deck was a white tablet resting atop a wooden crate. In the far distance, Mac and Dante could see a white blinding light rising like a sun on the horizon. Also, Ramos and Lilith were there, and Mac could see his kids on the wooden craft. The next scene illuminated an army of demons approaching them from the bright light, and Mac could see their features twisted with the ferocious scowls of war. In the next instant, the light faded, and then the images in the ball died, too.

"What was that?" Mac asked.

"I think it was our future," Dante said. "Take the Tablets, my friends. Shiraz will guide you back through the tunnels along a safer route than you came from. After dessert, of course!" King Leto said.

Two soldiers entered the room, each of them carrying a tablet in their hands. The whiteness of each Tablet was blinding, and they emanated raw energy. Mac wondered what magical portal these stone objects had been pulled from. There were inscriptions on each one, but he could not read them from where he was. From a distance, they appeared to be some hieroglyphic.

"The letters contain strength, but the vibration of speaking the words on these Tablets is where the power of each one comes from. Use these wisely, and get them to their destinations because when in the wrong hands, the Tablets of Destinies have been the doom of many star systems. My friends, they can either be saviors or terrible weapons of destruction." King Leto said.

"But how are we supposed to get the Tablet into the Tower of Kail with those harpies hunting us out there?" Dante asked.

"That's a very good question. I'm sure you will find the answer. Now, eat some cake before you leave." King Leto smiled. He was a warm, fatherly man, and Mac liked him very much. He felt at ease with the king.

The servants brought a green cake with pink icing that tasted like a strawberry shortcake.

"Why don't you and your people come to the surface with us?" Mac asked.

"We tried several years ago, but we've been without the sunlight for too long, and those who did venture into the light were permanently blinded."

"I'm sorry for you, king. I wish it were different; you'd like Eritria. It's a beautiful place now that the centaurs have been wiped out." Ramos said.

"Maybe someday. We've been alive a long time here, and I do not think this is our fate. We'll return to the surface one day." King Leto said.

To change the subject, Mac let his curiosity get the better of him.

"What's this cake made of? It's delicious." Mac asked.

"Cave beetles. They have a lovely flavor when ground into flour with parsnip juice, don't you think?" King Leto said.

That was the last time Mac ever asked anyone what was in his food on the planet Eritria.

After they ate, the party collected their weapons, and they were on their way out of King Leto's underground kingdom, following Shiraz back to the tunnels. Mac thought she had a pretty face, for a sheep anyway, and found himself conflicted about the people of this planet. Back on Earth, the differences in skin color had been one of the biggest obstacles. Still, on a planet forty million light years from home, species would be another issue if he knew his people and their tendency toward prejudice and discrimination.

As he watched the sexy, winged, dark angel stride by, he knew he was falling in love with Lilith: a creature like none he'd ever known. He felt reborn in her presence. Her alabaster skin was so soft he could hold her forever, and he thought she was perfection with glorious, feathered wings as black as a starless night. He walked beside her as they exited the city and entered one of the multiple tunnels leading out.

For some reason, he contemplated the universal order of things and the fascinating series of coincidences that led him to her. Was there such a thing as coincidence? Or was there a divine plan that he was an unwitting participant in? To Mac it didn't truly matter, he figured, and those from Earth who would scorn them, he would have no time for.

A rollaway door had secured each adjacent tunnel, and although Shiraz assured them the walls were at least two feet thick, Mac thought he heard the scratching of tiny feet on the other side. As Shiraz led them with her light gem, Mac, Lilith, Dante, and Ramos readied their weapons in case the ants broke through or they encountered them in the darkness ahead.

An hour passed as they walked around one corner and then another, winding their way to the surface.

"We need to devise a way to get one of the Tablets into that tower," Ramos said.

"As soon as we do, the harpies will either attack us and destroy the Tablet or use it against us," Lilith said.

"They'd use it against everyone they could, right?" Mac asked.

"The harpies are the worst-case scenario the King warned us about," Dante said.

"No one should have that kind of power for very long; it's not safe in the hands of mortals," Ramos said.

When he became a warlock, Ramos left the land of the living and became something in between. Now, a creature of dark magic, he could feel the power of the Tablet calling to him, whispering power inside his mind. He wanted it like a nicotine addict craves a cigarette after three days of withdrawal. With the power of the Tablet in his hands, he could raise a legion of the undead and wash over any enemy standing in their way. But at what cost? The Tablet could cause his undoing, but what if he could control it? Then he remembered the robe he wore and its anti-magic shielding. Would it protect him? The dragon said it would help. He thought.

"Did you hear what I said?" Dante asked. "I was, uh, what? Sorry." Ramos said.

"We have to get to the surface of Eritria and lead the harpies up there," Dante said.

"The harpies believe there is only one Tablet; they wiped my people out looking for it," Lilith said.

"We take one of the Tablets with us back up to Eritria, get the harpies to follow us there, and then when the coast is clear, I'll place the other Tablet inside the temple," Ramos said.

"I can draw their attention away because if they see me with the other Tablet, they'll be incensed," Lilith said.

"Dante and I need to be at the top of the waterfall when you pass by. As the harpies follow you through the tunnel at the top, you hand one of us the Tablet, and when they have gone up, we'll sneak back up into the temple and head for Wasatch Village." Mac said.

"Back up a second. We fell through the temple and landed in an underground river. How are we supposed to get back up? Also, why is Ramos taking the Tablet?" Dante asked. "I'm the one with an anti-magic robe, and I sense immense power from this Tablet. I believe placing it inside the temple may cause an energy field to usher forth that the robe might not even protect me from." Ramos said. "OK, massive energy blast that may kill you makes sense. Good luck, bro." Dante said. "To the left of the opening you fell through is an ancient ladder that was once used by the slogs to travel to the Eritrian surface. You could use that to get out of Valuria." Lilith said. "We're drawing the harpies to Wasatch Village? My kids are there. Isn't there something else we can do?" Mac asked.

"I am telepathically reaching out to the other tribes as we speak, to let them know we require their aid. I don't know if the signal is strong enough alone, but maybe inside the Tower of Kail I can reach them." Ramos said.

"Do you know for sure you can reach the other tribes? There are what, maybe two thousand people in your village, and how many harpies?" Mac asked.

"Forty thousand, my best estimate," Lilith said.

"I have a hunch it'll work," Ramos said. Mac shook his head and looked at the ground for a moment.

"Alright, fine. Our success or failure is on the edge of a knife blade, but what the heck! I didn't come out here to be bored. We only live this life once, right?" Mac said.

"That's the spirit!" Dante said. "We'll make a wolven out of you yet!"

"Don't you threaten me with a good time," Mac smiled. Dante looked at him quizzically before understanding another of Mac's dry jokes.

"You humans have an unusual sense of humor," Dante said.

"Can we continue forward, please? Even with thick doors, these tunnels are unsafe, and the ants always find new places to burrow through." Shiraz said.

"Of course, lead the way," Lilith said.

Shiraz led them back to the cave opening without incident and bid them farewell. Before they could thank her, she was down the tunnel and out of sight.

"Well, we've all got our marching orders," Mac said.

"What?" Dante asked.

"Sorry, old expression. Let's go get this done." Mac said.

"Good luck, brother," Dante said. He put his hand behind Ramos' head and gently butted his forehead against Ramos'. "Be safe." Then he let his brother go. Ramos nodded and smiled with understanding.

"Hey, it's me," Ramos said.

Ramos took one of the Tablets and vanished through the jungle, heading straight toward the Tower of Kail.

Mac and Dante began running toward the waterfall, and Lilith followed them to help in case of any unforeseen attacks. When they reached the nearly invisible staircase, Lilith waited until they were safely up at the top before launching her plan. This was going to be a long day, she thought.

CHAPTER 12

LILITH WATCHED THE CITY OF Calvalor from her perch high atop the waterfall as Mac and Dante climbed the staircase. Lilith knew the harpies were looking for her, but more than likely, they were relieved to have the last of the Egren gone. Lilith was sure they would have a welcome party waiting for her if she turned up again. Mac and Dante climbed the arduous staircase as Lilith grew impatient.

"I can carry you up here, you know?" Lilith said.

"We can manage, thanks!" Dante said, rolling his eyes.

Lilith shook her head and noticed several bands of armed slogs were walking through the forest near the cave where they'd met Shiraz. By her side was the Tablet, meant to go back to earth with Mac. She wondered how such a small stone tablet could be used as a deadly weapon.

"Come on, boys. Get your butts up here." She shouted.

"Moving as fast as we can," Dante said. He and Mac could have bounded up the stairs, but narrow as they were, and high above the ground as the staircase was, it was an awful risk neither felt like taking.

"Yeah, on second thought, why don't you come down and get me," Mac said.

"It's too late. You wanted to be big men and walk up the flight of stairs. So, you get what you asked for," Lilith said.

"I was just...joking?" Mac said. "Toooouchy," Dante said.

"You guys better hurry up because a band of fully armed slogs is heading toward the cave. If they find Ramos, he'll be alone down there." Lilith said.

"Yeah, but we already ran into those guys, and they seemed very helpful," Mac said.

"You were misled, Mac. The slogs are one of the fiercest tribes known to my people, far worse than the harpies. They most likely let you go so that you could find the Tablet for them. All that prevented those worms from going to war with us was our magical power. The harpies and slogs are the enemies of this little inner world, and they both seek power among all else." Lilith said.

"So, if they find Ramos with the Tablet they'll try to take it? I'd like to see that." Dante said.

"Don't underestimate the slogs; they're sly hunters and very dangerous."

Mac and Dante shot each other a wary look, and then they began to run up the steps.

Ramos was walking through a thick grove of trees with aggressive, biting insects swarming around his head, and not even the hood of his robe could keep them out. The humidity had matted his fur, and he was miserable and alone. He was startled as he heard the harpies screeching and mewling like feral cats not far from him.

They were looking for Lilith and the interlopers who had executed their queen. The power of the Tablet in his hands made his eyes glow radiant blue and purple, so he was on an electric high that had him almost gliding off the ground despite his physical condition. If the harpies found him, he might be able to kill them all with a single blast of power. Dark thoughts swirled in his mind as he contemplated incinerating the harpies in an inferno of purple fire, watching their ashes blow around in the breeze, or perhaps resurrecting them for his amusement.

The tower was in sight now, an ancient wonder from a time when great magic had ruled the land. It had once been polished ivory but was now covered with an overgrowth of vines and was browning with age. Tall grass and weeds grew along the path, choking the once beautiful stone walkway, but he ventured on the messy path.

Ahead of him, he saw an archway opening at the tower's base leading into darkness beyond. Ramos stopped outside the archway and looked around to see if anyone was watching him enter. Satisfied, he ducked his head and went inside. He would have to wait until the harpies cleared the valley before he could do his part, and he hoped Lilith had seen him go in. Walking inside, he saw a staircase leading toward the top of the Tower of Kail.

"Oh, you've got to be kidding me. Stairs?" Ramos said.

He looked up the center of the spiral staircase and shook his head in disgust before taking the first ten thousand steps. Then he felt the first arrow enter his back. Ramos turned in surprise as he instinctively reached behind to try and dislodge the painful missile from his shoulder blade. Then three more whooshed out of the forest, hitting his right lung in a perfect bull's eye ring.

Ramos stumbled forward, dropping the Tablet, his eyes glowing purple as he tried to block out the mind-rending pain. He could not find the adversary, and his vision was blurring. Two more arrows came from his left side, entering his neck and partially exiting the other side. He turned left, now entirely off balance. The fire in his eyes was quickly fading, and in a final desperate act, he conjured a weak purple fireball, but since he could not lift his arms, the shot was ineffectively directed into the dirt.

"You wolven are amazing creatures, Ramos. We would never have been able to get the tablet back if it had not been for you. Those ants are far too dangerous for my people." Omnious said.

"You bastard!" Ramos said. He was fading from consciousness as Omnious stepped over him and picked up the Tablet.

Dante and Mac were finishing their run to the top as Ramos entered the temple; it seemed like time was speeding up. Dante closed his eyes, using the power of his ogridite bracelet, and saw Ramos staggering out of the Tower of Kail. Arrows were sticking out of his chest like needles in a pincushion.

"Oh no! Ramos!" Dante said. "What? What's wrong?" Mac asked.

Mac used his bracelet to locate Ramos and saw the elder wolven warlock stumbling through the forest like a walking voodoo doll. His body was being wracked with wooden arrows and poison darts, and the Tablet was lying in the dirt. Mac could see slogs surrounding Ramos as he cast a purple ball of fire into the ground. Slogs overran Ramos, and although his robe could protect him from dark magic, it was constructed of cloth and had no defense against the piercing arrows.

Ramos took two more pained steps forward and fell to the ground. Dante could see the slog leader Omnious step over Ramos' body and walk over to where the Tablet lay. He picked it up and turned to face the emerging army of slogs, holding the Tablet above his head. He made a victorious gesture, and then he and his soldiers vanished into the forest with the other Tablet of Destinies.

"Crap!" Mac said.

"We have to get back down there!" Dante said.

"What happened?" Lilith asked.

"Slogs took the Tablet and killed my brother!" Dante said. His paws were balled into fists.

"I've still got to clear Valuria of the harpies, so one of you has to get the other Tablet into that tower. You guys take care of this. Dante, I'm so sorry about your brother." Lilith said.

"We'll come find you once we get the Tablet back and restore it to the Tower of Kail," Dante said.

"OK, you two get going," Lilith said.

"Do you know where to go when you reach the surface?" Mac asked.

"Fly east into Wasatch village and lose them in the woods. Our people will give aid to you when you arrive." Dante said.

"My kids are in that village. What if she's followed back there?" Mac asked.

"I'll be careful," Lilith said.

Mac switched to human form and walked over to the much taller Lilith, placing his hands on her shoulders as he looked deep into her eyes.

"Take care of yourself, and we'll be right behind you," Mac said.

"Don't worry about me; I'll be fine. Take care of yourself down there, and don't be too long. We need that Tablet back in place to stop the ick. We're running out of time." Lilith said. She raised the ring on her right hand, and the eyes of the snake gleamed with an evil light. "Besides, if things get too complicated, I'll call my old friend Lothrax. He loves a challenge." She stooped down and kissed him on the mouth, her soft lips brushing his as their souls touched. When she pulled away, Mac was stunned to see her eyes glowed red. Lilith grinned back at Mac with a mouth full of wickedly sharp teeth and a forked tongue. Her flesh had taken on a slightly green tone, which reminded him of stories told to him as a child of the succubus, female demons, denizens of the fiery pits of Hades who would lure men into falling in love with them and steal their souls.

"That's impressive," Mac said.

"We all have our little quirks don't we, Colonel? And I'm no damsel in distress. Just get up there and join me as soon as you can." Lilith said.

The stark change to Lilith's features made her appear demonic in a way that was both frightening and sexy to the shape-shifting mission commander. If she could accept him as a wolven, he had no problem with her as a nightmare from a children's story.

"Go!" She spoke.

Then the raven-haired beauty took to the sky, Tablet of Destinies in her hands as she flew toward the crystal city of her ancestors. Mac watched her fly, feeling a knot in his stomach, worried not for her safety, but that he would never see her again.

"You ready?" Dante said. "She'll be fine, let's go." He placed a hand on Mac's shoulder, and the two were more like brothers now than ever.

"Yeah, into the shadows we go," Mac said. Broad Axe floated above his people, levitating on an anti-gravitational disc outside the great three-mile-high pyramid, using his powerful magic to cast his voice into the clouds. Every reptilian within a hundred miles of the sky city would hear him speak. Initially, there was some confusion over why they had to move to the dead capital city of the Telerumian's, but the reptilians were told their questions would be answered after the pilgrimage. Today, for the first time in ages, Broad Axe was smiling. The sun shone on his face as he stood before the massive pyramid. His people had figured out how to use this ancient weapon, and if it came to a last stand with the wolven and their allies, he would use it to blow them apart like crumbling dirt. Asura stood behind him as he put his hood back to look at his subjects. Asura stood beside the cosmic portal with the controller in his hand, nervous excitement building as he waited for war.

"Reptilians! We have been exiled from our home for far too long, but today we will return and take back the rightful ownership of our land. Our race was forged from the crawling lizard on Eritria by beings from a distant universe, and from Eritria we shall recover our true power. Telerum has never been our home, and today, we will wipe out the wolven and Minotaur scourge that has threatened our way of life for so long." Broad Axe said.

A resounding cheer erupted from the massive crowd.

"Are you ready to return to Eritria?" Broad Axe yelled.

Another affirmative cheer erupted.

Asura levitated the cosmic portal a mile from the horde of reptilians and concentrated on the plains outside the Bog Lands while simultaneously pressing the button. The doorway opened, but this time, the gate had grown tenfold. Instead of a doorway big enough to allow three or four people to walk through shoulder to shoulder, this one was a mile wide and high. Asura was shocked at the sheer enormity of the gate. The reptilian army stood with mouths agape, adrenaline pumping, ready for war.

"Run through the gateway! Take back our homeland and rid our world of enemies!" Broad Axe commanded.

With a unified hiss, followed by a loud battle roar, the reptilians of Telerum ran through the gateway with battle axes raised, swords drawn, and giant iguanas pulling catapults and battering rams. Drums of doom pounded rhythmically, sending a message that the devil was coming and doom would be arriving with him.

"Father, I don't know how much larger this gate will grow. We may need to work fast; I feel it could rip this world apart if it gets too large."

"Keep the gate open for as long as possible. If we begin to lose the war, my man inside the pyramid will unleash the pulse beam, but we'll have to be back on this side of the gateway to survive. Stay near the gate, and I'll signal you. We won't have long to escape after I give the order." Broad Axe said.

As the valley emptied, Broad Axe and Asura mounted their giant iguanas and rode forth. "I have a very good feeling about all of this." Broad Axe said. Asura glanced his way, nodded, and rode on in silence. He wasn't as confident as his father, especially after his army's last confrontation with the wolven and Minotaur. Before he crossed over to the other side, Asura took one last look back at the monstrous pyramid rising far into the clouds, and he felt a pang of fear for the first time in his life.

Lilith carried the Tablet into Calvalor, landing in the courtyard of the queen, and stood alone in a ring of ghoulish harpies. They gathered around her, eyes gleaming, mouths twisted in evil grins. She was the last of her species; all others wiped out by an evil band of parasitic bloodsuckers. But what the harpies did not know was that Lilith was so much more than who or what they thought she was. Now she stood before Surya, the latest harpy queen, and glared at her with poison in her eyes. Power emanated through her as she felt the electric rhythm of the Tablet in her hands. The Egren were a benevolent and peaceful people, which had been to their detriment when the harpies arrived and began their hostile takeover. But Lilith was no Egren and had been born on a world many light-years away from Eritria. She was also now even more powerful than her ancestors because of the Tablet.

"Good morning, Surya. I'm not surprised they chose you as the next queen. You harpies are famous for poor decision-making skills." Lilith said.

Surya's cobalt black eyes flashed at Lilith as if the remark had caused her more than a little embarrassment. A jagged scowl spread across Surya's face that incensed Lilith. The harpies were challenging to look at, with their sallow, aged, pale skin and deep-set wrinkles that reminded Lilith of spoiled melons in the hot summer sun.

"You should not have returned here because you're about to experience the same ruin as your dear mother and father. They begged for death, you know. I remember your mother crying as she watched us slice your father's neck open very slowly. Their pain was so delicious; it's a pity there won't be more of you around to maim after today. We'll have to go after those slogs for entertainment from now on. I see you also brought the Tablet of Destinies. You're an idiot!" Surya said.

"You done talking? Because time's up." Lilith said.

"Get her!" Surya said to her minions. Lilith's rage rose in a tidal wave of hatred.

She could not clearly remember what happened next, but as Surya's vile servants surrounded her, Lilith felt the fire in her eyes glowing brightly, and she spread her onyx wings. Like the fires of Hades, heat swirled around her in a tornado of flames. Lilith stared into Surya's shocked face with cold eyes, baring her fanged teeth. Like an angel of death, she stood against the forces of darkness and consumed her enemies like tinder in a dry summer forest. Lilith compressed her strength, and as the harpies of Surya's guard screamed in torment, she pushed her palms forward releasing two orbs of whirling flame into Surya's eyes.

"Noooooo!" Surya screamed. She burst from the ground, spinning on burning wings, as wicked orange flames burned her to the core. Spiraling out of control, she crashed into a grove of trees.

When it was all over, there were over a dozen smoking skeletons lying around Lilith in a circle, and the Tablet was laying on the ground next to her. Other harpies were nearby, regrouping for another attack. She could smell their diseased rot and felt their hateful eyes watching her from the bushes, buildings, and shops.

"I've got the Tablet of Destinies! If you want it, come and get it!" Lilith said.

Lilith took to the air again, and as she did, the sky filled with screeching, mewling harpies. She bolted toward the waterfall as the harpies gave chase. They cleared out the valley, enraged by the death of their new queen and the gall of the Egren castaway to come back and dare to challenge their coven. Lilith hoped that Mac and Dante could recover the other Tablet in time, and thought about the fire god, Lothrax.

She could summon him at any time, but he did not work and play well with others, and it had been hundreds of years since her mother last conjured the demon. Once that door was open, it would be not easy to close. Lilith burst through the cave opening and found the entrance to Eritria as the tunnel filled with harpies. They followed her up into the temple of Ostrid and away from Valuria. The crazed monsters vanished up the hallway tunnel, leaving Mac and Dante to seek out the Tablet of Destinies stolen from Ramos. The two of them had reached the bottom of the waterfall by the time Lilith had her violent outburst and had scorched the harpies and a good amount of the forest in her rage.

Ramos had seen the harpies clear out in his wounded and near-dead state. Alone now, he began to recover from his defeat slowly. What the slogs did not know, and what Ramos had not been told by Inga, was that if he wore the Robe of Dragaz, he could not be killed by anything other than fire. While Dante and Mac were making their way to him, he stood and began pulling arrows out of his body, wincing as each one dragged through his flesh like a hot poker. The slogs had his Tablet, and although he understood their desire to capture the magical artifact and respected the sneak attack, they would pay for shooting him with poison-tipped arrows.

"Alright, Omnious, I'm coming for you," Ramos said, whispering.

Movement in the trees set him on alert, and he sent two purple orbs of pure energy into the dense forest in front of him. Trees and bushes exploded into a violent shower of splinters, raining down and creating small fires in the dry twigs.

"Crap! Stop that; it's us!" Mac said.

"Yeah, we're the good guys!" Dante said. The two appeared from behind a large tree, and they could see the relief in Ramos' eyes as they walked into the new clearing.

"Sorry about that, but I've had some recent trouble with our little buddies, the slogs," Ramos said.

"We know; thanks to these handy bracelets, the two of us were able to see you," Mac said.

"We saw what Omnious did!" Dante said.

Ramos looked at him with a raised brow. "I've been learning some of the earthman's slang," Dante said.

"Yeah, well, I'm ready for some payback," Ramos said.

"Let's rock and roll then," Mac said, baring his claws.

"See, he says such cool, strange things," Dante said.

Ramos rolled his eyes. "Let's go. They think I'm dead and that you're all long gone. We can sneak up on them now. But we must hurry. Time is shorter now than it was a minute ago," Ramos said.

"Let's go get that Tablet and save my little girl!" Mac said. He could not stand the thought of losing Serena because of the slogs after everything they'd already been through. His feral anger began to set in.

They crept through the woods, knowing that slog archers could be anywhere, stalking them from the trees. However, unbeknownst to them, a celebration occurred in the slog village, and everyone in the kingdom attended. The cliffs were almost in view now as the trees began to thin out, leaving them more exposed the further they walked. They could hear voices.

"We need to find cover as soon as possible," Mac said.

"I say we get up a little higher and see what they're up to," Dante said.

"There's a ledge up there that winds around the corner, see it?" Ramos said. Ramos pointed to the right, about forty feet up to a ledge just wide enough to hold the three of them.

"It looks like there are some footholds on the way up. Let's go." Mac said. A resounding cheer rose from the slog city.

The three were on the ledge in twenty minutes and crouched behind a giant boulder. Down below, Omnious was holding the duplicate Tablet of Destinies in his hands and preparing to place it in a wooden box as his loyal subjects watched. His speech made them into a frenzy, and they all carried weapons. Spears, swords, knives, crossbows, and polearms pointed into the air as the audience cheered. Omnious began to speak again, his voice booming through the canyon.

"Today, with this artifact, we will dominate the land. Our first goal is to rid Valuria of the ant menace. For too long, they have been a threat to our way of life, killing us in the forest as we hunt for food and blocking the cave entrances to our ponds of spiritual renewal deep within Valuria. Even as I speak, the ant army approaches from their hiding places underground. They expect weakness, an easy target, but they will have no such luck! Today, we fight!" Omnious's eyes were glowing like two bright orange lamps as he surged with the power of the Tablet.

Ramos, Dante, and Mac could all hear a rumbling through the forest below them as an army of six-legged, enormous, and incredibly organized ants marched toward battle with the slogs. Omnious looked even more demonic with the Tablet in his hands, and the ring of horns around his head emanated a vibrational energy that spread out among his people like a wave, empowering them, strengthening their resolve, and transferring the power into them. The first ants arrived in the canyon within seconds, and the king sounded a battle cry as he shot an orange stream of energy from the tips of his fingers toward the ant hoard.

He had become a beacon of power for the slog army, roasting legions of army ants as they stormed the canyon. His soldiers rushed forth, bringing down sharpened steel blades on armored bodies as the melee began. Stingers punctured slog warriors as serrated mandibles chomped through legs and arms while archers from the cliffs fired volleys into the onslaught.

"Looks like we arrived just in time for the show," Dante whispered.

"I don't feel good about this," Mac said. "Mac's right, this is bad. We have to get that Tablet away from Omnious and escape without being seen." Ramos said.

"To battle! Kill every one of the bastards!" Omnious yelled.

"I've got an idea, but we'll have to work fast. We can use the ogridite bracelets to track each other, and the talisman Gregor gave me allows for close-range teleportation. You two get to a safe spot, and I'll teleport to where Omnious is standing. He won't be able to harm me with his magical abilities if I wear the Robe of Dragaz. I'll slit his throat, take the Tablet, and teleport to where you guys are hiding. Without Omnious and his power, the ants will overrun them." Ramos said.

"Then we get the Tablet to the Tower of Kail and get out of here, right?" Mac said.

"Yes, and once the Tablet is in place, I'll collapse the staircase leading up to it and seal the entrance," Ramos said.

"Great plan, brother. Let's see if we can execute it as smoothly as you described it," Dante said.

"Go toward the tower now. I'll meet you there in a few minutes." Ramos said.

"Here, take this. You'll need it to kill Omnious." Mac said. He handed him the ornate knife he had taken from Resha after her demise.

"Thank you, Mac," Ramos said.

"It's not much more than a letter opener, but it should do the job for you," Mac said.

"I'll make sure it does. Now go, and don't get caught." Ramos said.

Ramos closed his eyes and watched them disappear into the forest in his mind's eye, and when they were far enough away, he opened them and watched as the battle continued below him. This was going to take cracker-jack timing, and he knew it because if anything went wrong with his plan, the ants might steal the Tablet, and he did not think the three of them would stand a chance against their army. Although he was no longer truly among the living, Ramos still had reservations about his safety as he prepared his mind.

"Here we go," Ramos said.

To give himself a barrier, he raised several slogs from the dead and instructed them to form a ring around Omnious. Then, his talisman activated, and in the blink of an eye, he was behind the enraged slog king. The undead slogs battled the approaching ants, but the living nearest their king panicked when they saw Ramos appear. Before anyone could react, the blade of Mac's knife was deep in Omnious's throat. Ramos cut a sickening grin across his neck, separating Omnious's head from his body in an expertly timed slice. It fell backward, held on by the skin from the back of his neck, like a demented Pez dispenser. Omnious fell, Ramos grabbed the Tablet, and in a flash, he was in the forest's center with Dante and Mac.

"You did it!" Mac said.

"We'll stand guard outside the tower. Do what you came here to do." Dante said.

The tower was in sight, and the coast was clear, so Ramos ran inside with an overwhelming sense that his time was running out. In less than five minutes, he reached the final step and entered a round room with a pedestal in the center. The roof was a pyramidal crystal glimmered with prismatic beauty in the sunlight, casting rainbows on the floor. Ramos walked over and placed the Tablet on the pedestal, not knowing which way it should face or if he had even done it correctly. His mind was racing, and he hoped he had not been a fool when his family and friend's lives were on the line.

As he backed away from the pedestal, Ramos held his breath. The Tablet rose from the pedestal as if lifted by an invisible hand, spinning around in the air. White light sprung forth, and the stone artifact rolled in place as it spun, creating a blinding strobe effect. Ramos turned up the hood of his robe as the Tablet's brilliant magic filled the room, causing the crystal to glow. He felt the radiation of powerful energy outside his robe and suspected that if he uncovered any part of his body now, the magic would consume him. The fire raged on, and before Ramos began to descend the tower, he watched a beam of solid light fire from the crystal into the ceiling of the land of Valuria.

It spread across the continent of Eritria, reinvigorating all the ancient, dormant pyramids. Ramos had done it. Unknown to him then, the tower rested directly below the three pyramids outside Wasatch. They had been built on an energetic lay line tracing north along the coast, and when the Tablet's energy touched the pyramids, their capstones magnified its power. Raw positive energy moved worldwide, igniting other pyramids and reestablishing the long-lost global energy grid. The trees felt a renewed, peaceful sensation that had been gone from them for so long. The bushes, insects, enchanted rocks, and every sentient race of Eritria also felt the change. The ick turned to ash as the light flowed through it, negating its effects, and for the first time in two days, Mac's daughter Serena sat up in bed, feeling much better.

The king and queen of the naga were instantly aware that the Tablet had been replaced but saw, through Ramos' eyes, that their son had been lost in the quest to retrieve it. A bittersweet win for the future of their planet, the queen broke down in tears as her husband consoled her, his sorrow mixing with hers. Carp's loss created a void in them that would not soon be healed, but because of his sacrifice, the queen would be pregnant with triplets within the month, and the naga could begin again.

More powerful than a star, that light circled the planet of Eritria in less than a minute, and when it was done, the free people of the land felt an energetic release. Ramos stopped on the third step down and cast a destruction spell on the staircase. As he walked, the stairwell crumbled behind him, one stair at a time, and when he stepped outside, the remaining stones crashed down, sealing the tablet inside, safe for now from the rest of the world. "We have to notify the other chiefs that war is upon Eritria once more," Dante said.

"I know. I tried to do that inside the Tower of Kail, but the magic was too strong, and I had to escape." Ramos said.

"Let's form a meditation circle. Mac, join hands with Ramos and me." Dante said.

"OK," Mac said.

The three formed a ring and joined hands. As Ramos and Dante closed their eyes, so did Mac.

"Let yourself drift, clear all thoughts, and feel the vibration of the universe speak through you as we combine our energy to communicate with the others," Dante said.

Mac felt an energetic bond with Dante and Ramos, like having a small electrical charge pass through his hands, bonding him to the other two.

"Alright, chiefs. I hope you can hear me." Ramos said.

Ramos concentrated on the five wolven tribes and their chiefs, for everything would be lost if they could not hear him or mobilize in time. First, he thought of Double Head of the Gore Paw, who were mighty hunters and warriors of the plain's region, and then the Terran leader of the Frost Blight clan, warlocks of the Polar Regions. Next, he concentrated on the Dark Claw, a clan of assassins from the southeast led by Nicodemus the Wise. And then he thought of Belial, a demonic wolven from the chaos realm, who was the leader of Arcane Fist, a clan of fire and ice mages hailing from the northernmost Fire Lands, the only region not controlled by Asura.

One of their many abilities was that they could open portals to anywhere in Eritria when summoned. Ramos reached out with their combined aura, and as he did, his face appeared in the sky above each tribal city.

"Great chiefs, I, Ramos of the Blood Paw tribe, request your aid in the war against an invading army of harpies far below Eritria. They seek to destroy us as they have other civilizations, and our time grows short. We bring good news, however. The Tablet of Destinies has been restored. Our people may once again gather strength from this ancient artifact of great magical power. Join Dante and me on the field of battle and protect the citizens of our world from encroaching evil." Ramos said.

His plan worked; each chief nodded to the image of Ramos and lifted his fists high into the air in allegiance, as did his tribal followers. The warriors of Wasatch Woods also saw their chief speaking and mobilized for combat.

"Meet Dante and me today on the plains between Wasatch Woods and the Bog Lands," Ramos said.

He broke the communication and heard a squawk from high above them. It was Saki! She had somehow managed to find him down in Valuria. Ramos called to her, and she flew down.

"Need a ride?" Saki asked.

Her multicolored plumage looked even more beautiful to his beleaguered eyes, as none of them were looking forward to walking across Valuria and climbing that waterfall.

"How'd you find me beautiful?" Ramos asked.

"You were on my mind. When the pyramid began functioning again, I located a small ventilation shaft on the side of a cliff along the beach, a little further north of your village." Saki said.

"I am glad you're here, my friend," Ramos said.

"Well, come on, the three of you, hop on.

I'll get us out of here." Saki said.

"It sure is good to see you," Ramos said. "Don't go getting gushy on me. But yeah, nice to see you too, hot stuff." Saki said. Dante and Mac exchanged a quick, knowing glance and mutual frown.

Ramos, Mac, and Dante climbed onto her back, and although the weight was substantial, Saki never showed it. Beyond the forest, the three wolven could see the ants and slogs still fighting with one another as they bid Valuria farewell. Saki climbed into the sky and found the ventilation shaft, carrying them to freedom. She flew up into a small point of light at the end of the shaft, and then they were soaring above the ocean. All of them could see the magnificent light emanating from the largest of the pyramids. The other two were humming in vibrational resonance with the bigger one.

"By the gods! We're back!" Ramos said. "There's something else you need to see, Ramos," Saki said.

In the distance, they could see something shimmering in the midday sun. As they adjusted their eyes, they realized it was the cosmic portal's portal, and it was opening back to Eritria from some other world, but this time the opening was massive. It must have been miles wide, Mac thought. Through it, they could see a pyramid more enormous than any on Eritria. It was so large that they could not see the top, even though the gigantic opening the cosmic portal had created. Something else was also there, and as Saki drew closer, they could see a mass of millions of bodies moving across the plains.

"Reptilians!" Ramos said.

Then he spotted Lilith flying toward the forest, followed by an angry army of harpies. Lilith bolted toward Wasatch Woods as the winged demons chased her. What happened next was even more unexpected. The reptilians began firing into the squadrons of harpies with arrows and laser weapons, and the harpies, in turn, engaged the reptilians in combat. On a sweet, cool day in Eritria, the war had begun once again just when the planetary grid had been repaired.

Mages from Arcane Fist appeared on the field, exiting their teleportation portals, and with immediate urgency, they began flinging ice and fire spells at the reptilians and harpies. Double Head's Gore Paws arrived from the north, and seeing that the Arcane Fist was under siege, they joined in, their ferocious warriors hacking and cleaving with bladed battle axes, long swords, and teeth and claws. From the trees, Nicodemus's Dark Claw assassins fired volleys of arrows into the reptilians, sneaking through bushes and running behind trees to kill their prey as the reptilian scourge ran into them like battering rams. Lilith flew directly for Ramos; the surprise was written like a tattoo on her face as she neared.

"I thought for a moment you had all been killed!" Lilith said. She held the second Tablet tightly in her arms.

"We had help from a friend, or the three of us would probably be fighting our way out of Valuria right now," Ramos said. He stroked Saki's neck.

"Ohhh, you always know where to touch me," Saki said.

Ramos blushed with embarrassment. "Look!" Lilith said. She pointed to the woods below, where thousands of Blood Paw tribesmen ran toward battle and barked mad.

"We have to get this tablet secured and join them!" Ramos said.

Flying in on steam-powered airships were the Frost Blight clan, and the warlocks brought a legion of the undead. Undead soldiers were parachuted into battle at the gateway to Telerum as their warlock masters mounted pterodactyls and soared through the air on wings of leathery speed. They cast regeneration spells on the wounded wolven below, reviving them for more battling, and raised the dead reptilians to fight against the living ones. Saki landed outside Wasatch Village. Ramos hid the Tablet of Destinies inside a deep well in the center of town. Mac's children rushed to see him, hugging Ramos around his neck.

"Ramos, where is our father?" Bobby asked. With no time to explain, Mac motioned for Ramos to say nothing.

"No time, young sire. The battle for Eritria has begun, and all I can tell you is that your father is fine and one of the finest soldiers I have ever fought alongside. We'll return once more when our planet is safe." Ramos said.

He brushed a paw across Serena's cheek. A single tear was falling from her right eye. "Fear not, little one. This will be over soon, and it is good to see your recovery!" He smiled, and without another word, he mounted Saki again. She rose high into the sky with Ramos, Mac, and Dante on her back, and the beautiful Lilith joined them for the battle.

As they disappeared beyond the tree line, Serena wondered who the pretty woman was with Ramos.

Stephanie Brandt left the medical building, drying her hands off after scrubbing up from a recent surgery. She watched Lilith vanish over the trees. Far away, Stephanie could hear violent roars as the warriors of Wasatch Village followed the path of their destiny toward another battlefield of war.

A general in the human army stopped beside Stephanie. For a moment, he considered the wolven might require their aid again but contemplated passing it by the New World Congressional Committee and thought better of it. Stephanie looked at him and tilted her head.

"You going to mobilize and help our friends out?" Stephanie asked.

"So far, this is not our war. The wolven are big boys and can handle this on their own, " the general said.

Stephanie rolled her eyes at his lack of action and returned to her duty. Eventually, the human elite who journeyed forty light-years from Earth would have to face off in combat against the people who helped them learn how to survive on their planet. The General's decision was the beginning of strained relations with their neighbors. It was democracy in action all over again, she thought.

CHAPTER 13

ALL SENTIENT BEINGS LIVING IN the Bog Lands were fleeing for their lives as war destroyed their home. A thirty-foot-tall bog giant named Gwart, set ablaze by a flaming tar ball, trundled through the thick silt, stumbling over fallen trees and boulders as he burned. Gwart, one of many unfortunate casualties of Eritria's latest war, succumbed to his injuries and fell dead face first into the swamp as he continued to burn.

The plains were filled with warring bodies, making friend and foe challenging to locate. Mac, Ramos, and Dante entered the battlefield from Wasatch Forest, confronted by a panoramic view of devastation on an epic scale. Bodies clambered over each other, slashed with swords, gnashed with razor teeth, tore at each other, and ended life in a dance of death unparalleled in recent times.

"It seems that we arrived late to the party. Good lord, look at all the reptilians! There have to be millions of them." Mac said.

"I never imagined Asura would come back so soon and never with this great an army!" Dante said.

"Is it only Asura that leads those coming through that gate, or did he bring his father with him this time?" Ramos asked.

Dante shrugged and punched a reptilian rushing at him, breaking his jaw and dropping the lizard man to the ground. He knelt with lightning reflexes and tore out the man's throat, tossing it to the side. With the bog's foliage in flames and the swamp burning out of control, visibility quickly became a problem on the battlefield.

Choking smoke floated like a fog of death as warriors on all sides ran through, slashing and hacking with wild abandon. Blood soaked the grass in a maroon rain as one warrior after another slipped and fell into the sticky fluid. Screams and shouts of rage and agony were the battle hymn, and it rose to the heavens in a discordant cacophony. Shadow warriors dodged and parried through the smoke and flame.

"It looks like the gates of Hades opened up here," Mac said.

"Look up," Dante said.

Lilith was engaged in aerial combat with three harpies, firing bolts of red flame from her hands, striking them as they attempted to get at her with their swords and bows.

Wolven assassins from the Dark Claw were removing harpies from the cover of bushes and capturing reptilian war wagons. The reptilians had been bringing large wooden war wagons over from Telerum, all filled with weapons and supplies to be used for the takeover.

Nicodemus commanded his troops to flank the reptilians' left and right sides as they came through the cosmic portal, while the warriors under the command of Double Head rushed forward in hand-to-hand combat.

Ramos controlled the Wasatch wolven, leading them from the front as their battle cries rang out. The Arcane Fist spread along the high ground, casting fire and ice spells at the harpies and reptilians. Yxx and his Minotaurs were notified of the battle, and he arrived with three hundred thousand angry bullmen from Davendale.

Shouts and battle cries erupted around Mac and Dante as they fought tooth and claw through the mobs of reptilians and harpies. The libmok's, having heard that Broad Axe and Asura were returning to reclaim their homeland, joined in to fight with the reptilians. Lond, the king of the libmok's, sent his remaining army from the previous war back into combat, what was left of them. This time it would be all or nothing for the libmok's. Wolven and Minotaur forces had so decimated their numbers after the Centaur war that it would mean extinction if they failed this time. Lilith was dodging arrows as she fought the oncoming harpies, but she was beginning to tire, and the ring on her finger cried out for her to summon Lothrax.

"Need some help?" Mac asked. He aimed his rifle and fired a blue laser bolt into the shoulder of a harpy, raising her sword toward Lilith.

"I'm fine. You boys run along and find something else to do." Lilith said. Fire leaped from her hands in arcs, and she knew it was a gift from the Tablet of Destinies.

An arrow whooshed by her head from one of the Dark Claw, hitting a harpy in the leg, and as it lost flight control—attempting to pull the arrow out— Mac shot it in the neck. The portal had never been this wide, and he could see it growing larger by the minute. How long would it be before it caused a gravitational rift between Eritria and Telerum? The corpses of reptilians lay scattered as wolven warlocks raised them from the dead to fight again in an almost comical display of violent theater.

Mac turned and spotted a large reptilian in a black robe racing from the field of battle toward the cosmic portal on what looked like an overgrown iguana on steroids. In his hands was the cosmic portal.

"Gotcha!" Mac said.

He would get that device back, even if it meant his demise. Too many ill-intention people had used it, and enough was enough. He raced through the fog of war on fleet feet and followed the mysterious iguana rider through the gate. As he crossed over, Mac felt an odd sense of déjà vu running through him, as if he had been there before and had no idea he was stepping back in time.

His adrenaline pumped like fuel through a jet engine, and the excitement of retrieving the door back to earth was overwhelming. As a wolven, he could run faster, harder, and farther than he ever could as a human. A group of sword-wielding reptilians got in his way, blocking the view of Broad Axe riding his iguana toward the gigantic pyramid, which infuriated the already irritated white wolven from Earth. Mac stood before three of them as they stood in attack stance, grinning toothless smiles and brandishing their thick swords. They looked to him like three old men with green, leathery skin, oblong black eyes, and leather armor.

Mac ducked down low and rolled forward, coming to one knee, and fired two rounds from his rifle at the first reptilian, dropping him in his tracks. But he had not counted on their lightning speed, and before he could fire again, a sword caught him in his right shoulder. As it did, an exquisite blossom of pain exploded from the wound as he squeezed the rifle trigger with his good hand. The middle reptilian fell to the ground, half of his face disappearing in a spray of blood mist, and then Mac reached up, pulling himself along the sword blade toward his enemy, a ferocious howl of rage escaping him. Nose to nose now, the reptilian wore a mask of horror as Mac turned his head to the side, ripping out his windpipe with one menacing chomp.

"Gross!" Mac said.

The reptilian slid away from him, flopping on the ground as Mac spit his throat out beside him. Mac was horrified and in pain, but now, he had a sword to go with his ancient rifle. Shaking his head at the three bodies around him, he pulled the sword painfully out of his shoulder and put the dead reptilian's scabbard around his waist. He took a glance at the sword. It had a katana look and feel that made Mac think of ninjas swinging down from trees under the cover of darkness. The gift left him by the sword, and as he pulled it out, there was a painful throbbing in his shoulder. The shoulder would heal, he told himself and ran on.

The robed figure arrived at the base of the pyramid and dismounted. Next, he disappeared inside a doorway that blended into the overall structure so well Mac would have missed it had he not watched the man enter. Mac arrived moments later, blood trickling from his wound, looking warily at the giant iguana creature looking for signs of aggression. It merely sat there eyeing him with disinterest and captured a passing dragonfly. It was satisfied munching the multi-winged insect while Mac sidestepped around it and entered the pyramid.

Inside was a long stone staircase leading up to the massive structure, so Mac followed it, keeping his rifle pointed at the top of the stairs. After about fifty steps, Mac saw a platform and a light glowing ahead of him.

"I'm getting that case back and getting the heck off this planet," Mac said.

Surprised, he heard footsteps from behind and turned to see Ramos had followed him.

Lilith was flying across the battlefield when a harpy spear hit her back, and she tumbled to the ground. The blade had pierced her right shoulder just above the blade, and as she hit the ground, the spear tip broke off, leaving the point sticking out just above her skin.

"Agh!" She spoke. "Enough of this!"

Lilith stood, feeling the spear tip move inside her shoulder, and chanted the sacred words to bring the fire god. The ring's jade eyes glowed brightly as her voice vibrated with each syllable.

Thunder clapped in the sky above as dark clouds rolled in, blotting out the sun; lightning flashed across the battlefield as a gigantic two-hundred-foot-tall stone door, with a brass ring doorknocker appeared on the south end.

"Wolven warriors, clear the battlefield! Lothrax is coming." Lilith said, her voice impotent in the noise of battle. She walked toward a hill on the northern side, wounded, with her ability to fly now hampered by her wounds.

The wolven was startled when the massive stone door appeared, and most soldiers were now gawking at it. Fighting between the races stopped as they stared through the smoke and small fires covering the plains. The stone door began to open, and immediately, the sickening odor of sulfur erupted from the portal, mixing with the battlefield smoke.

Towering over the stunned warriors, the door stood like a monolithic nightmare, and then, like a horror, a demon composed of pure fire stepped through the entrance to their world. Lothrax, the god of fire, was on

Eritria once more, and as he entered, the wolven scattered for cover, leaving the reptilian army and harpies to face him. Asura was the first casualty of the demon's wrath; he was standing closest to the entrance when Lothrax entered, instantly incinerated by the blast furnace of heat rising off the demon. Broad Axe saw his son's demise in his mind's eye and became even more eager to see the planet destroyed. All he had to do now was reach the mechanical room of the massive pyramid.

"Did you just see what happened? I'm not hallucinating, am I?" Ramos whispered. "I think that fire god from the mural in the Temple of Ostrid might have been more than just an artistic musing," Mac said. "Do you think Lilith caused this?" Ramos said.

Mac nodded and remained silent as he watched the two-hundred-foot-tall walking wall of flames stomp on the reptilian army and crush harpies in his powerful hands. "Remind me never to piss her off," Ramos said.

"Agreed. A large, robed reptilian man on the back of an iguana rode toward this giant pyramid with my cosmic portal in his arms." Mac said.

"That's Broad Axe, Asura's father. Nothing good can come if he has your cosmic portal." "I have to get it back to return home and save my world," Mac said.

"I'm here to help you. Broad Axe is a dangerous enemy; if you try to fight him without protection against dark magic, it'll end badly." Ramos said.

Ramos found an entrance at the bottom of the massive construction. The door was ajar, but there was no sign of Broad Axe.

"Look at the size of this thing; he could be anywhere inside it," Mac said.

"Well, we have to stop whatever he's up to.

Let's get this over with," Ramos said.

"Lead the way, partner," Mac said, stepping to the side. A long corridor of stairs led up into the pyramid as Mac followed Ramos.

Mac and Ramos entered a rectangular room at the top of the steps, but there was still no sign of Broad Axe. Instead, they were confronted with the statues of three golden gods. This room appeared to have only one way in and out, and as they entered the door behind them, a brick wall slid shut, trapping them inside.

"Looks like we're all in for this now," Mac said. Ramos gave him a silent nod and lit a torch mounted on the wall.

The statues of the gods were posed, each performing a separate action. The god on the far left had the body of a man and the head of an ibis, was dressed in black iron battle armor, and held a lightning bolt in his hand. On his face was a ferocious sneer as he glared skyward. The middle god was a sheepman garbed in a Roman toga, aiming a crossbow directly at the entrance. It was so lifelike that Mac secretly hoped it wouldn't spring to life and attack them. The final god was a Minotaur holding a large diamond in his outstretched hand, and as the torchlight danced around the room, the precious gem glittered and shone like a star in the dim light.

"Strange room," Ramos said.

"This has got to be a test or trap of some kind," Mac said.

"Sure, why not? I wonder how Broad Axe got through here, though." Ramos said.

"When I was a kid, my friends and I would all sit around the table and role play in Middle Earth. Most of that game involved dungeons, traps in every other room, and monsters that threatened to eat us at every turn." Mac said. "You had to solve the puzzle to get into the next room."

"What do we do first?" Ramos asked. He was walking around, looking curiously at the gold statues.

Mac walked over, eyeing them with suspicion.

"One of these statues opens a door. I know which one it is, but if I'm wrong, we could get dropped into a pool of acid or something." Mac said. He had mentioned this too late, however. Ramos saw that the Minotaur's hand appeared to be a lever, so he pulled down on the hand of the diamond-wielding god. It clicked as the lever released, and a hiss entered the room a moment later. "What was that?" Mac said.

"Great. It's probably poison gas." Ramos said.

Mac followed his hunch and pulled on the lightning bolt god's arm. It released, and as the room filled with choking fumes, a previously unseen brick wall door on the other side of the room rumbled open. The two looked at each other and exited the gas chamber into a hallway that suddenly turned around a blind, forty-five-degree corner. A blackened doorway was across the hall, and Mac could smell rotten meat from somewhere in the room ahead.

Ramos looked in with mistrust, feeling the eyes of the undead watching him from the darkness, hearing their whispers in his mind. He answered their calls, telling them to rest and go to sleep. Then he cast a protection spell on himself and Mac before moving on. Rounding another corner, Mac saw what looked like a supply closet and opened the door.

"Did people live in this pyramid?" Mac asked. He was speaking to himself.

"This is a machine designed to produce energy if it's anything like the pyramids back home," Ramos said.

"I think it's probably a massive weapon, and Broad Axe may be getting ready to use it on Eritria," Mac said.

At the end of the hall, another stone wall greeted them, only this one opened with a push. Inside this room, three ladders led up to three separate platforms thirty feet above their heads. An onyx statue of a man with the head of a jackal stood in the corner, and his hand was a long spear.

"I'll bet there's treasure up those ladders. I'd go up there and see for myself if we weren't pressed for time, but we should keep moving and return for it if we can."

Mac said. There were two other doors besides the one they had entered in this room.

"This statue looks a lot like the Egyptian god Anubis from my home world, but there doesn't appear to be anything to press or pull on him," Mac said.

They chose the door to their right, and Mac pushed it open while Ramos held the torch. As they left the room, the statue turned its head, and its legs began creaking into life. Mac and Ramos found the hallway they had entered bent again at another ninety-degree angle, and when they came to the end of this one, a stairway lay before them leading up. As they ascended, it spiraled away into the darkness, and after a few more minutes of creeping, they came to another room, but Broad Axe was not there either. Behind them, something moved. They stopped to listen, but neither of them could smell anything except for the musty odor of the ancient building rife with cobwebs and reclusive spiders.

"Let's keep going," Mac said. "Something's not quite right," Ramos said.

He walked over and raised his torch, considering the deep dark of the stairwell.

Satisfied they were alone, he turned to join Mac in the room. This chamber had a single door on the south wall, and inside the room were pieces and parts of machinery from some iron hulk but nothing else of interest. Mac walked over and pushed the door, but it would not budge. The sound came again like a brick sliding over gravel. Their ears pricked up, and they turned to see that the statue from downstairs was staring at them with a stoic expression. Mac looked at the statue's chest and noticed he wore an ankh on a gold chain. When he turned back to the door, he saw that the same symbolic shape had been carved into the door.

"He's got the key," Mac said. "Wonderful," Ramos said.

He launched a ball of purple fire at the Anubis statue, which bounced off harmlessly.

"Ummmm, that didn't work. At all!" Mac said.

Mac fired his rifle, hitting the golem in the leg. The tiny laser bolt bounced off Anubis and around the room a few times before dissipating. Anubis began to walk toward them with his spear pointed outward, but he was slow.

"We need another idea," Mac said.

While the statue crossed the twenty-foot space between them, Mac decided to take aim again, but this time at the ankh necklace. With calm nerves and a smooth trigger pull, he hit the target, and the key fell from Anubis to the floor with a clang. The statue kept coming.

"I have a plan. I'll roll over there and kneel behind him, and you push him over. He's close enough to the staircase that we could roll him down it and get away." Mac said.

Ramos motioned to his shoulder.

"Do you think you should be rolling around with that injury to your shoulder?" Ramos asked.

"It's just a flesh wound," Mac said.

How he wished that the people of this planet had access to Monty Python's Holy Grail movie.

In a flash, Mac ran at the monster, and when it stabbed at him, he ducked and rolled along the hard floor, getting behind it. Then he got on his hands and knees and braced his body into a frame. The Anubis statue began to turn, and Ramos dashed into it as it did. The statue was off balance instantly and flew over Mac, but instead of rolling down the staircase, it slammed into a wall, shattering like a clay pot. "Looks like he had a glass jaw after all," Mac said. He picked up the ankh and went to the door, placing it in the carved recess. The door opened.

"A what?" Ramos asked.

"Nothing. It's just an old boxing expression." Mac said. "It means he went down easy."

They were in a diagonal hallway now, and at the end was another stairway leading up, so Mac and Ramos followed it. Daylight shone into the stairwell as they climbed up, and when they got to the top, they saw a doorway leading into another room. This one was much larger than the others and had a machine inside that reminded Mac of the Hadron collider he had seen in pictures long ago.

Large transformers are ready to deliver power, steel girders are bolted to the floor holding it up, and coiled tubes and wires are filled with viscous fluids. And then someone turned it on. The monstrous machine whined as if something inside of it were gaining speed. At first, it was a small electromagnetic whine, but soon, it rose to a deafening roar as they walked through the chamber. Mac estimated that the machine was more than a football field in length and width and reached high above them into the pyramid where, at the top, they could see the sky and just a hint of outer space. Then, near the edge of the machine, they finally found who they'd been looking for.

Broad Axe was working the controls on a large metal panel configured with buttons, knobs, and switches. Mac wasted no time and fired a round into Broad Axe's back, which seemed to do nothing to the lizard king. Broad Axe turned toward him, annoyed. Mac wondered if his rifle had lost power, and when he looked at Ramos, the wolven warlock motioned for Mac to stand out of the way as he covered his head with the hood of his robe. They could no longer hear each other speak because of the volume of the machine, so Mac took Ramos' direction and stepped behind a corner.

But when he did, he got on all fours and crawled along the floor toward where Broad Axe had set down the cosmic portal. He crept to it and picked it up, checking to ensure the remote control was also there.

Ramos and Broad Axe faced off against each other, warlock versus warlock in a battle of energetic magic. Broad Axe had many tricks up his sleeve and was shocked when his spell of living death reflected off the young wolven and slammed into a wall nearby. A family of roaches living inside a crack in that wall was killed instantly. Ramos used a life drain spell on Broad Axe, but the old warlock was too wily for him. He deflected the spell with his anti-magic shield, sending the life-drain spell back at him. Ramos dodged out of the way, receiving only a small bit of the spell, while his robe absorbed the rest of the magic.

Broad Axe countered him with a bolt of lightning, which caught Ramos in the only exposed part of his body, his feet, as he began to stand. For an instant, Ramos felt like his entire body was riding on a colossal current of pain, and had he been genuinely alive, it would have stopped his heart. He sprang to his feet again, the fur smoldering under his robe, and quickly cast two balls of pure purple fire, which hit Broad Axe in the stomach. The old man was sent reeling into the control panel, and as he slid across on his butt, he shut it down, silencing the machine.

"Nice try, warlock, but your skills are not yet perfected. I can tell by your strength that you've not been at this long. You should have approached me with more than just a human and some parlor tricks. You'll die here, you know?" Broad Axe said.

"You're the legendary Broad Axe? If you were, I'd be dead already." Ramos said.

He grabbed the talisman of teleportation around his neck. Reaching into his pocket with the other hand, he grasped the hilt of his sword and concentrated on the magical talisman. Ramos envisioned himself standing behind Broad Axe, and as the great reptilian king prepared to send all his hatred and malice toward Ramos in one final spell, the other vanished. Broad Axe was so stunned that he dropped his hands, and the green ball of energy evaporated. A second later, he felt a presence behind him, but before he could turn, a fiery blade pierced his back and exited through the front of his body. Broad Axe let out a cry and fell to the floor. The great reptilian warlord stopped breathing a minute later.

"Mac, let's get out of here and return your cosmic portal to Eritria before something bad happens. I don't like being on this planet and cut off from our people." Ramos said.

"Great, I'm ready to go. That was an excellent trick, my friend. You'll have to tell me how you did that sometime." Mac said.

"You got it," Ramos said.

The two found a door on the side of the pyramid that allowed access to the outside and took it. Saki saw them emerging and flew up to greet her friends as they did. Meanwhile, inside the pyramid, Broad Axe struggled to his feet one final time and reactivated the energy weapon in a final act of malice against the inhabitants of Eritria.

"Ready to go?" Saki asked.

"Yes, please, as fast as possible!" Ramos replied.

She allowed them to climb aboard and took to the air. Behind them, Mac and Ramos could hear the machine starting up again.

" I should have checked twice to see if he was dead, but at least we got the cosmic portal back!" Ramos said.

"We've got other problems as well. Lilith summoned a two-hundred-foot-tall demon, and it's over there right now, burning the plains to charcoal." Saki said. "She's also pretty badly hurt."

"Please, take me to her, Saki!" Mac said.

Mac had the controller and case in his possession once again and had never felt so relieved. The portal was growing closer as Mac looked back to see the pyramid crystal glowing white. A vortex of light swirled around the top of the magnificent capstone, shooting off lightning bolts of pure energy in every direction.

"Saki, we don't have much time," Ramos said.

Saki picked up the pace, and just as they passed through the portal, Mac pressed the button and closed the cosmic portal to Telerum forever. Broad Axe, bloodied and bruised, fell face-first into the control panel, accidentally firing a laser beam so powerful that it would have ripped Eritria in two. Instead, the beam shot straight up with titanic strength and blasted Telerum's sister planet Krypton. The resulting explosion shattered Krypton into billions of fragments, which in turn caused a death rain on the surface of Telerum. Giant chunks of debris slammed into the oceans. As it flash-boiled most of the water, the remaining ocean rose in a five-mile high, planet-wide tsunami that washed over its surface, knocking over dwellings, destroying spaceports, and burying everything in its path with red dirt.

Krypton spread across the Milky Way galaxy as an asteroid cloud that stayed there for another million years. Telerum was dead, and years later, the people from a little blue planet called Earth would begin to explore her surface to understand what could have happened to change the course of Telerum's fate.

Lothrax had already reduced the reptilian ranks to little more than ashes. Lilith was unconscious and bleeding in the grass. Saki landed next to her as Lothrax walked across the plains, decimating everything in sight as darkness covered Eritria. The last of the harpies went up in flames and feathers, while the reptilians and some of the wolven army succumbed to white fire unleashed from Lothrax's hands.

"Consume, burn...join me in the hot winds of the chaos realm," Lothrax said. His voice was guttural and low.

"Lilith, sweetie, you have to wake up now and put the monster back in his box," Mac said.

He knelt beside Lilith, cradling her head in his hands.

She opened her eyes and smiled. She reached up to stroke the fur on the side of his face.

"That's what she said. Hey, stranger..., I don't feel so well...I think there was a spear on that poison." Lilith said. She was incoherent and delirious.

"You have to call that thing off," Mac said. He pointed toward Lothrax, who was on his way toward the Faerie Lands and spreading a swath of fire in his wake.

When the remaining reptilians saw that their path back to Telerum had been cut off, they quickly dropped their weapons and surrendered. Dante reemerged from the smoke and shadows, covered in blood and breathing heavily from fighting. Lilith held the ring high and mumbled an incantation that caused the jade eyes of her twin snakes to glow with radiance again. Lothrax was suddenly pulled back toward the stone door as if in a vacuum. He screamed into the black clouds above as Lilith relieved him of his duty.

"Goodbye, old friend. Until next time." Lilith said.

The door shut and vanished. As it did, the darkened clouds drifted away, and blue skies hiding behind them reappeared.

"I can get her to your village, Ramos. Do you have a medicine man there?" Saki asked.

"My crew doctor, Captain Stephanie Brandt, is there. She can look at Lilith." Mac said.

"I'll take her, but I can only take one more of you on my back without risking a crash. Getting you all out of Valuria was tiring." Saki said.

"You take her, Mac," Dante said.

"Yeah, we'll be along in a day or two. I think the worst of this is over, and once the fires are out, the healing can begin." Ramos said.

"Thank you, my friend," Ramos said. He stroked her neck.

"You're welcome, as always. Are you ready, Mac?" Saki asked.

"I am. Thank you for being so kind." Mac said.

Mac held Lilith in his arms and carried her over to Saki, holding her after he mounted the great bird. The contrast between the powerful demon princess and her now vulnerable unconscious state was stark, and he was honored that she needed his help. He just hoped they were not too late.

The dead littered the battlefield, and a stench of decay hung like an intense, malodorous tapestry over Dante and Ramos as they stood watching Saki taking to the sky carrying her passengers.

"Gregor would have been proud of us, Dante," Ramos said.

"He is proud of us, big brother. Let's go home." Dante said.

Saki flew Mac and Lilith to Wasatch Village. Mac dismounted and carried Lilith to the small building used as a hospital to return the war-wounded. Inside, he found Stephanie treating a wolven warlock from the Frost Blight and asked for an empty bed for Lilith. Serena, who had entirely recovered from her illness, was assisting Stephanie.

"Captain Brandt, can you please help Lilith next?" Mac asked. Stephanie turned around as, before her and Serena, Mac transformed into human form once again.

"Daddy?" Serena said. "What happened to you? You just changed...back?"

"It's a long story, but suffice it to say, I'm half-wolven now. You think it's strange?" Mac asked. He was almost wincing after asking her. "No, I think it's cool!" Serena said. "Are you staying with us now?" Serena was almost twelve and had grown up fast in his absence. He could see the young woman in her eyes and thought about how much she resembled her mother.

"Welcome back, Colonel. Of course, I'll help her out." Stephanie said.

"You're not staying, are you?" Serena asked. "It's complicated, sweetie. Where's your brother hiding?" Mac asked. As if on cue, Bobby entered the room and hugged Mac. "He's not staying. He's leaving again, just like always." Serena said.

"It's not like that. I think I know how to save our planet. I can do it; then we can go home." Mac said.

"Back to Earth? Why in the heck would we ever want to go back to that crap hole?" Bobby asked.

"Watch your language, young man. Ah, you're not a kid any more than your sister is at this point." Mac said.

"Answer the question, Dad," Bobby said.

"I had a vision one night. I think I'm meant to go back and save Earth from destruction and institute a reversal of our neglect."

"I call those delusions of grandeur," Bobby said.

"I don't have time to explain it now, but I've got to go, and Dante's joining me," Mac said.

"Dad, you have a serious problem with family commitment. We're going with you this time, like it or not. You're taking us with you since you can't stay with your family." Serena said.

Stephanie cleaned Lilith's wound and placed some herbs inside the gash. When she did, smoke rose from her skin as the poison from the spear evaporated, and Lilith began to come around.

"What a day. I feel like I was thrown off a cliff." Lilith said.

"Bobby, Serena, I want to introduce you to a very good friend. This is Lilith." Mac said.

"Well, a little more than a friend," Lilith said.

Mac transformed back to wolven form, and as he did, Bobby's mouth dropped open like a hatch.

"That's awesome! I want to do that, too!" Bobby said.

"Sorry, buddy. This might have been a one-time deal. Say hello to the pretty winged lady," Mac said.

"Sorry, it's very nice to meet you, Lilith," Bobby said. He was red with embarrassment.

"You're gorgeous, Lilith. Did you help Daddy?" Serena asked.

"We helped each other. I wouldn't be here now if it weren't for your father and his friends." Lilith said.

"Daddy, I want to go home," Serena said. Mac could sense the urgency and a tear in her voice and felt the same way. It was time to go back.

That night, Mac dreamed of Earth again, a place in the sun for him and his children. It was a new world, and Lilith was a part of it. The four of them had serenity for the first time in their lives. She soared through the air on her onyx wings, floating around like a dark angel in the sunlight. Mac woke up the next morning and felt refreshed for the first morning in an exceptionally long time. They all called him a fool when he notified the new Congress that he was returning to Earth. The new elite political establishment from Earth had no desire or intention to ever return to their broken world. They had already planned on moving away from the wolven to rebuild their society in the mountains north of Wasatch Woods.

Around noon, two days after Mac and Lilith arrived, Dante and Ramos entered the village with their remaining soldiers, war-weary and glad to be back in the forest. A celebration was held in their honor, and not one wolven or human went to bed that night sober. Thanks to their ability to get the Tablet back to the Tower of Kail, the birth rate would spring to a new high that year, and most of the conceptions would happen shortly after the celebration ended that night.

During the party, a pact was formed between the wolven brothers and Lilith that since Mac had been so noble to help the people of Eritria in defense against Ragnok, Broad Axe, Asura, and the ick, all of them would travel to Earth and assist Mac in his quest. The following day, Dante, Ramos, and Lilith joined Mac and his children as he prepared to open the cosmic portal back to Earth. Mac took the cosmic portal down to the shoreline to prevent a catastrophe and opened it near the ocean. Mac had to strengthen his resolve quickly when he opened the portal and saw the turmoil- ridden Earth again. Serena grabbed his hand nervously, and the others stood by him with silent, open-mouthed shock.

"I knew it would be bad, but...my God!" Mac said.

They stared at an abandoned shoreline where large pockets of seaweed clogged the once-sandy beach. On the Earth side of the portal, the tired skeletal frames of more than twenty hotels jutted out of the ocean. Harsh waves crashed against them as the sea fought to claim the derelict buildings with her salty arms.

Mac's dream returned when he recognized a large horseshoe-shaped hulk of a hotel with the words *Avi ta* written on the sign and knew it as the Avista Resort he and his family had stayed at frequently during his childhood.

"Daddy, this is scary," Serena said. "Welcome to Myrtle Beach, kids," Mac said.

"You ready to get started?" Dante said. He placed a hand on Mac's shoulder.

"You bet, let's go save Earth," Mac said. All six of them stepped through the gate, and as they took one final look back at Eritria and those who had come to see them off, Mac gave a final wave and closed the portal.

One hundred and fifty years had passed in Earth time while Mac had been helping to save Eritria. Although he did not know it, many foul creatures had risen without man's control, and humanity's remaining survivors hung by a thread to existence. If he and his team could not reverse the damage, humanity would blink out of existence in that sector of the Milky Way galaxy forever. As Mac stood on the beach, gawking at the destruction, he knew their success or failure was something that only time would tell.

Mac, Dante, Ramos, and Lilith will return in:

In the Company of Wolves: Anathema